MAGIC HEADACHES

Megan Allen

Disclaimer

This is a work of fiction. Names, characters, businesses, places, events, locales, and incidents are either the products of the author's imagination or used in a fictitious manner. Any resemblance to actual persons, living or dead, or actual events is purely coincidental.

I am a christian and I am writing a book about magic and God. I know the Bible says people who do witchcraft will burn in a fiery lake but I like to imagine worlds where there are no rules and where 'magic' (supernatural abilities) can come from God. After all, Peter walked on water. Daniel and Joseph interpreted dreams. Elijah called down fire. Moses parted the red sea. Impossible things are possible with God. Don't try witchcraft on Earth but it's fun to imagine other worlds. Because if there are other planets with life, God made them also.

ISBN-13: 978-0692063217 (Allen Books)

ISBN-10: 0692063218

Cover design by Nathalia Suellen

edited and updated 6/23/2021

Big thank you to my first readers: Matt, Mom, Britt, Lauren, Kelli, Sheila, Bri, Candace, Autumn, & Teresa. I'm lucky to have you all.

<u>Magic Headaches</u>

Magic Headaches

The Morland Prince

Morland Blood

Chapter 1

Derek

Derek Jensen closed his laptop and rubbed his raw eyes. He could see the afterglow of the screen burned into his eyelids. And when he opened his eyes the contrast of his dark bedroom made him feel blind.

He'd read it again. He was such an idiot.

He should never read his own blog, especially at night. *Rookie mistake.* Night blurred the lines of reality.

Derek raked his hands through his too short hair. He sometimes forgot which version of himself he was. He hated his short hair but it was different from how he'd had it before so he kept it.

Now that his eyes had adjusted, he saw how true the night was. There was no moon and he sat in the pure vast dark. He could have been anywhere it was so dark. He could have been back on Morland.

He knew he wasn't.

He knew it but his hand rose to his right side all the same. He traced the cursive tattoo of her name and took a deep breath. That tattoo was his touchstone, his one truth in a life of lies. That tattoo told him three things: that he was alive, that he was on Earth, and that his sister was dead.

He ran his fingers over the thick black letters that spanned his right side from his lower ribs down to his waist covering up exactly where she had stabbed him: B-r-i-g-t-t-e. He never should have reread his stupid blog. He slept poorly enough as it was.

He'd written it out a couple years ago so that it didn't have to live in his brain anymore. But now it just lived in two places.

His best friend/only friend, Peter, had been the one who'd encouraged him to put it on the internet. Derek did and didn't want to find someone who had been to Morland before. He lived with a constant background fear running along his spine that something or someone would drag him back to that horrible nightmare of a planet.

Why did he keep opening up the same can of worms. The worms were still dead. He kept checking. He poked them, still dead. No new comments on his blog. No new emails. He exhaled the breath he was always holding. He'd put his story out there in case someone was looking for him, for Morland. But no one was. That was good, right?

But... he also craved finding some link. He needed to know how he had fallen into Morland in the first place. And he would have given a lot to talk to someone else who had been there and back, a fellow veteran of the Queen's reign of terror.

But the only people who left comments on his blog were fantasy nerds who said his story was 'A-mazing! But...I wish there had been more descriptions of the battles!" and other such nonsense.

It made him roll his eyes whenever that stuff happened. He didn't want praise on his autobiography of pain and suffering. They didn't need more details of the horrors of his past and he didn't want to remember them well enough to write them out. Derek had only hoped to find a *little peace* in writing it all down but peace wasn't a commodity easily found for murderers like himself.

Derek had read it again because he felt something coming, some storm off the coast or some slumbering giant starting to stir. He was sure it was nothing. He was sure it was just a soulless man's paranoia. But he'd found himself reading his own story like a treasure hunter looking for clues. As if he didn't know every word. As if he could forget even one. As if it didn't haunt his every nightmare. *Morland, pah!* Morland was the bloody worst.

He'd thought about writing an addendum to the blog. But it would take away the feeling of victory. It was better that it ended with him escaping. People might think 'Oh good he's okay now. He's home on Earth. Home in Waxhaw, North Carolina. Everything is okay. I don't need to worry about him anymore.'

But Derek was not okay.

He never would be. And he was pretty sure no one really believed that his blog was based on his life. The best place to hide the truth was in plain sight, right?

Who could ever believe that a tree had taken him to another world and a bright red flower had brought him back? He hardly believed it himself.

Derek knew Morland was far away. So far Earth's telescopes couldn't see it and it definitely couldn't see him. But sometimes, like tonight, it was as if Morland was breathing over his shoulder, up his neck. He couldn't run from that. He couldn't run from his own mind. He'd tried. Sometimes the loneliness and the fear locked inside himself made it hard to breathe.

But there was one thing a soulless man was good at and that was making himself feel nothing. So Derek took a breath and forced himself to shake off the feeling of unease and coming disaster. Because *nothing* ever happened in Waxhaw, North Carolina. Everything would stay the same and that thought was a comforting little nightmare itself. He was absolutely unpleasable.

Elinor

There was something wrong in the woods.

Elinor slowed her steps to listen, to find whatever it was. But her younger siblings's romping and laughter drowned any forest sounds. They were a long walk from their house and from any road. Her mind knew everything was *probably* fine. They couldn't have chosen a quieter, safer town than Waxhaw. If she were still in downtown Atlanta it would be wise to head any misgivings. But here...

She tried to shake it off as she sped up to keep an eye on Katie and Colton. But the more she walked the worse she felt. Something was wrong here.

7

The ill-at-ease feeling was turning physical. She sank to her knees to catch her breath and to feel the solidness of the earth. She raised her hand to her head trying to squash her growing headache from the outside but that didn't help.

She looked around and couldn't see them anymore. "Colton! Katie," she yelled. Nausea was rising as she frantically whipped her head back and forth trying to find two little heads, one dark and one fair.

"What is it?" Colton asked appearing before her as if he'd teleported. He leaned closer, the young Sherlock always looking for clues. This time he sought evidence as to explain her current position on the forest floor.

"El, are you okay?" Katie asked kneeling down, locking her little fingers between Elinor's.

"I... I," Elinor said bringing her free hand to rest on her forehead again. "My head... I don't feel so good."

She tried to stand but the feeling of wrongness slammed into her like a tidal wave. Her head was pounding so violently it made her stumble like the ground was having an earthquake. Her vision was blurring and the colors seemed off, dimmed. One minute her little sister and brother were right beside her and then they were gone as if they had blinked out of existence.

Colton took charge and sent Katie running for the house. Elinor tried to stand again but she only got worse. Her vision started flashing gold, like a strobe light was going off and it felt like fire was raging through her skull. Waxhaw, North Carolina was trying to kill her.

Chapter 2

Elinor

Her trip to the hospital was a haze. The violence of her sudden afflictions had sent her in and out of consciousness. But the pain in her head wouldn't let her sleep for long and the *other* problem kept her too scared to sleep.

So she tried to focus on the pain.

Her head hurt like poison bombs were exploding in her veins and filling her head with pressure and making her temples pound like a marching band. It was a colossal pain that made it hard to catch her breath.

But the headache was the best of the *new* things that were happening to her. Because no matter how she avoided it... she was also going mad. And the madness was in the form of trees, a whole forest of them.

Elinor studied her surroundings carefully before she tried *it* again. The hospital was one shade of cream: walls, floor, and ceiling. Her dad had his eyes closed in the chair next to her, the stressful hours finally catching up with him. She took a deep breath and then closed her eyes. She waited there a moment, in the in-between. Then she let her breath out long and slow and opened her eyes.

Well, crap, Elinor thought, *I really am going crazy.*

When Elinor looked around she didn't see her hospital room with its boring walls, floor, and ceiling or her sleeping father. She was now seeing a forest with trees as far as she could see in every direction but not normal trees.

As if hallucinatory imaginary trees could be normal.

No, the trees and everything else around her was sepia colored like a filter on an old photo. The sky above was obstructed by the forest canopy and the floor below was littered with leaves and small plants. There was no one in the woods but her and she wasn't even *really there.*

Because despite what her eyes were telling her, Elinor knew she was still in the hospital. She could feel the bed beneath her and hear the noises of the hospital with its incessant beeping and hurried steps. She took one last look around and blinked her eyes trying not to flinch at the sudden appearance of her hospital room. A sigh escaped but it sounded more like a soft moan to her own ears.

Every time Elinor blinked, her vision shifted from forest to hospital and back again.

Blink. Hospital.

Blink. Forest.

Blink. Hospital.

Blink. Forest.

Repeat.

But it wasn't just the trees that changed when she blinked. She did too. She was all misty and see-through. Her long blonde hair looked like fog blowing in a breeze she couldn't feel. But she didn't feel see-through. She didn't feel different. And she couldn't touch the trees that were inches from her shoulder. She passed right through them like they weren't there.

It made her breath catch in her chest and she covered her mouth to keep in a terrified cry. What was happening her?

But her madness wasn't why she was in the hospital, no one else knew about that yet. It was the pain. Maybe she had a tumor that was sitting on her optical nerve causing the headaches and the hallucinations. Or maybe she was going crazy. There was no happy explanation for what was happening.

She didn't want to wake her dad and have to tell him why she was crying. She didn't want to be crazy. She also didn't want to see a forest every other blink. None of this was normal.

She studied her sleeping father as if the answers were somewhere on his face. George Lirdin looked tired, aged somehow. He'd always been a handsome man with fair hair and the face of a Disney prince but that pose of exhaustion made him look *other*. It reminded her instantly of how he had looked when her mother had died.

Empty. Vast. So far from her.

"Dad," Elinor said calling him back.

"Oh thank God!" he said waking in an instant and running forward to kiss her forehead and hold her hands. "Nurse!" he yelled without taking his eyes from her.

"How are you feeling?" he asked with furrowed brows.

"I don't know. But my head hurts so bad. How can my head hurt this bad?" she asked her dad, her voice coming out scared as tears instantly pooled. Her tears made her blink rapidly which sent her vision shifting from reality to madness so quickly it made her a little nauseous.

She thought for a moment about telling him what she saw when she blinked. The two of them were so close. After her mom had died, they'd been alone for a while and their bond had solidified into something deep and strong. But when she opened her mouth, she couldn't find the first word to start it. *Later,* she told herself cowardly.

"I don't know what's wrong but we'll figure it out. I promise, baby," he said pulling her into a hug.

"Oh Elinor!" her stepmom said entering the room, probably summoned by their talking. She had tears already rolling down her cheeks. "I'm so glad you are awake."

Rebecca Michaels-Lirdin had dark hair knotted in a messy bun at the back of her head and the stress bomb of having a child in the hospital made her look like she hadn't slept in a week.

When her stepmom's arms locked around Elinor. A peace settled over her. Being held by her made Elinor feel like everything *might* be okay. A mother's hug was a kind of temporary magic but then Elinor blinked and gasped. Trees everywhere.

She had forgotten for a moment.

"So what's the plan?" Elinor asked pulling back. She needed a plan. A plan would distract her. A plan would fix all of this.

"First, they want to do an MRI just to make sure everything is okay," her dad said. "Then they will also take a blood sample to check some things. They've got a long list of things they want to test for."

Elinor took a deep breath and felt calmed. She always felt more at peace when she could see the next several steps laid out like stones on a garden path. This one and then this one and then we will be there. She flipped through the medical knowledge that every future pre-med student obsessively amassed and wasn't happy with the diagnoses that came easily to mind. But she still had one more year of high school before pre-med. If she already knew everything then there would be no need to go. She let her ignorance be a comfort. Or she really tried to.

While her parents held her in a protective huddle, she heard her dad's soft spoken prayer into her hair about God being in control and asking for healing and wise doctors. And it helped ease the panic of the sepia woods to remember that her God was bigger than whatever else was going on.

The doctors said there was nothing wrong but when the headache still didn't go away, they told her she needed to stay the night. They also told her that she was probably having a migraine and that seemed to mean *something*. It meant something more than just a headache.

Maybe if the doctors knew about her switching forest vision it would help them cure her but the words kept getting stuck in her throat. There would just be no taking them back after they were out. It would change everything.

She'd known the madness was probably coming for her one day but she'd deluded herself that it was just a silly childhood fear, nothing substantial, nothing she'd needed to worry about. She wondered if being aware she was going mad meant there was still a little hope for herself.

Even though she had repeated that experiment a thousand times, Elinor was still so disappointed each time she saw the forest again. She was only seventeen. A wave of aloneness hit her hard and she was still deciding if she should tell the doctor about her madness when a young man walked through the sepia forest.

He just ambled along without noticing her. He had red hair to his shoulders and he was wearing some sort of leather clothing with a sword strapped to his waist. She guessed he was about twenty or so. He looked like handsome trouble. Was she sharing her delusions with someone else? If she was he wouldn't be such a bad companion. She blinked on accident and when she looked back at the forest he was gone.

Though she'd only seem seen the man for a moment, he set her resolve. She wasn't going to tell anyone about the trees. Seeing him, seeing anyone, in the forest made it feel real somehow. She knew it wasn't. It couldn't be, right? But it just didn't *feel* like a hallucination, whatever they felt like.

And if she was honest with herself, the other reason she didn't want to tell anyone was because she was so scared, scared that she was really and truly crazy. And if that was true, where was she supposed to go from there? Because craziness was a... *sensitive* topic in her family.

Her grandmother, her dad's mom, had gone crazy. She'd just lost all her marbles one day, the day her husband left. He'd walked out the door, barefoot, without a word and had never come back. He'd left his wallet, keys, and every pair of shoes.

Elinor's dad *hated* to talk about it. He'd been twelve at the time but the wound was nowhere near healed. She'd only seen one picture of her grandfather. Her grandmother had kept it on her nightstand at the care home she lived in before she had died a couple years ago.

Elinor had pieced most of the story together. Her dad had found his mother sobbing on the floor, crying that her husband was gone forever. He had wanted to call the police, to get everyone out looking for him. But his mother had been insistent. She had said no one would ever find him and they might as well not look.

The mystery had torn at her dad but he had had to start taking care of his mother instantly. She'd been unable to handle what her life was and she had retreated inside herself. She never made another lunch or went to another baseball game.

She was gone.

Elinor wondered if her father had ever really forgiven his mother for quitting on him. Maybe he had. He was a kind man with no traces of bitterness that she could see.

But... her dad always had a haunted look in his eyes when his parents come up in conversation. And Elinor knew while she contemplated her possible madness that she could never tell her father. She knew she didn't have what her grandmother had but this could just be her own unique strand of madness.

She slept peacefully through the night, the medicine they gave her was supposed to 'break' the migraine. It didn't but at least she felt rested.

She'd decided to put some makeup on as an outward defiance of her symptoms. If she looked better, she'd feel better. *Science.*

She blinked and saw the forest, which was especially unhelpful when she was pointing something at her eyeball. So she only blinked one eye so she could at least partly see what she was doing when she saw *it.*

Her eyes were different colors.

One was blue and one was green.

It wasn't a shocking difference and when she blinked her eyes to get a closer look she saw them change. The eye that was seeing the mirror was the normal blue her eyes always were but the eye seeing the forest was green. And they switched instantly when she blinked.

It is pretty cool, she thought grudgingly.

She spent a good ten minutes studying her eyes in the mirror as she sat on the sink counter. The eye that was seeing the forest was still her eye but there was a difference. There was a gold ring in the iris that mixed with the blue to make her eyes look green. Her other eye didn't have a gold ring.

It was fascinating.

It was proof. Proof of what, she didn't know. But it was evidence that something was really going on.

She stopped herself from calling her family in because it didn't actually prove anything. It was just another weird thing her body was doing. It was unexplainable. Maybe she was only imagining the yellow ring. She didn't think so but she ultimately decided to keep it to herself for now. She could always tell them later but she couldn't take it back.

All the tests came back inconclusive and Elinor was sent home after a thirty-six hour stay. Nothing was wrong that anyone could find but her head hadn't stopped hurting. They referred her to a neurologist which sounded scary. Maybe they suspected she was keeping a secret. She saw the forest man once more before she left the hospital. It had been just as fleeting but it held steady her resolve. Maybe she wasn't crazy... Maybe it was something *else*. If only she could find him, maybe he had some answers.

If my life was a book, Elinor thought, *this would be the part where my mentor finds me and tells me I'm the chosen one or at least that I'm a witch and I'll get to go to an awesome magic school. But real life is, alas, not like books. And this is my real life. I'm not imagining this.* Those thoughts were jarring.

This was all real and it was really happening to her. So it *had* to mean something then. *Right?*

She relived the previous week over and over in her mind. She kept hoping she'd find the trigger that started the pain and the hallucinations but nothing stuck out.

They had just moved to Waxhaw, North Carolina from Atlanta, Georgia on July third. Her parents had wanted the little ones to grow up around trees instead of the congestion of Atlanta. Her dad had found a job at a manufacturing plant and her stepmom found a job as a chef for a large catering company.

On the fourth of July they'd stopped their unpacking and went to the fireworks festival in downtown Waxhaw. Then the next day Elinor had gone on a walk in the forest behind her house with Katie and Colton and she'd broken. In an instant. In a moment. It didn't make sense. She just didn't know what had gone so horribly wrong. What was off with the woods behind her house? And why had it only broken her? Though surely it was just coincidence. Woods didn't attack people with madness and migraines.

Chapter 3

Ryan

Ryan Michaels looked over at his step-sister and had to take a deep breath to calm down.

This wasn't supposed to be her life.

Elinor looked absolutely pitiful. Seeing her in pain was torture for him. It had been two weeks since the hospital trip and Ryan had tried to spend as little time as possible at his summer internship in Raleigh. He wanted to be home.

Everyone was a mess.

Colton had dived off the deep end. Elinor was the greatest, most important puzzle he'd ever seen and he was obsessed with curing her. He currently had her neck bent over a foam pillow and her forehead strapped backwards so she was looking upside down at the far wall.

The ten-year old doctor wannabe scribbled in one of a seemingly endless supply of notebooks while he straightened his glasses like a little villain. Ryan would have laughed if it weren't so heartbreaking. Elinor tried every stupid migraine cure Colton found and he found many. Ryan was pretty sure that Elinor tried them mostly for Colton's sake.

Ryan wouldn't let himself hover. Their parents were doing enough for everyone. They were always touching her forehead as if migraines were a fever they just had to break. Katie was usually at Elinor's side holding her hands and shooting Elinor with the biggest puppy dog eyes the world had ever seen.

Elinor. Wasn't. Doing. Well.

He could see the trapped fear in her eyes. She needed peace. She was a strange first born/middle child mix who needed a surprising amount of alone time to function, to recharge. He couldn't give her that yet but he could get her close.

"Had enough attention for one day?" Ryan asked with a smile during one of the rare periods where they were the only two in the bonus room.

"Is this how you feel all the time?" she replied with a smile to match his.

"Yes," he sighed dramatically. "You were never meant for the pressure of a firstborn. It's a good thing I came along to help you out. Get up. We are going for a walk."

Ryan headed straight for the backyard and Elinor followed along cheerfully. They walked for a couple minutes in companionable silence.

"How are you really?" he asked.

"I don't know. Not super. It'll be better when school starts. When the machine of our family starts whirring again into routine. And it'll probably be better when I have my appointment with the neurologist next month. They will know what's wrong with my dumb head. When do you head back to Chapel Hill?"

"A couple days. But I'll be sure to come back for my fall break."

Elinor stopped walking and pointed to a tree ahead of them. "What is that?" she said turning her head to the right.

"What do you mean?" Ryan said trying to follow her finger. "That big tree? It's a little bigger than the ones around it, I guess. Oak tree? I don't know. Maybe we should have brought Colton. I bet he's got this whole forest charted."

"No, it's glowing. Don't you see?" She walked to the base of it and started to pull herself up to get a closer look.

"Okay. You are pushing your luck, nature girl. If I bring you back with a scratch, I'll never hear the end of it," he said as he climbed the tree in her stead. "What am I looking for exactly?"

"The pretty shiny area in-between the branches."

Ryan climbed up and stuck his head through the branches looking around. The small amount of sun that was able to filter through the leaves and branches made the light look dappled and dark, almost brown.

"Sure is pretty," Ryan said looking down at Elinor but he couldn't quite see her.

Elinor

"Ryan!" Elinor yelled tugging on his pant leg. He disappeared before her eyes. His torso was fading in and out as she blinked. He was saying something but she couldn't hear him. She tugged harder on his ankle and he climbed down. Elinor hugged him.

"What was that?" she said assessing him to make sure he was all in one piece.

"What was what?" he asked.

"You disappeared for a second. I couldn't see you from the waist up..." she trailed when she saw his face.

"El... I think you were just at a weird angle around the tree. I couldn't see you for a second either but here we are safe and sound. I think we should head back inside," he said grabbing her shoulder to herd her back to the house.

She took a last look over her shoulder watching the gold shimmering light between the branches. It was probably just light reflecting off something or maybe she had fully crossed over into crazy land.

"Hey El, maybe you should stay away from that tree, from these woods. Don't go messing around here when I'm not around," Ryan said.

"Yeah."

She had enough to worry about besides one real tree in a forest of hallucinatory trees. It was starting to feel like too much. There was a wrongness here. It was an easy promise to say she'd stay away.

Chapter 4

Derek

Derek paced the forest. His oldest least favorite pastime. He'd spent so many hours running the forests of Morland trying to find the way home and here he was looking for the way back. The irony was not lost on him.

This time though he was on the defensive. When Morland came calling, when destiny stabbed him in the back again and forced him back there, he would be ready. He was not a scared thirteen-year-old kid this time. No, when Morland came to get her pound of flesh she'd be facing a different creature.

He hadn't always been so concerned with going back. There had been times when he'd, almost, forgotten about his lost years. Moments when the possibility of his past catching up with him seemed laughable. It had taken him so long to get back that it seemed so unlikely that anyone would spend the effort to find him. Who would want him? He only ever made things worse.

But he knew better. His mother would not drop the case so easily. He had disappeared right in front of her, after all. She wasn't done with him yet and by now she would have guessed all he had done to stop her.

Their blood would surely be traced back to him.

So he paced the woods with two long knives strapped to his thighs, a rations bag on his back, and a mental map that he added to tree by tree each trip. Not like he'd recognize it. He hadn't when he'd tried to find it on the other side.

It had been a while since he'd walked the woods. But some piece of him was waking up. A part that he had hoped was gone forever was stirring. He hadn't slept in months and he had no idea why.

Not that he'd slept great since he'd been back. So often he dreamed of *her*, of wringing the life from her neck and watching as the Darkness receded and she was golden-eyed once again.

Free.

Free but dead. He unconsciously brought his hand to his side.

What had changed? What was wrong now? Maybe it was just him. It wasn't beyond the realm of possibility that his obsessive paranoia had transformed into delusions or schizophrenia. Maybe he was finally going crazy. He sighed. It might actually be a relief.

But the sunshine glowing through the tree branches was even able to chase away his darker thoughts. Who could wish for death or madness on such a bright, lovely day.

Elinor

"How is that?" her dad asked as he slid heavy dark curtains over the beautiful windows that looked out into the woods behind their house. Elinor smiled as the light was pushed back outside where it belonged. But no curtains could keep out the *other* woods, the imaginary hallucinatory ones that plagued her at every blink.

She stopped the sigh that wanted to escape and locked it down.

After months of this new life, she had to accept that there were only some things she could change. She needed to be grateful for the little reliefs. And her head *was* instantly better at the new darkness that the curtains provided. Light sensitivity was one of the worst parts of migraines.

"Lovely," Elinor said trying to smile but she wasn't sure it reached her eyes.

She had finally allowed her family to commence 'Bunkerization of the House' as Colton had named it. Elinor had fought it as long as she could. She hated that her migraines were changing her family but she had to admit that it made her life easier.

Every window was now barricaded with curtains.

Sun: 0 Elinor: 1

Then Elinor's eyes slid to the floor and she noticed bright white light leaking free from where the curtain didn't *quite* hit the ground. She eyed it like it was a spider but she decided to let it stay.

Sigh. Sun: 1 Elinor: 1

The living room didn't *have* to be blacked out completely, not like her room, which could trick anyone to what time of day it was.

"Sure is dark in here," Katie said biting the inside of her cheek as she looked around.

Elinor felt guilt slam down like an anchor. Maybe she could just never leave her room in the daytime and let the rest of the family have a sunny, bright house. *I'm a monster for making them live in the dark like this.*

"I'm sorry, Katie. Maybe we can…" Elinor started to say but Katie interrupted her with a tiny bear hug.

"Nope. We had a family meeting about 'Bunkerization' and we all decided that we love you more than the stupid sun that makes you head hurt worse," Katie said into Elinor's stomach.

"I love you, little bear," Elinor said kissing the top of Katie's head.

"I love you, medium-sized vampire," Katie said beaming up.

"Ha ha," Elinor said bringing her hands up to tickle Katie's neck.

"We should call it 'vampirization' instead," Katie giggled and squirmed away.

"You did not think of that on your own. Who is the culprit for poisoning my own sweet sister against me? Was it Ryan?" Elinor asked. Katie's silent mad-dash from the room was confirmation.

It was nice that Ryan wasn't forgetting Elinor while he was away at college but how he managed to annoy her from three hours away was a skill only given to older brothers. Elinor had the best family in the world. But even that couldn't fix her.

She felt the pain start to flair and she wondered if it was even worth it to turn the house into a bunker if the pain still came to life whenever it wanted. Elinor didn't make a sound or change her face as the pain roared to life because it was already an acquaintance if not yet an old friend. It felt like daggers and pulsing. It felt like pressure and tenderness. It felt like poison dripping through her veins. *I could write some really depressing poetry*, Elinor thought.

She headed to the kitchen for the supplies she'd need. One of the other new changes to their house was the freezer. It no longer held only frozen chicken breasts and popsicles. Now half of the shelves were dedicated to ice packs and some days it didn't seem like enough.

"Getting bad?" Colton asked as he ate one of said popsicles. His free hand reached across the table and magically pulled out a moleskin notebook, from somewhere.

"How many notebooks do you have about my migraines?" Elinor asked smiling. She tried to smile as much as she could. *Don't worry about me. See I'm smiling*. But her action of taking an armful of ice packs broke her cover.

"I have *enough* notebooks. That's how many," Colton said flipping it open. "Okay today is October nineteenth and it's two thirty-six p.m.," he said looking at his watch. "Did it just start now? That's curious because dad is bunkerizing the house. Hmm I should probably chart this under "Bunkerization" as well as the daily pain charts." He said pulling out a second notebook from seemingly nowhere but Elinor's mind was on other things than her little brother's sleight of hand.

Hearing the date sent a little jab through Elinor's heart. *October nineteenth.* Over three months of daily migraines that were well on their way to four.

October nineteenth.

She should have already had a month and a half at Cuthbertson High School. She should have been starting her senior year. Instead she'd spent that time in pain, in the dark, and alone.

She'd started homeschooling as a temporary measure until she got better. Temporary seemed on its way to becoming permanent. Elinor couldn't fall behind when Chapel Hill was so close. She had to get better. She had to be at the University of North Carolina Chapel Hill next fall. It was part of the plan: pre-med, then med school.

Colton was staring at her and Elinor realized she'd been silent for a moment so she made a joke to take the attention off of her building despair. *That's right, Middle Child. Repress and deflect,* she told herself.

"How old are you? You do know that most ten year olds don't get a thrill over charts and graphs? Are you Merlin living backwards? Are you Benjamin Buttoning?"

Colton rolled his eyes. He'd been an old soul since the day he had been born. He acted no more like a ten-year now than he had as a five-year old when he'd been five. She didn't know where he got his brains from. Ryan and herself were normal. So it must have been the combination of their parents that made such an amazing child.

"Okay bye," Elinor said kissing the top of his head as she headed to her room.

"Oh no, you don't," Colton said following her.

"I'll tell you all about it when I get up later."

"Just tell me the level," he called after her.

"Level eight," she said over her shoulder as she hurried to her room.

The hospital had recommended that she start keeping a pain journal, a daily number to express her pain level for the day. They said it would help her future doctors to understand what she was feeling and to notice patterns and changes.

Colton was completely on board with the idea, of course. He had charts printed and journals ready for her use and his study as soon as she was home. But Colton didn't just want numbers. He wanted to know what every level *felt* like. So Elinor obliged him. It had been surprisingly hard to write out an honest description but she'd done her best:

Level 0: This means no pain at all, I assume. I don't think this is a thing.

Level 1: There is a tingling sensation behind my eyes and at my temples. The phantom beginning of things to come. Because they are coming. My head never stays at Levels 1-3 for the whole day. It will dip down for a while sometimes but it always gets worse. I try to enjoy it while it lasts.

Level 2: Along with the tingling comes tiredness. A wave that comes and goes. My body is tired already and the show hasn't even started yet. But I can still do most things at this low level.

Level 3: Along with the tingling and the tiredness is neck soreness. It feels like I've done intense neck workouts or I have a weight around my shoulders. I turn my head from side to side and stretch like that will fix it. It will not.

Level 4: The pain is real. I can ignore it. I can still do things like reading but the pain is a program running in the background. It has started and it has brought its friend, nausea. It is subtle at first, almost confused with hunger but it'll differentiate itself soon enough.

Level 5: The soreness, pain, tiredness, and nausea are all walking hand in hand winding each other up.

Level 6: The pain is now its own creature. It has its own wants and needs. And it makes demands. It needs the curtains to be closed, smells to go away, and all sounds must be turned down. It will not negotiate or compromise.

Level 7: I can't ignore the pain easily. It doesn't help that I need to rest in between tasks. My batteries are so low that I constantly have to lay down with icepacks to recharge to be able to do another task. I can't read without making it worse. This might be the worst part!

Level 8: The pain cannot be ignored at all. I still try sometimes by listening to a movie or audiobook quietly in the dark but the pain pulls me out of it. The nausea has blossomed. It leaves me reeling and I try rocking from side to side to assuage it. I don't want to move, but I still could if there was a fire or something. But until then I'll just lay right here, maybe forever.

Level 9: It hurts a lot. Really. Pounding, pulsing. All consuming. Unavoidable. It can't be escaped.

Level 10: It's now at a level that I can't bear. I'm going to the hospital. It has to end now. They need to make it stop.

Elinor's migraine was currently a level eight. She often downplayed her symptoms but she always told the truth about what level it was even if her numbering system felt like a joke sometimes.

The visual record of her pain journal was supposed to be helpful and encouraging. But it was horrifying. It was one thing that Elinor just felt bad all the time but it was chilling to see the days of pain laid out side-by-side unceasingly. But she faithfully recorded her pain and hoped the doctors would see something in the numbers that she couldn't.

But even the charts and graphs didn't explain to her family and doctors what a migraine *really* felt like, how it made her feel. And she found she couldn't ever find the right words. It was sensitivity to light. It was pain all over her head. It was rolling nausea. It was so much more. But numbers were tangible. Numbers could be understood. And even if a number fell so short, it was a language they could all speak. But Elinor still felt sure that things were going to get better soon.

Anytime now.

But not *right* now. A level eight was a time bomb and she didn't have long to get in the dark.

Her room was dim with the door closed but the light at the bottom of the door was not allowed here so she slid the curtain installed just for that problem over the closed door and pure darkness caressed her eyes.

It felt better in the dark.

Elinor laid on her bed and opened her eyes into the cool icepack but the forest greeted her instead of the dark. And her despair, that had been building as the school year had started and she had stayed home, crashed down on her like a suffocating wave. Tears fell freely from her eyes and her vision cycled between a pitch black room and the stupid sepia forest. Most of the time she couldn't even think about the madness.

The migraine pain was consuming enough so she just tried to ignore her ever-switching vision, as best as she could anyway. She closed her eyes tight but the tears still found their way free. She clenched her fists as a prayer poured out in an intense whisper.

"Why God? It's already been three months. Please make the pain stop. I'm missing school. I'm missing everything. Please. Please. Oh God. It's all passing me by. I'm being left behind. Please. Hear me! Is there anyone who can help me?"

Peter

Derek stormed into the game store in an angry rush which was how he went everywhere. Peter Lawrence was really used to it. Being Derek's best friend was not unlike befriending a tiger. Tigers did sleep a lot and most of the time they didn't care enough to bother their human trainers but sometimes they tried to maul off their faces and eat their insides. Some days it did feel too high of a risk.

But Peter wasn't a normal person and his own issues had alienated more than one friend so he smiled at the angry red-head and said "Hey buddy. Did someone park in your favorite parking spot or murder your dog? It's really hard to tell."

Derek slammed his bag on the counter and pulled out his laptop. Peter just raised his eyebrows and went back to shelving the new Magic cards that had come in. Peter already had his booster box below the counter waiting for him. Thirty-six packs of cards were in that box and opening each one was like unwrapping a Wonka bar and looking for a golden ticket.

Peter had the best job ever. The game store where he worked, Game Night Every Night, sold board games, card games, figurines, comic books, movies, and every nerdy accessory that a guy could want to buy.

It hosted tournaments and meet ups. No matter the time of day or day of the week there were always people milling around. It was where *his* kind of people hung out: nerds, geeks, gamers. Peter couldn't have dreamed of a better place to work. It helped that his boss, Nick, was super laid back and that the store was the only place Peter was ever happy. So there wasn't a lot Derek could do that would upset Peter there.

"Need help with your homework?" Peter asked smiling bigger, poking a stick at the tiger.

"Did you think I wouldn't notice?" Derek said typing deliberately and aggressively loud on the keyboard of his laptop. Peter wondered how often he had to replace the keyboard.

"Notice what?" Peter asked but he already knew what it was. It could only be the one thing.

Derek turned the screen around and Peter sighed. *Yup, looks like we are gonna talk about this here. Awesome.*

"So I cleaned up your blog and made it easier to find. It's not a big deal," Peter said but he knew that it was.

Derek was super touchy about his blog and Peter got it. Being trapped on another world for five years was *some* people's idea of a nightmare. It wasn't Peter's. Getting away was one of Peter's favorite daydreams especially to somewhere *else*.

Peter had read *a lot* of fantasy and sci-fi novels before he'd met Derek but after finding out that there was actually another planet out there with life on it, and that it was a magic planet at that, Peter had been *all in*.

Maybe some of his favorite novels were about real places too!

Derek was not amused by this. Derek was not amused by much and Peter's fascination with Morland especially upset Derek. But Derek was a hypocrite. He had long ago crossed over into paranoia and obsession over Morland so Peter did not trouble himself over Derek's double standard. Peter had read Derek's blog many times and he did believe that it was true but he also knew that Derek hated everything so it was hard to trust his opinion on things.

Derek's blog was real and raw and awesome. It recorded, in often bloody details, the dark years Derek had spent trapped on the magic planet of Morland. His story had everything. A mage takes in a young boy. The boy grows up to be prince. But wait, the Queen is evil and becoming a prince was a trap! He can't find his way home. Oh no, his sister has embraced the Darkness. Maybe killing all his siblings will help. Maybe...Nope. Okay, maybe the mage knows a way home. He does! Hooray. Classic.

Peter had recently taken it upon himself to fix it. He'd really only fixed some grammar and changed the format. He just wanted it to look cool and legit. He hadn't planned on telling Derek. And he also was not going to tell him that he had started working on some illustrations to add to it. Nothing fancy, just some charts and graphs probably. And he'd probably self-publish it but Derek did not need to know any of that.

"It just looked so boring before," Peter said, "and it didn't even come up when you googled 'Morland'. How was anyone ever supposed to find it? Isn't that the point? That if someone wanted information on *that place* they could find your blog? And I thought you never read it so does it even matter what it looks like?"

Peter was pretty sure Derek read it at least once a month but Derek claimed he *never* did. Peter used to be able to tell by the spike in the views but now that it was easier to find and listed on a couple different sites, which Derek did not need to know about, Peter couldn't tell when Derek looked at it now.

"I've been reading it more often lately," Derek said. "I just... I don't know. But you had no right to mess with it. It's not your story!"

"What's not his story?" Nick said walking over, probably to make sure that Derek didn't inflict any harm to his store or employee. Nick was forty-years old, at least, with gray streaks in his brown hair and an awesome long beard.

"Working on some fanfic?" Nick said raising his eyebrows at Derek. "I hope it's raunchy. I bet it's a story about Hermione and Draco. Their secret love affair hidden under Harry and Ron's nose. I'd read that. I've read worse from these guys. I'm talking specifically to you, Jack," Nick said making eye contact with the shy, emo-looking kid who jumped in his seat and flushed.

"I'm sorry, kid," Nick continued, "but no one wants to read a story about an alternative universe where all the Avengers are dinosaurs."

"I'd read that," Peter said smiling at Jack but Nick, ignoring him, continued on, "See no one. But Jack, I did really like your short story about if sharks had a 'Human Week' every year where they studied and caught us. That was funny and clever. So what's your story about, Derek?"

"Nothing!" Derek said grabbing his laptop and moving to an empty table. Nick looked to Peter.

"It's fine, Nick," Peter said. "This one was probably, actually, my fault."

"It's usually not your fault?" Nick asked laughing.

"One time! I accidentally dropped a case of Mountain Dew and then forgot to tell you and suddenly everything is my fault," Peter said with a fake huff as he walked over to talk to Derek.

"I'm sorry, okay? I shouldn't have done it without asking," Peter told his best friend. "I didn't think it was that big of a deal." *Liar.*

Peter knew it would be a big deal. "It's not like I told anyone in real life about it. And everyone online thinks it's just a story. I can change it back if you really want."

"No. What does it matter?" Derek said.

"Well that's as close to a 'good job, Peter' as you are capable of and I'll take it. What's your deal lately? You've been super irritable and that is saying something."

Derek rolled his eyes, which was his equivalent of breathing, but then said, "Do you ever feel like something is coming for you or waiting for you?"

Peter knew what Derek was saying. Derek felt like Morland was coming for him. Had since the day he'd been back. Derek worried that somehow the Queen would find him and he'd be trapped there again. Peter answered Derek's question with a nod because Peter did worry that something was coming for him.

But Peter didn't worry about planets and evil queens coming to kidnap him. His worry was more tangible and took on the shape of his father and the shape of the bruises he left. Derek nodded back and dropped it. That was one of the reasons why they'd become and stayed friends. They just let each other be as damaged as they were. Neither tried to fix the other because it was impossible.

So Peter went back behind the counter and brought over his new booster box of Magic cards and let Derek open half. Friendship was weird.

Chapter 5

Elinor

Elinor lay in a tomb of ice packs and tried to hold onto herself. But she was losing herself slowly and in pieces. The forest had stolen so much from her. It was happening before her very eyes but she didn't know how to stop it.

It happened at doctor's offices and in the light.

It happened when the sun was shining and her siblings were laughing.

It happened when the school year started and she didn't.

It happened when one by one her friends trickled away from physical distance and misunderstandings, until it was just her family, herself, and the pain.

She lost herself when the migraines didn't stop. She admitted to herself that it felt better sometimes, for moments, for hours. But it was always just moments and it was never gone. It was every day. All the days of the week. All the weeks of the month. And the months were adding up. One constant migraine that ebbed and flowed like the tide. Building up and crashing down but never gone. Constant.

"We've seen a lot of doctors," her stepmom told the alternative health doctor at their first appointment with him.

This new doctor was a kind of chiropractor/eastern medicine/ physical therapist mix. Her stepmom did not pull her punches. She was a bulldog when it came to doctors. Her approach was to be direct and honest and see how the doctor responded.

Elinor wished she was more like her. Elinor liked to think she was becoming worldly and savvy of the medical field but mostly she was becoming bitter and it wasn't nearly the same thing. She had to start protecting herself, to lower her expectations, to prepare for failure as she waited to make them all liars. Elinor didn't tell her stepmom that but she was a smart woman and she too was becoming less trusting.

"And we are a little hesitant about trying alternative treatment but we are open to trying anything that will help Elinor with her migraines," her stepmom said.

"I appreciate your honesty. It's important that I understand where you are coming from," the doctor replied calmly with his notebook ready. "Are you hesitant as well, Elinor?"

Elinor nodded and said, "But I wouldn't be here if I wasn't hopeful, if a part of me didn't believe that you could help me. But it just hurts too much to give it more of my heart, if that makes sense."

He sighed a little and said, "I know you've seen a lot of doctors and specialists but I'm going to do my best to help you."

"Thank you," Elinor said.

"But you need to have a good attitude about this. If you are sending out bad vibes it will be your own fault when it doesn't work. I can only do so much and we can try my treatments but if you don't believe than I'll just be wasting my time."

Elinor watched her stepmom's face change. Her eyes narrowed and she smiled a cool dark smile. "Now that's a new one. I think we are done. Thank you for your *time*," she said nodding to Elinor as she stood to leave.

"Wait. What?" he asked incredulously.

"You are copping out already," her stepmom said. "You are giving up and blaming Elinor already. No, thank you. That's not supposed to happen till the end. So I guess thank you for your forthrightness? You've saved us a lot of time and money."

Elinor and the doctor both stood open-mouthed as Rebecca Michaels-Lirdin walked towards the door. She turned around to raise an eyebrow at Elinor who hurried to follow.

"Well that was frustrating!" her stepmom said exhaling as they got back into the car. "I'm sorry but that doctor was the worst. I can't believe his attitude. Lunch?" she said changing the subject but Elinor knew she'd be right back at that bone. They pulled into a little bistro down the street and as soon as the waiter brought them both a sweet tea her stepmom was back on the subject.

"I can't believe that guy," her stepmom said shaking her head as she pulled her dark hair free from its bun and then put it right back up. "I'm sorry if you wanted to stay but... He was just too frustrating. I mean his whole spiel about how if you have a bad attitude it's not his fault that his voodoo witch doctor treatment won't work. I mean..."

They were both surprised when tears fell suddenly and silently from Elinor's eyes. Elinor had thought that she was alone in her frustration and anger at doctors. Her stepmom was always so stoic and calm but today her shell had broken and it broke Elinor a little bit.

It was somehow harder when they were both disappointed and frustrated. Elinor realized how helpful it was when she was forced to put on a show that everything was fine because when she didn't have to pretend she apparently cried at restaurants in the middle of the day. *Great. This is a super awesome new development, Elinor. Way to keep everyone guessing.*

"I'm sorry," Elinor said unable to stop the flow of tears. She kept her eyes down. Elinor knew they must be changing colors like crazy while she cried, her eyes blinking between blue and green as she saw the forest. "I... I'm just having a hard time lately."

Her stepmom reached across the table to hold her hand, ignoring the waiter who awkwardly left a basket of bread at her elbow.

"What can we do to help you, El? I know it's hard. I wish I could fix you. I wish that so much, my girl. Your father and I pray for you every morning and every night. We'll find it. I promise. We aren't giving up. I love you so much." Elinor nodded but even knowing that she wasn't in it alone didn't stop the bitter taste in her mouth.

Over the next couple of months and the next doctor and then the next. Elinor felt her seed of bitterness growing slowly and steadily in the fertile soil of her pain. It had taken her awhile to realize that she had changed. She had trouble holding her temper and she suddenly saw only the worst in people. She was unappeasable and unpleasant to be around. But even being aware of it, she couldn't seem to change her attitude. It felt outside herself. She was just a victim of the circumstances.

One Saturday, Elinor was laying down on the couch in the bonus room with her eyes closed unable to even listen to music to stave off the boredom that came with the pain when Colton came in his excitement a palpable force.

"Okay, get up," he said tugging on her sleeve. "I've found these stretches that are supposed to help." Elinor opened her eyes and then closed them.

"Elinor!" Colton said. "Get up. Come on, lazy bones. Yoga will be good for you. These poses are just for migraines," he said shaking a piece of paper in front of her face.

She opened her eyes again and closed them again.

"You need to try these right now! What if this is the thing that will fix you and you are too lazy to even get up? You are giving up. You don't even want to get better do you?" he said as he started to storm out of the room.

"Wait," she whispered. With one hand holding her forehead and the other pushing off from the couch she said, "Let me see." He brought the paper over hesitantly. She saw that his eyes were rimmed with tears. She studied the papers to give him a moment to collect himself and to show him she did care about his efforts. His perseverance often helped her to keep going.

"Thanks. I'll try these a little later today, okay? Colton, I will never give up. I promise. Thanks for not giving up too." As she patted the side of his face, tears burst forth and his words were thwarted with hiccups.

"I'm… so…sorry. I didn't mean to yell at you. I-I know you don't feel good. I don't like making you feel even worse but I need to get my sister back. And this is all I can do. I can find anything out remember, you said I could discover the meaning of the universe if I wanted to. I'll keep looking, k?"

"Okay," she said pulling him close for a hug. "Everything is gonna be okay. I'm still here." She closed her eyes and took a deep shuddering breath, trying not to cry in front of him. His hope was so sweet and loving but it was also poison in her veins every time it didn't work. Because in trying to support Colton she would start to believe that this smoothie, exercise, or herb *would* fix her as promised. And then when it didn't she had to hide her own bitter disappointment and assuage his without crushing him. It was exhausting. But what else could she do?

In that moment, holding Colton, she came up with a goal for herself, a mantra she would repeat when the pain wanted to make her into an unfeeling monster. She would tell herself, *Let it make you kind. Let it make you kind and not bitter or mean.*

She was going to let it bear down on her like a river and allow it to smooth away all her rough edges. She wasn't going to let it break her or beat her. She would face it with a smile and let it make her kind. So Elinor just had to get used to the pain and visions and somehow she did.

She marveled at the human brain's ability and proclivity to make constant horrible things normal and commonplace. She adjusted to her headaches first. It helped that her family knew about them and were so helpful and understanding. And people had heard of migraines before.

The visions of the forest were isolating and terrifying. But somehow they became her new normal too. Three things kept her from diving off the deep end and completely losing whatever marbles she had left.

The first was the man in the woods. When she saw him it reminded her that she wasn't alone and that he was there with her somehow. She saw him almost every day usually just in quick snatches.

The second thing that helped was closing her eyes as often as possible. She was likely to do this with her migraines anyway but closing her eyes was like Schrodinger's cat. Her brain didn't know which reality she was seeing and so it went quiet. She wished she could just bite the bullet and live her life with her eyes closed. But those moments were enough. They charged her up and felt like a balm to her brain.

But she had to eventually open her eyes and that was her final trick to keeping sane. She found a super sketchy Russian website that sold intense moisturizing eye drops. Whatever was in them wasn't legal or available in the US but they made it where she was able to keep her eyes open for ten minutes straight without her eyes drying out. It was a small miracle because on her own she could never go more than a couple minutes. The eye drops meant that she only had to see the woods six times an hour. That was acceptable and it helped her keep her eyes a secret from her family. And she had nearly mastered the double blink.

She tried to always blink twice rapidly whenever the forest was due so she only had to see it for a second and then she was seeing Waxhaw again. It worked fairly well and all of her techniques combined made it where she could *just* make it. She thought she might just survive it. She only had to see the forest six times an hour.

She was reminded of a quote by Robert Louis Stevenson "Anyone can carry his burden, however heavy, until nightfall. Anyone can do his work, however hard, for one day. Anyone can live sweetly, patiently, lovingly, purely, till the sun goes down. And this is all that life really means."

Six times an hour. That was only one hundred and forty-four times a day minus all her sleeping hours. It was endurable. *Anything was endurable,* she told herself. If only the pain came only six times an hour.

But the months were stacking together into the shape of a year and she just needed a break. She had lost some of her softness and grace. She had lost her patience and her hope. She felt like an empty shell of herself, like a girl watching as her life flashed by unlived. She had to get out of it.

As one year of constant sorrowful pain came rolling around, she decided it was time for change. She had come to silent terms that the old Elinor was gone. Maybe not forever but at least for now. And she had to pull together the broken shambles and make a life out of it.

She couldn't live for a cure. She was tired of four days a week at a doctor's office. She needed to accept that this was her life. She wasn't going to die from it. It definitely wasn't the worst thing that could have happened. It was very far from it. She had the best family she could imagine. She had enough to eat and a roof over her head. She would live a long, long life.

She would not have classified herself as a particularly morbid person but that didn't stop her from burying herself, well, her old self or more aptly her once future self.

She held it in her hand. It only took up one piece of paper. She had taken a lighter and a spade not sure if she would rather be buried or cremated but as she reread it, she decided to let it burn. She had gotten the original idea from Vampire Diaries, the T.V. show, and when she first saw it she realized it was exactly what her soul needed, it was why she had been slowly dying inside.

On the show people were always dying or becoming vampires or hybrids or werewolves or whatever without their permission and they were obviously having a hard time adjusting to not being human anymore. So there became this tradition of saying goodbye to their old selves, to all the things their human selves would have done like have kids, die of old age and boring human stuff. It helped them have some closure. Once they were done, they could face this new world as their new selves. And Elinor hoped to do the same. *Fresh start.*

She held the paper containing herself.

"Elinor Marie Lirdin

She would have joined her brother at Chapel Hill this fall.

She would have been an amazing doctor.

She would have been able to leave home and live on her own.

She would have been a help to her parents and never be a burden.

She would have lived all her days in the bright sun.

She would have never had cause for despair or bitterness.

She would have done everything.

But she is gone with this paper, leaving behind the shredded broken leftovers. But those pieces live. And they will forget the other parts and form new dreams, lesser dreams. But enough to live on. It's okay those pieces are gone. I'll be okay. Unattainable, impossible dreams must be laid to rest or they will destroy everything.

Good Bye."

She flicked the lighter on and the paper spread with flames. She let them lick her fingers before she dropped it to the ground. Embers broke free and floated slower to the ground. And she thought the free embers were her. They weren't as big as the whole paper. But their bright pain and grace made them something special.

Later that night as she evaluated her new life, she decided that she would go to Central Piedmont Community College, the local school. It was far from her dreams of UNC Chapel Hill with Ryan and her career as a doctor. But it was starting something and she needed to be doing *something*.

And so a year and a day after it first started, Elinor announced at dinner that she was going to college. Katie spoke first.

"You can't leave." Tears were already filling her eyes.

"Honey," said her stepmom, "there would be no harm in waiting one more year. Dr. Booker said…"

"Oh and I'm going to take a doctor break. I can't live my life stuck here. I finished my senior year homeschooling and I did fine. And I'm not going away. I'm going to go to community college here, Central Piedmont. Just to try it, okay?" she said hating the sound of defeat in her voice.

Her dad spoke up next saying, "I think that's a great idea. You could do some of the classes online since you did so well this past year and maybe go a couple days to the Levine campus. I think it would help you to get out. You haven't had much of a chance to make friends since we moved here."

Elinor smiled. She was so glad he understood. She had been suffocating with the doctor's offices day after day. And she was so lonely for people her own age. Ryan was off at school, Colton was ten and Katie was only eight.

"What will you study?" Colton asked, whose envy was poorly hidden. He talked almost daily of everything he would study when he went to college.

"Something medical. Maybe medical assisting. I think. I'll need to do the general classes first no matter what I pick. So that's what I'll take this semester."

She couldn't look at anyone, especially her father. She had always wanted to be a doctor. Always. And then specialize in obstetrics, later maybe. She remembered holding Colton and Katie right after they had been born and she'd been shocked by the beauty and magic of birth. And that dream had been very painful to give up. She didn't want to see the look of heartache on her father's face.

Besides the constant pain, she could never be a surgeon now with her shifting forest vision. Even a nurse wasn't a great choice. She would still be around sharp instruments and given responsibility over sick people but she couldn't give up medicine completely.

"Sounds perfect," said her stepmom too brightly, dashing her eyes away too quickly. "This will be a great new start."

Maybe things would really change.

Chapter 6

Derek

It was starting again, fall semester and community college... Derek felt so old and so tired. With how time had messed with him by taking five years and yet also taking none, it had made him feel one hundred and nineteen instead of just nineteen. Or was it twenty-four?

What did it matter anyway? He was stuck here at community college. Waiting out the clock, waiting for it all to begin or end. It felt like things were never going to change and that shouldn't bother him but it did.

He just had to make it through another year. But that felt impossible. Just today then. He just had to keep his head down, try not to draw attention, and just make it through another day. Oh god, how many times had he said that in his life?

He leaned back for a moment and closed his eyes. It all just felt so pointless. He shook himself. Feelings were for fools. He was alive, wasn't he? He wasn't a child solider in an army for a dark queen anymore. He wasn't scared and alone and cold and hungry anymore. He needed to stop whining and be grateful, dammit!

There was absolutely nothing wrong with his life except himself, who he could hardly stand on the best days and wanted to murder on the self-pitying nostalgic days like today. His hand rose to his side, touching what was real. No scar, just a tattoo. Morland didn't deserve one second of his time. *She* didn't have any power over him anymore. So why did it feel like the Darkness was just out of sight, waiting for him?

Elinor

Elinor held her printed schedule in her hands. She knew it wasn't cool to have it out but she kept feeling the need to check the room numbers again. Her softly pounding head kept trying to distract her.

It wasn't too bad today, a level six, and she was determined to keep it from getting worse. *Like I have any control of it,* she thought rolling her eyes.

She had a full day of classes Monday, Wednesday, and Friday. Two before lunch and one after. And then one online class. How hard was that to remember? She sighed and took one last look at her sheet: ENG 111 Expository Writing: Room 1317: 9:30 a.m-10:20 a.m.

The campus was small, like a medium-sized high school. But her campus, the Levine, was not the main campus. That one was located in uptown Charlotte. That campus was bigger and probably felt more 'college' like, whatever that was. The Levine campus was shaped like an 'L'. It was three stories tall and was a mix of red brick and large rectangular windows. It looked like a modern museum inside with glass and sharp black lines. *It isn't Chapel Hill but...it is pretty,* she conceded.

She hadn't been paying much attention to the other students and when she looked up a guy was directly in front of her. She wasn't able to hold in her gasp. *Impossible.* She took a step back and he walked by unaware. Elinor stood staring because she'd know him anywhere.

He was the man she saw in the woods.

He had been standing right in front of her and he was walking into *her* class. She blinked. The forest was empty. He was in her real world. Could he move from one reality to another? She mechanically followed the other students into class. She looked for him to make sure he hadn't disappeared back into the woods but he really was there, sitting in the back row.

She studied him a moment. It was him but... he was different. His red hair was short and his face was clean-shaven. He was obviously wearing normal clothes without a sword. He looked a little younger but she was sure that he was the same man.

She wished she could sit next to him to study him all class but she admitted that would be weird. So she made herself sit in front of him to avoid the temptation altogether. She would use her time to think of what she was supposed to say to him, which as the minutes passed by proved to be an impossible task.

Elinor could not find a thing to say that didn't sound absurd.

Hello, stranger. I've been watching you in my imaginary forest and it's nice to meet you in-person. Creepy.

Hey, did you know that you have a medieval-looking doppelgänger that I see sometimes in a sepia forest? Stupid.

Hello, Did you know that you are proof I'm not crazy? Ugh

Hi, I bet you look really handsome with long hair. Want to know how I know that? Bleh.

Elinor tried to follow along with the teacher, an older woman, who attempted to rouse the class to engage but only succeeded in barely keeping them from complete apathy. But Elinor couldn't focus because the adrenaline rush of confirming that he was real and the mystery of it all was too much. The man from the forest was real and he was sitting in her class. She wasn't crazy. Well there was now a *chance* that she wasn't crazy. And she'd take it. She thought she must be vibrating with anticipation.

When the class was dismissed, Elinor was one of the first out the door. She wanted to be able to get him alone to say... something, something that would open up a conversation at least. She needed to talk to him. She might not be crazy after all. And with a big smile Elinor followed him down the hallway.

"Um, excuse me?" she called out after him, her stomach literally quivering. She didn't know his name because the sign-in sheet had started at the front of the room and had ended with him.

He turned around, looked her up and down, and then kept walking.

"Hey, can I talk to you for a second?" she asked catching up with him, mentally and physically shaking herself from his strange reaction.

"What? Are you lost? The stalker's support group is that way," he said as his eyes pierced her to the wall.

"What?" she said confused as she searched for the words.

"Ugh," he said rolling his eyes as wide as humanly possible as he spoke in a patronizing voice. "I don't like you. I don't want to go out with you. Get a life or better yet wait for a guy to ask you out. It's so unattractive. You aren't in high school anymore." And then he was gone and into another classroom before Elinor could blink.

Her mouth dropped open and her cheeks flushed crimson. She turned around and walked the other way, any way that was away from him.

What a jerk! she thought, *What a total and complete narcissistic idiot. Ask him out! Ha! Un-believable. What world does he live in?*

She huffed and pulled out her schedule. She had an excuse this time because every thought but rage and humiliation had fled from her brain.

HEA112 First Aid and CPR: Room 1320: 10:30 a.m-11:45 a.m.

She still had ten minutes before her next class so she stopped in the restroom. She looked at herself in the mirror and sighed.

Her face was as horribly red as she feared. She pressed her cold hands to her cheeks willing the color to fade as she cursed her pale skin. Elinor pulled her long blond hair into a bun to get it off her neck, took a couple deep drinks from her water bottle, and decided it would be best to wait it out in the bathroom until she looked like a normal person again.

Shaking her head, she couldn't really believe that had happened. She felt like Elizabeth Bennet at the ball. But *she* had only overheard the rude things said about herself. Elinor had heard it all to her face and had responded with nothing. Nothing! It was so frustrating. But Elinor could not compare *that* terror to Darcy. This red-headed stranger could have no secret heart of gold, she was sure.

Her next classroom was pretty full when she walked in with two minutes to spare. There were two open seats. One was next to a black-haired girl and the other was, of course, next to the stupid idiot boy from the woods. She chose the seat by the girl which was, so unfortunately, only an aisle away from him and even with her back to him she heard his snicker. *Lovely.*

But despite his antagonist presence she loved the class. The teacher was energetic and loved his subject. She successfully kept her eyes from wandering over to the boy, Derek. She learned his name because he answered just about every question. She grudgingly accepted that he was very handsome.

Not as handsome as he looked in the woods, she told herself.

But it could have just been the scowl and the murderous glint in his eyes. Everyone else had apparently taken heed because he was the only person without a partner.

She had lunch after that class which was nice. She needed a break. If he turned out to be in her next class she'd request a schedule change, Edward Cullen style.

The lunch area was small. There were only twenty-five odd tables, a Subway restaurant, and a bunch of vending machines.

A band was playing cool jazz music near the doors that led outside to the courtyard and it was low enough that it didn't worsen her headache which was a small miracle. She didn't have the courage to approach someone again so she ate alone and listened to the jazz band play.

Although she tried not to, she noticed Derek the moment he walked into the lunchroom. He sat at a table full of guys, which was shocking. How could he have so many friends? Maybe he wasn't horrible to them. Or maybe they didn't really know him.

Because there was something off about Derek.

She wondered if his friends noticed the *something different*. But maybe she couldn't see him impartially. She either saw the sword bearing man in the woods or the hard creature in front of her. Because there was nothing soft about Derek, not his chiseled cheekbones or the firm set of his mouth. He looked like a statue of a man, cold marble. But he breathed and he sneered at Elinor's attention before turning back around to his friends.

Her last class was Sociology and she thanked God that Derek wasn't in it. She'd take even the small blessings. The class went quickly enough and she was homebound. She hadn't been assigned any homework so she had nothing to keep her mind from that stupid boy.

Tuesday was a blessed relief from school. She started her online class. When she looked over her college experience so far, she was more than a little relieved that the workload would be doable, if not easy. The syllabi painted a steady pace and few really large projects. And if her head started to get bad while she was on campus then it was really nice knowing her next day would be at home so she could recover. It. Just. Might. Work.

She had worried if she'd be okay to drive everyday with her vision but she had practiced the double blink all summer. She limited her driving even though she felt like she could do it safely. She always gave it her full one hundred percent attention. No talking on the phone or texting. And no music. That was surely acceptable.

She reasoned that she was probably the safest teenage driver in town. She really only lost her sight for a second, which was the same as sneezing or slow blinking. She did wish a little bit that she could take the bus like she used to do in Atlanta. But they didn't have college buses here and the nearest city bus stop to her house was seven miles away. And school was only eleven miles away so it wasn't worth it.

As the day waned, her curiosity grew and grew, unchecked in the stillness. It was an insatiable need to just know what was going on. The mystery of seeing Derek was building into too much pressure. Who was he? Was Derek the same person as the man in the forest? Was the forest man his ancestor or descendant? Was he from another reality? Was magic involved or science? The questions pounded unanswered in her mind.

Elinor decided that it had to be the past. It was the only thing that made a little bit of sense. Some crazy time machine gift had let her see the past with Derek's near identical ancestor. Or the far future. Or his twin? Her head felt like it might explode.

What did it all matter? This was the least useful magic gift she could think of. So she could see the past or future or parallel universe but she couldn't interact with it. And it seemed its only occupant was Derek's doppelgänger. What a dumb power to have.

Chapter 7

Elinor

"You didn't have to come home just to check on me," Elinor said as Ryan unloaded his bag in Colton's room.

"What are you talking about? I came to pick up a book. I've really been needing to read..." he said scanning Colton's shelves and pulling one book down at random. "*Taber's Cyclopedic Medical Dictionary*. What is this kid reading? I think he's the only one of us that's actually in college."

Elinor wasn't put off. "I'm fine, Ryan."

"I know you are. But I just wanted to check with my own eyes. And I've been having trouble getting back into the swing of things. I'm still recovering from having to clean out the basement of the previous tenant's junk."

"Are you really still complaining about that?" her stepmom said as she came into the room. "I didn't realize I had raised such a delicate son."

"It was really dark and nasty down there. I got bit by like a million no-see-ums. Look at this nasty cut," he said showing them a deep cut on his elbow. "And I'm pretty sure I still haven't gotten all the spiders out of my hair," he said smiling before shaking his head at both of them.

That night the kids went out back to the screened-in patio for their poker game. It had become routine for whenever Ryan came home. He had taught everyone the game a year ago and now they had a fancy tabletop and chip set. It amused Elinor to no end how they each won pretty evenly and played so different.

Colton was pure psychology. He studied everyone and everything. If there was no chance involved he would always win.

Katie was a sly little fox. She always looked like she had something up her sleeve, which made her impossible to read. This drove Colton crazy because she had no discernible tells. She was simply loving every second of the sibling bonding and the cards she received in her hand made no impact on her enjoyment of the evening.

Elinor knew she was a bit of a mess. She was unstoppable some nights and others she was out of the game in an hour.

Ryan was good. He played more than the three of them combined. And it had become almost instinct to him.

But as different as they played, the time was theirs.

And it was precious.

It meant the world to the little ones that Ryan still made an effort to hang out with them, letting all pretenses down and pretending crunchy cheese puffs were cigars just like they were doing. Elinor would be lying if she didn't admit that it meant a lot to her as well. He had moved on to college and was living his perfect life. Everything was going according to his plan. But he hadn't allowed her to be left behind. He had always been the one to push her to test her headache limits and remind her to live her life.

Colton and Katie headed to bed after a couple hours. The game had gone to Ryan and he had won the pot, which was only ever four dollars. Elinor and Ryan stayed outside, watching the white Christmas lights sway in the strong wind. Katie had commissioned they be hung inside the screened-in patio months ago and the effect was so nice they stayed up all year long.

"What's going on?" Ryan asked her after a couple minutes.

She just looked at him. "I could ask you the same question."

He sighed, "Fine. I'll go first but that doesn't mean you won't have a turn."

"I hope you've been getting into lots of trouble because I need some heat taken off me."

"Yep. Loads of trouble, just for you."

"You are the best older brother I have."

"Anything for you. But as a tip, maybe stop passing out in the woods from horrible migraines, it's kind of a cry for attention, middle child."

"One time…" she said rolling her eyes. "Never live it down." She turned to look at him, eyebrows raised expectantly.

"Okay, okay," he said. "I'm not sure what it is. Maybe it's just a junior slump or something. I just feel tired and aimless. I still like my major. Political Science has always felt right for me. It has gotten more challenging since I've gotten through the general education stuff. But I enjoy it. So I don't know. I just feel off. I sure wish you were there with me."

She smiled sadly.

"You wouldn't have hung out with a lowly freshie anyway," she said.

"You're right. It would have totally blown my cool. So really it's all worked out for the best," he said with mischief in his eyes.

She threw the box of cards at him.

"You are up, Miss Lirdin," he said giving her the imaginary floor.

"Okay, Mr. Michaels," she said playing along. When she didn't speak right away he sat back waiting.

"It's not that the work is too hard. I mean it's only been one week. In one of my classes it feels like we are still just reading the syllabus," Elinor said.

"Is it your head then?" he asked.

"Yes and no. It's been bearable so far. It's more the dead dream that's the problem. I know. I know," she said raising her hand to stop his popular mantra that her migraines didn't have to define her and that they would end one day but she needed to start living now.

"But there is a thing called realistic expectations. You may have heard of them. And I've adopted them so I can do *something*. Because I can't do all those other things. I'm not at Chapel Hill with you. I'm not starting premed. I'm at a community college taking pre-reqs for some medical degree like assisting or office administration.

"Most of the time I'm grateful I can just be in class. Grateful for whatever path my life ends up taking. But sometimes the bitterness is so bad I can hardly breathe. I'm working on it. I really am. I feel this constant cycle of fury that everyone my age is doing what they want, followed by forgiving myself for my limitations, and forgiving God for not healing me when I know He could. Don't look at me like that," she said seeing his pity and sad puppy dog eyes. At times like this it was so obvious where Katie learned the look.

"This is why I don't talk to them about it," she said pointing to the house. "You wanted to know." She breathed out heavily trying not to cry. "I'll be fine. It has gotten easier, being in college. I feel like I have a path. Homeschooling was fine. It served the purpose of getting me a GED but it was easier to feel sad. It feels like I'm finally back on track. I have no idea where the track is going but I'm optimistic. Just optimistic enough," she said with raised eyebrows. "Your unattainable dreams for me will kill me, Ryan. I have to have low expectations and just be grateful... I can see in your eyes that you disagree."

Ryan had been pushing her since her migraines had first started. He kept trying to make her do the things she used to do. He encouraged her to read as voraciously as she used to and to go out and make new friends. He tried to get her to go on hikes and stay up late. His was a totally different approach than everyone else in the family. But she just couldn't do what she used to do. She tried but all those things she used to do tried to kill her now.

Then after a while, Elinor had started to fight him on it and she knew he didn't understand why.

She wished he knew about her forest visions. She thought about telling him a million times. But he would tell their parents and he definitely wouldn't believe her. Ryan didn't like Harry Potter. He didn't like any novels actually. He didn't secretly wish he was magic or the chosen one. And if Elinor told him that whenever she blinked she saw a magic-looking forest, he would be quick to 'get her the help she needed'. So Elinor stayed quiet again. But she was glad she'd spoken her mind about the other stuff.

"You think I can do anything if I try but Ryan..." she said tearing up finally. "I really can't. Maybe someday. But I've explored the depth and width of my limits and it's not very big. I'm struggling here and you keep tossing me a life jacket and instead I feel like it's weighing me down. I know you only mean well."

Ryan

He took a minute to steady himself.

He felt like she'd dropped a nuke on him. Ryan really thought he'd been doing the right thing. Everyone else was babying her to death and she had needed him to push her but he'd obviously gone too far. He didn't really have any idea of the depth of her pain. Colton and Katie kept him informed in their own ways. Colton sent him charts and status updates and Katie sent vague yet helpful texts like "She looks like she's under a cloud today" or "There is no sparkle in her eyes."

But he wasn't around all the time and he couldn't know. He didn't think anyone in his family really got it because she was so darn good at locking it down. He knew she was protecting everyone, and that she really hated complaining. But he wondered if she was more honest, like she was tonight, if it wouldn't help the rest of them know how to help her better.

"I'm sorry, El," he said after a minute. "I only wanted to push you out of that hole you'd fallen into. But I get it. I was putting my own expectations on you just like the rest of the family. I do think that we could find a way to help you be whatever you want but I support the plan you are on now. You are starting slow and getting the hang of things. Colton showed me a video from a headache specialist and one of the things he said was that you have to keep living your life. You have to find ways to be in the world and do things even if it's hard. I'm sorry if I've been too pushy. I can't help but dream for you but I'll try to tone it down. I know you are going to have a great life," Ryan said.

He loved his stepsister like they were flesh and blood. They had had an instant camaraderie and connection when they'd met as kids. Ryan had hated being an only child and it had become unbearable after his dad had left. When his mom had started dating again he'd hoped that it would be to a guy with a kid. Elinor and he had been an unstoppable duo of trouble and fun until the little ones came.

Katie and Colton had made them grow up a little bit but only in a good way. *The bigger the better*, Ryan had thought. He loved being the oldest of their pack. They looked up to him and he protected them. And so it killed him that there was absolutely nothing he could do to fix this. He mentally decided to visit home more often. Maybe he was the only one she could talk to.

"It's okay," she said. "I'm sorry I dumped all those feelings on you. Thanks though. I'm glad you came home." So was he.

Chapter 8

Elinor

Elinor needed to find a way to make it go away. It seemed like every other thought she had was a begging, pleading prayer. *Please God. Please. Make it stop, all of it. You are all powerful and You could make it go away if you want. So why not? Please. Please God.*

If at least one of the horrible things would go away it would be bearable. If she had just her headaches she could totally live with that and if she had just her forest vision that would be bearable. But both... It was just too much. Too many unbearable things. It was getting harder to hold on.

The next week Elinor decided to make it her mission to figure out what was broken in her brain. She was going to find someone to talk to about her ability. This Derek kid was *the* worst. He was clearly not the right choice. She ignored him in her first two classes but tried to be casual about it like she wasn't doing it on purpose.

At lunch she studied the room. Who could really help her? What kind of person had the kind of skills or knowledge she needed? A teacher? No, they might be just as bad as a doctor.

She needed someone like Giles from *Buffy the Vampire Slayer*. He knew everything about supernatural magic stuff and could find the answer to any problem in his endless mountain of books. But she probably needed someone that wasn't fictional. She was distracted from her musing by shouting at Derek's table. Surprisingly it wasn't centered on how Derek was a horrible human. It was between two other guys.

"You are such a cheat, Peter! No way you got all that mana fairly just as you needed it. I'm never playing magic with you again!" yelled a muscular guy to a tall thin guy.

The boy being yelled at, Peter, laughed like they were joking. His smile made his glasses rise up on his nose. He had blond hair that fell in a curly mess around his face almost hiding his blue eyes. He looked... nice. He was handsome in a soft way. The kind of handsome that was missed with a too-quick glance. He didn't stand out in a crowd.

"I am the magic master," Peter said. "None can beat me. Plus, you just don't really get all the rules. Magic is more rules than actual game, Jerry." He then gathered all his cards together still chuckling to himself.

Elinor had found her man. Who better than the 'magic master'? She watched Peter for a couple more days. Now that she was looking for him she found out he was in her Sociology class.

Outside of class he was always doing different geeky things: cards, board games, comics, novels. One day he spent all lunch watching his favorite Lord of the Rings scenes on his laptop. He was perfect. He would know enough about magic and other worlds.

And there was no way, she told herself, that the same thing would happen as the last time she had approached a guy. She decided she'd talk to him Friday at lunch. Derek didn't usually stay the whole time, so that would make it a million trillion times easier. Then she'd just have to get him away from the rest of his friends.

Peter

Jerry ended his turn without attacking which was strange because Peter didn't have a flying creature to block his attack and it would have been an easy three points. But then Peter realized why Jerry had done it and Peter became distracted as well.

There was a beautiful girl walking straight towards them. Peter didn't know her name but she was in his Sociology class. Maybe she was lost. Maybe she would turn around. But she didn't. She was staring directly at him. He should've looked away but he just studied her as she walked up. She was really pretty with long golden blonde hair loose at her back. She was wearing a jean jacket that was covered in patches and a sundress that settles above her knees... he made his eyes quickly travel back up to her face as she walked over.

"Peter?" she asked when she got close, very close and with her came the faint hint of lavender and mint.

"You know my name," he said. When she just stared at him in reply, he realized that wasn't the smoothest thing he could have said.

"Can we talk for a minute?" she asked. He brought his hand casually to his chin to make sure his mouth was closed.

"Yeah," he said standing up.

"Hey! Wait a minute. Peter, we're in the middle of a game," Jerry said in protest. It seemed his voice had returned to him now that the female was only interested in one of them. Jerry stood up trying to intimidate the girl but she just raised her eyebrows and led the way to the outdoor patio area.

"Jack, fill in for me, k?" Peter said as he followed the pretty girl outside.

After she sat down at a table in the empty courtyard, she said "Thanks. I'm sorry to take you away from your game."

"No. No. Don't worry about it. We play every day. It won't kill Jerry if I leave this once."

He suddenly regretted admitting to playing it *every* day. But she must have seen him around. No point trying to be someone else this late in the game.

"So umm..." she said as she scratched her head and then ran her fingers through her hair to smooth it down. "This is harder than I thought it would be..." she laughed nervously.

Peter tried not to smile but it made him feel really good that she was just as awkward and uncomfortable as he was. *And she looks really cute all nervous.*

"Well, let's start with your name? I've seen you around and you know who I am," Peter said coolly. He was so impressed with himself for taking the initiative. He even leaned back in his chair, a little.

"Oh. I'm sorry. I'm Elinor Lirdin," she said extending her hand.

"Peter Lawrence," he said shaking it.

"I have a couple classes with your friend, Derek. And *we* are in Sociology together," Elinor said.

Oh. Peter thought sighing a little bit. *That's what this was about.* She has a crush on Derek and wanted him to smooth it over.

"If you're interested in dating him you should just talk to him yourself," Peter said looking at his shoes.

"Mfffh," Elinor said with wide eyes. Peter leaned forward, worried. He couldn't tell if she coughed or almost threw up.

"Oh goodness. No," she said quickly. Then repeated firmly. "No. It's not like that at all. He's kind of a big jerk. No, I wanted to talk to you about something."

Peter pulled his head back to re-examine the strange specimen in front of him.

"What about?" he asked.

She rubbed her forehead.

"Magic," she said staring him straight in the eyes.

"Magic?" he asked with raised eyebrows. "We could have talked inside then. It'll be much easier to explain with the cards in front of us. But basically..." he said but she raised her hand to stop him.

"No, I mean *real magic*," she said looking sheepish.

"Is this some kind of joke?" He looked around for whoever had put her up to it, probably Carlos.

"No. Please, I need your help. Do you believe that there is real magic? That there is more than just the four walls of this world? That there is more than what the average person can see?" She leaned forward, her eyes wide and unblinking.

He couldn't doubt her sincerity. She really wanted to know. No, it looked like she needed to know.

"Really?" he said. "Okay."

Now he was the one scratching his head, thinking. After a couple seconds he said, "Okay, so it sounds like you are talking alternate realities, dimensions, or like other worlds. Hypothetically there could be infinite parallel universes with all our different choices, with all of history happening at once, things like that. There are lots of theories about how at times the walls between the dimensions are thinned and if one had the right kind of force you could, say, *melt* through to the other side. But that is only theoretical. That kind of stuff probably isn't *real*."

"Okay so that's possible," she said ignoring his qualifiers. "What about, like, magic abilities or powers?"

Peter was just floored at how this conversation was going. Never in a million years would he have thought...

"Okay, that's a really broad subject. I mean we've got man-made abilities: Captain America or the Hulk. Stuff like that. Then we've got natural talents: being a wizard, stuff you are born with like being a mutant. Then there are alien powers: Green Lantern, Superman. And then literally a million more things. I just don't know what you want to know about specifically..."

Elinor stared him in the eye for a solid couple of seconds before she said. "I ask because... I..." She looked down at the table and then pulled her eyes up look at him as she said, "because I have an ability."

"What?" Peter said unable to hide the skepticism in his look and voice. "Are you sure you aren't messing with me?"

"I really, really wish I was," she said as a single tear began to fall from her eyes.

She wiped it away hurriedly. When she blinked a couple times, Peter jerked back in surprise. If they hadn't been having the conversation they were having and if he hadn't had his attention drawn to her eyes he never would have noticed when her eyes subtly changed back and forth from blue to green as she wiped her tears.

"Oh God," he said staring at her. "I saw it. I saw you. I saw your eyes." He brought his hands to his temples. "I can't believe it. I can't believe it. Get out of here!" he said.

Elinor rose to leave. "Well thanks for listening. Sorry to take you from your game."

"What?" he said grabbing her arm. "Where are you going? This is the greatest day of my life. Sit back down. We've got a lot to talk about."

Elinor

Elinor never imagined things going as well as they did with Peter. He was so excited and he believed her from the very start. She had made the right choice. She let herself smile as he rambled on about the *possibilities*. He was writing in his notebook only glancing at her for a moment before scribbling away again like mad. She caught a vision of what a future Colton might act like.

"Slow down," she said reaching over to tap his arm. He looked like he'd been shocked, his eyes going straight to her hand. She pulled it back quickly. She chided herself. She shouldn't flirt with him, even on accident. She couldn't even think about liking any boy with her head in a constant vice and madness on the fringe.

"So when you blink?" Peter said looking up from his writing.

"Yes. Every time I blink my eyes change color and I see a forest."

"What kind of forest?"

"It's sepia-colored and it just looks like a normal forest with trees and stuff. I think I'm seeing a forest from another time or place."

Peter eyes bulged and his smile went all the way up.

"Whoa," he said. "That's really cool."

"That's one word for it," she said smiling in spite of herself. But even the revelation that she was seeing some kind of enchanted forest didn't stop his rapid questions and notes. This guy was unshakeable.

"How long has it been going on? Were you born like this?"

"No. It's been a year. It started all of the sudden like being struck by lighting. And my headaches started the same time." Peter was slowly filling his notebook and a thought suddenly hit her. "You aren't going to tell anyone are you? Or show anyone that notebook?"

He looked up smiling. Peter was usually smiling she discovered quickly. "No. Not unless you tell me to. I'm a good secret keeper. Although, Derek would be very interested to know this. He's always looking for magic things."

"Ugh. No way. I already tried to talk to him."

At Peter's surprised expression she added, "I didn't get two words out before he verbally abused me in the hallways. Berating me for trying to ask him out and telling me I was unattractive. To set the record straight with someone, I was not trying to ask him out. Ew. I only managed to say, 'Hi, excuse me. Can I talk to you?' Terrible, terrible mistake," she said shaking her head.

"Why would you want to talk to Derek about this?" Peter said looking almost hurt. They'd been friends for a total of twenty minutes and he was already staking his claim. She would have smiled but she still hadn't told him the other part.

"Oh, well I guess I didn't explain everything yet." His face fell. "Come on, Peter! It's not like that. The thing is that sometimes when I blink and I'm looking at the forest, I see someone. Just walking around. It wasn't someone I'd ever seen before until... I know it's crazy. Well it's gonna sounds crazier than what I've said so far. But it's Derek I see in the woods. He looks different though. Longer hair. Old looking clothes. He has a sword at his side. Sometimes it's like he can see me looking at him but he usually just walks off." Peter was looking at her with eyes as wide as saucers.

"That's how I felt," she laughed. "When I saw Derek on the first day of school, my heart stopped. He was the man I'd been seeing in the forest. But it's like it's his twin or something. They are the same person but so different. I don't know. Maybe I'd seen him before and my brain attached onto him as the subject of my delusions. I don't know," she said leaning back, looking at the sky. Peter remained quiet and she looked back to him. His face was pale and he looked drawn out.

"What it is?" she said reaching out for his hand. She pulled back. Why couldn't she stop touching him?

"Elinor," he said quietly, "I know what you are seeing."

Peter

Derek was going to freak out.

He was going to lose his lid.

He was going to burn the whole city to the ground.

Elinor could see Morland. How? How? How? His mind was processing the different paths from here. How to manage Derek. What this ability could mean. How this could have happened. Peter made himself take a deep breath. He ran his fingers through his hair.

"What do you mean?" she asked.

Peter wished he hadn't spoken. He couldn't tell her about Derek. Not yet. It was going to be bad when he did. And she was so sweet. He just needed time to sort it all out.

"Oh," he said stalling for time. "I think your situation is starting to seem familiar that's all. It reminds me of something I read. I'll have to find it and see if it really has anything to do with all this." He started to gather his things. "Hey, why did you come to me with this? Was it because I know Derek?" he asked, hoping she said no.

"No. Your knowing Derek was a big minus. It was a lot of little things, I guess. You seemed to know the most about things like this." She blushed a little before she said. "You were always doing some different geeky thing. I don't mean that in a bad way. But I just hoped that would mean you would at least be open to the idea and maybe you might have even heard of something like this before."

"I can't say it's exactly my field of expertise. I'm planning on majoring in computer science."

"Wow. That's cool. I know nothing about any of that," she said.

"I don't know everything. Not half as much as Derek probably."

"Is he studying computer science, too?"

Peter laughed a little and stopped himself. She wouldn't understand why that question was funny.

"No. He's not. He's just always had a knack for it but he wouldn't major in it. He'd say it's not practical," Peter said trying to find a veiled way to answer without lying. What Derek meant by 'not practical' was that it would be useless in Morland. Morland was the filter he used to view everything.

Derek hated Morland more than anything in existence but he had this dogged certainty that he was going back. That something was going to pull him back. That they had a trap laid. But for all Peter knew, maybe they were coming for him. Maybe there was a trap laid. He didn't fight Derek on it.

"He's studying nursing. Or taking his pre-reqs. I'm not sure that he'll apply to the program. But he's interested in medicine. So who else have you told?" Peter asked pulling the conversation back.

"You are the first," she said.

The first? I'm the first person she's told. That thought settled deep inside him. It felt lucky and heavy. Something about his face made people tell him their darkest secrets. But he was very grateful for it today.

"Why haven't you told anyone before me? Like your parents? It's been over a year, right?" he asked. "I mean wouldn't they have noticed your eyes? It's pretty crazy when they switch."

She was silent for a moment and he worried he'd gone too far. They'd only known each other for an afternoon.

"I work really hard to keep my eye changing a secret from them. And really it's not as drastic if you aren't looking for it. And even with my eyes how could they ever believe me? I know you do a little but... It's not a hallucination. It's not a side effect of some medicine or something. I'm not crazy. It's real..." she looked down for a minute, as she closed her eyes and took a deep breath. "But I'm so scared it isn't. My grandmother went crazy. No, no magic. She couldn't see a forest when she blinked," she said raising her hand to answer the question his eyes were asking.

"She went regular people crazy. She went the kind of crazy that makes you fade away. My grandfather left her and it was like suddenly no one was home. She was an empty shell, unable to really function. My dad had to put her in a home when he went to college. So I didn't tell my family partly because that pain is still very real and very present. And partly because of seeing the other Derek. I knew there had to be something to that. I don't know that I could have convinced myself that I was sane if I only ever saw an empty forest."

"This is fascinating. I'm so glad you came to me. But we should probably head out if we are going to make it to class," he said zipping his bag closed.

"Thank you, Peter," she said standing as well. "I can't tell you what this means to me. To have someone to talk to. To have someone believe me. It's like I can breathe again."

Oh great, no pressure, he thought. He was between a rock and a hard place. He hated to keep anything from her but he owed it to Derek to keep his secret.

"You're welcome. It's been very illuminating for me. I've got, um, a lot to think about."

She smiled up at him. There had to be a way to help her and not betray Derek. Then an idea struck him.

"Hey, we are all going to a movie tonight. Would you want to come?"

If Derek got to know her it might be easier to breach the topic.

"Really?" she said her face literally beaming and guilt slammed down on him for his ulterior motives and didn't ease as she added, "It's been so long since I've been out. What time?"

"Uh I think it's a nine thirty showing. Is that too late for you?"

"No, it's fine. It's Friday night. Awesome," she said turning to head back inside. "Thanks again, Peter. I'll see you tonight. Oh but I'll see you in class. Bye."

"Yeah. See you."

It's going to be fine, he told himself.

So what Elinor was seeing Morland? No big deal. There were probably tons of people who could see distant planets every time they blinked. It was statistically a guarantee that Elinor was seeing the only magic place he knew was real.

Peter sighed. He wasn't convinced. It was a really horrible coincidence.

He pulled up his laptop and started to skim Derek's blog. Maybe it wouldn't be so bad. Derek still had some good in him. He'd seen it. But as he scanned the familiar sections, he felt less and less certain. He closed the laptop and went to class. It was probably all going to end poorly.

Chapter 9

Elinor

"Some friends asked me to a movie tonight," Elinor said trying to downplay her smile as she looked at her stepmom across the kitchen. *Be cool, Elinor.*

"Are you going to go?" her stepmom asked.

"Yeah, I'm kind of excited to go out."

"Is there anyone *special* going?"

"Ugh. No, mom. Just some guys. Who are *just* friends."

"Which theater are you going to?" her stepmom asked.

"Stonecrest on Rea Road," Elinor said.

"Are you okay to drive so far? I mean it's thirty minutes," her stepmom said. Elinor smiled. *Everything* was almost thirty minutes away from Waxhaw. Waxhaw was nestled south of Charlotte and conveniently far away from everything but trees.

"How are you feeling? Do you want us to drive you? We don't mind picking you up," her stepmom said then looking down at her watch she added "even if it's late."

"No, I'm fine. I mean I'm normal for me," Elinor raised her hand before her stepmom could protest. "And I'll call if I need you to come get me."

"What are you going to see?" Colton asked walking into the kitchen.

"I'm not sure," she said pulling her phone out to read Peter's confirmation text. "It's called... *The Blood Bomb.* Eh."

"Sounds really great," Colton said sarcastically shaking his head. "Are all your friends boys?"

"Yes," she mumbled. "Maybe I'll get to pick the movie next time."

The movie theater was slowly becoming unpacked when Elinor pulled up. She was glad because trucks had had to park on medians and grassy slopes because of how full it had been. But it was getting late and the seven p.m. movies were slowly emptying out. Even in autumn, the whole shopping center was lit with Christmas lights at the top of the buildings and around the trees. It was really pretty.

Elinor got there early and waited in the car. She didn't mind being a little early. The butterflies in her stomach were going crazy and she wanted to give them time to settle. She hadn't been out with people who weren't her family in ages. She actually hadn't been out somewhere that wasn't a doctor's office in ages. What if she was really weird and awkward? What if the guys didn't want to hang out with her again?

She checked her phone to see the time and then opened and closed a dozen apps. She opened her text messages and had to scroll down to see the last messages from her old friends.

Old friends.

That thought made her a little sick. She'd had such a tight knit group of girlfriends in Atlanta and she'd been sure they would survive the distance and stay close. But she hadn't counted on her migraines.

They just didn't get it.

Lucy had tried the hardest and had been the last to fade. Elinor knew that if she called an emergency they'd drop everything and drive up to see her but she needed friends for everyday life not just emergencies. She wondered if she still would have lost them if she was well. Probably not because she'd be rooming with Lucy at Chapel Hill and they'd be exploring everything together. Elinor took a deep sniffling breath and pulled herself out of it. If she came into the theater crying, she'd never get invited again.

She waited as long as she could but at ten till she decided she should go up. She bought her ticket and then walked in. She shouldn't have been worried about being weird.

The guys had a concession table covered in cards and dice and were laughing as they tossed cards onto the table.

"Hey guys," she said tentatively, walking up.

"Ah, she's finally here," said the guy who had been playing with/yelling at Peter at lunch, Jerry.

"Hi Elinor," said Peter. He hesitated a moment as if he wasn't sure if he should hug her or not and they ended up in one of those side hugs that said 'hey there, buddy?'

Peter introduced everyone.

"You remember Jerry," Peter said. Jerry grunted, his big shoulders shrugging. "And you know, Derek. And this is Carlos," he said pointing to a Latino guy. He nodded his head and smiled. "And this is Jack," Peter said. Jack was a shy looking guy barely able to make eye contact with her. His dark hair hung over half his face.

"Hey guys," Elinor said again. Derek was pointedly ignoring her as they walked towards the theater. Jerry wanted some candy so the rest of the group hung back trying to sort out the new group dynamics.

"So… What's the movie about?" Elinor asked.

"You came to a movie and you don't even know what it's about?" Derek asked irritated.

"Um yep. Sorry. I was just glad for an excuse to get out of the house."

"Well it's about…" started Jerry throwing his arm including the candy box around Elinor's neck.

"Hmm," she said uncomfortably and it looked like Derek almost smiled. "I'm stopping at the restrooms. Meet you guys in there," she said ducking under his arm, narrowly avoiding being trapped in a headlock as Jerry's other arm came over to open the candy box.

She washed her hands and then took a couple deep breaths. She barely stopped herself from saying, "you can do this" to her mirror self and settled for pressing her cold hands to her cheeks. When she got to the theater the open seat was in the middle, of course. It was between Peter and Jerry. She walked past Derek and Peter to get to her seat.

She didn't need Derek to stand to let her pass like Peter did but it was very possible he stretched out his legs to make it even more difficult. Thankfully, the movie started shortly after she got herself settled. The previews were all for violent horror and action movies, and she was starting to get a little concerned as to what she had gotten herself into. She wished she had listened to Jerry's movie description.

It turned out to be a pretty average action movie with lots of shooting and cussing and exploding of things. All of which were exactly Elinor's worst migraine nightmare.

The scenes kept flashing from white to black quickly while being accompanied by very loud noises. She almost started counting down to her personal time bomb. *I can probably finish the movie*, she thought fifteen minutes in.

She hated herself that after only fifteen minutes she was already giving herself pep talks just to finish a movie. Who can't just sit through a movie? She was determined she would.

After another thirty minutes she was doubting her abilities. Was there no dialogue in this movie? No times without flashing lights and machine gun sounds? But what would she do? Leave? Wait the movie out in the bathroom? What would she tell the guys? Her stressing was only irritating her already freaking out muscles so she just tried to relax.

She closed her eyes for a minute hoping that the darkness would relieve some of the growing pressure. She pulled her knees up to her chest trying to compress her stomach to stop the growing nausea. When she opened her eyes again to check the movie she saw the forest, of course. She was about to blink again to switch to see the movie theater when she saw movement in the moonlight.

It was him, the other Derek.

He walked around for a minute and then sat down. He looked up and it felt like he was staring straight at her. They each sat there staring at the other for a while. She thought about waving a misty hand at him but she thought better of it. Eventually he turned his head to the side and then got up and walked into the trees. She closed her eyes and waited.

How much more could be left of the movie? Surely everyone must be dead by now.

Finally, after an eternity, the movie ended.

The boys started to stir making comments about how awesome the movie was and then the lights came on. Elinor couldn't stop the hiss that slipped out of her lips. She pulled on her sunglasses against the fluorescent lights and then realized all the boys were watching her.

"So you really hated it, huh?" Peter asked looking apologetic.

"What? No. I mean probably," Elinor said.

"Girls!" Carlos started in "All they ever want to watch is chick flicks. Can't appreciate a classic. Why did we even let her come?"

"I don't think this could be called 'a classic'," chimed Jerry.

"No, I mean it's not that it's an action movie. It's just... I'll be right back," Elinor said as she pushed her way between the guys and promptly threw up in the ladies' room. Her turn had decidedly gone for the worse. How was she going to get home? She hadn't thought this through. *I'm such an idiot.*

Sticking the movie out seemed like the best plan one hundred and five minutes ago but now she was stuck with a high level migraine at a movie theater at eleven thirty at night with a bunch of guys she didn't know very well. She wiped her face with a paper towel trying to wash away this stupid night of thinking she could be normal and go out with friends and leave the house. Who was she kidding?

"Hey..." she said when she came out to see all five guys waiting for her.

"Are you okay?" Peter asked.

"No, I don't feel well. I need to go home. Sorry."

"Is it your head?"

"Yeah, I've got a bad migraine."

As they reached the parking lot, she fumbled in her purse. Peter touched her shoulder. "I think I should drive you home," he said.

"I wasn't going to... I was going to call my parents to pick me up." She brought her hands up to her cheeks as they flushed.

"I can drive you. It's no big deal."

"You really don't have to. It's probably not on your way."

"No, it's fine," Peter started to say but Derek interrupted him, "No, it's not on the way. That's dumb. It's the opposite direction. I'll drive her home. She lives five houses down from me."

Peter and Elinor stared at him.

"I saw her checking the mail one day," Derek said to Peter. "I'll drive her car and we can come back for mine later." Derek then stared at her, waiting for her to object.

"Oh, okay. That does make sense. If you are fine to leave your car here overnight?" Elinor said.

"I wouldn't have said it if I wasn't okay with it," Derek bit back.

"Okay," Elinor said.

"You good, Elinor? It does make more sense." Peter said.

"Yeah, I'm fine. Thanks. Sorry again," Elinor said.

"Why are you sorry? I'm the one who dragged you to a movie that tried to kill you. Get some rest. I'll see you later." He gave her a hug. Elinor and Derek walked in silence to her car. She unlocked it and then handed him the keys.

"Thanks again," she said walking around to the passenger side then pausing at the door she said tentatively, "Would it be super weird if I laid down in the back seat?"

"It's your car. I don't care."

As he adjusted the driver's seat, she buckled herself into the middle seat belted and curled in to face the seat. When the car started the radio turned on and she quickly said "Sorry but can you turn that off?"

Silently he obliged her and when she looked she saw him looking back at her in the rearview mirror. She turned back into the seat in too much pain and nausea to care about anything. *Thank God, I don't have to drive myself.*

Derek

Derek stared at the silent girl and was amazed that she could transform to look even smaller. She was curled in on herself, unmoving. He could see she was stabilizing herself with her left hand and a set of toes that were tucked into the seat crease. She was one with the car. She didn't rock an inch. Even so he found himself unconsciously taking extra care with turns.

He was relieved he didn't have to talk to her on the way back and he didn't mind the lack of music. It gave him time to think. He wondered how she had found her way into their group.

After the encounter on the first day of school, he'd been dismayed to see her again as she checked the mail at a house several houses away from his. The discomfort her presence gave him was a warning. He'd become too comfortable in his life, almost a normal guy. He chastised himself for his lapse.

He could never allow himself to become comfortable, to forget, or to think he was just a normal guy hanging out with friends. Forget and those years would be in vain. Forget and next time he'd be at *her* mercy again.

He thanked the girl for this wake-up call but she wasn't welcome in their group. He was glad he'd found this plausible reason to distance Peter from her. He didn't know why but there was something about her that put him ill at ease, something that removed his thin veil of civility. It would just be easier if she weren't around. And the thought of having her always around made him irritated.

But Derek was irritated by everything. Not having a soul does that to a person. It was like living a twenty-four/seven hell. It was having that something-wrong-hair-standing-up-on-the-back-of-his-neck feeling all the time. Derek constantly felt ill at ease and could never really relax. Because something was wrong and he couldn't fix it. His soul was gone and he sure as hell wasn't going back to get it. So he'd just bear the consequences of being without it.

The best way he could describe it to Peter was comparing it to leaving his cellphone at home. He'd keep checking for it but it wasn't there. And he knew that people were trying to communicate with him but he had no way of knowing what they were saying. But Peter didn't really understand. If he did, he wouldn't have dragged a stupid girl into Derek's life.

Derek could tell Peter liked her. He told himself that Peter deserved to be happy. But it didn't mean this girl would do that. She was so weak. She couldn't see a movie without puking in the bathroom. Peter was too much of a caretaker already. It was in his nature to want to fix things.

But this girl had some real stuff going on. He'd seen the pain in her face as they walked to the car. No, Peter needed a girl who could take some of the stress away from his crappy life. What he really needed was to leave Waxhaw and everyone in it behind, including Derek.

Waxhaw wasn't really that bad. It was small and quiet and almost in South Carolina. The town was mostly trees. And it felt almost haunted as he drove home. There was thick fog over the ground and he had to turn on the fog lights, the lone driver on the winding roads. Waxhaw was a place for forgetting. It was thirty minutes from everywhere and it was for people who wanted land and trees and solitude. The soft rolling mist that covered the road was there most nights and it suited Derek.

They arrived in their neighborhood without a word spoken. The neighborhood was full of brick houses and large wooded lots. It had changed since he'd moved there in elementary school when it had been mostly empty lots but it was all filled up now. Derek heard the distant horn from the train that ran through downtown Waxhaw and wished suddenly he was on it going anywhere away from here.

Derek pulled up to her house and slowed to a stop. He didn't know if she was asleep or not. He glanced back unsure what to do now. Was she asleep? He was uncomfortable.

She didn't stir. Was he supposed to wake her up? Leave her there? Carry her up to the house? He was regretting ever bringing up this idea. He hated having to evaluate social obligations.

"Elinor?" he asked.

"Yes, I'm awake," she said as she unfastened her seat belt and slowly uncoiled herself as she rose to a seated position. "Thank you," she said vaguely to the front seat. "I appreciate it."

She looked and sounded like a hollow cage. No one was home. Her eyes didn't focus on anything and her movements were slow motion.

He handed her the keys after he locked the car and she walked towards the house without a word or a look. He walked home in the dark wondering if his hollowness was as visible as hers was tonight.

Elinor

Darkness. Delicious, cold darkness.

Elinor inhaled deeply as though the darkness were a sensation to be breathed in. She had taken all her necessary medicine the moment she'd gotten home but they might take forty-five minutes to work or they might not work at all. That's why she had other supplies. She laid the frozen ice pack on her face, the heating pad on her stomach and breathed. She knew she had a very unpleasant stretch of time ahead.

At first her prayer was words. *God, why? Why couldn't I have one night free from this? Why do I have migraines at all? Why? I feel so alone. I know You are with me but I wish you would answer me.* After that her prayer became a wordless plea, a desperate cry in her heart as she begged for healing or at least relief.

She felt so alone and didn't want to be alone but she wasn't going to be able to get up and get anyone. And if she did they would only worry.

She wondered where the man in the forest was. She moved her eyes mask to flip it over to the colder side. When she blinked, she saw a flicker of movement and knew it was him. It made her release a breath and she felt a little less anxious for some reason. It somehow mattered that she wasn't *all* alone. He was sitting in a tree not far from her. His gaze seemed kind and watchful. Maybe he didn't want to be alone either.

And thankfully sleep eventually swept in to end the awful night.

But then came the morning. And with the morning came the sun and she'd forgotten to close the curtain behind her door so bright white sunshine rays were piercing the room.

Her face was so sore. She had never been punched in the face but it really must feel very close to this.

Everything hurt. Even her hair was somehow sore.

She'd really considered chopping her hair off recently. When her head hurt bad, her hair felt like it weighed a million pounds. But she'd always had long hair. It reminded her of her mom and even when it added to her headaches she could never quite make the chop.

The ice pack was warm and imagining having to walk downstairs in the lights was an insuperable barrier. She stretched wildly for her phone and finally finding it, she texted her stepmom.

"SOS. Need supplies in my room."

A couple minutes later brought a knock at the door.

"Come in," Elinor said. She was surprised when Katie came in carrying a tray of goodies. Katie was a dark haired little Elinor. She had her mother and Ryan's dark hair while Colton's hair was more a mix between his parents. But even with her darker hair, Katie looked surprisingly like Elinor for their only sharing a father but maybe Elinor saw what she wanted to see in Katie.

"Mom is on the phone with someone. She told me about your text. Is it very bad?" Katie asked unloading some of ice packs.

"It's not the worst ever," Elinor said truthfully. It was really bad but she hated to worry everyone. So she tried to be honest while downplaying it.

"Lay back, Nurse Katie is here. Just tell me what to do." She was going across the room to Elinor's drug box. It had started as a shelf in the bathroom but there were just too many now and it was easier to have it in her room.

"Okay. I need my nausea medicine; It's blue. And my pain pills, two green ones. Thanks." Katie came over with the specified items. She had brought a sleeve of crackers and a glass of water on her tray.

"You are the best, Katie. Thank you."

After Elinor had taken the pills, she lay down. She had one ice pack on her neck and the other one over her eyes.

"Do you want some Bengay?" Katie asked.

Elinor smiled. Her little sister was just as perceptive as Colton. She didn't know why that still surprised her.

"Yeah. Can you hand it to me?" Elinor said as she reached out blindly.

"I can do it." Katie said "Just sit back." Katie massaged the cooling gel at Elinor temples and forehead. She sighed. It was nice to not have to do it herself.

"I'm sorry you are feeling bad. Did it start at the movie?" she asked in a soft voice as she rubbed the Bengay down Elinor's neck.

"Yes. But don't tell Mom. I had no trouble getting home."

"Zip," Katie said. And Elinor could imagine the invisible zipper sliding across Katie's lips. Katie started to massage Elinor's head and it felt so nice. Katie was the only one who could do it without making it worse.

"Try to get to sleep, okay?" Katie said. Elinor could hear that she was still in the room. She was probably sitting on the floor with her iPad. Katie must be staying close in case she needed anything. She was a sweet girl.

Chapter 10

Peter

Peter sent Elinor a text on Sunday morning. "Hey Elinor, how are you feeling? Better I hope :)"

"Better. I still hate the sun though :/" she replied.

"I'm glad you are better! Let's grab coffee tonight. (No sun out at night) I'm a genius."

"Lol yeah sounds good. 9 at the place by school?"

"Deal!"

Peter got there early and was waiting outside when Elinor walked up. He went straight for the hug and he was glad it wasn't weird. Peter was glad to hold her for a moment because she looked bad. Like a washcloth all wrung out and left to dry crumpled. *And this is what 'better' looks like?* Peter thought.

"Hey, how are you?" Peter said making himself let go. "I'm glad you could meet me."

"Yeah, thanks for checking in on me," she said smiling. He opened the door and they walked to the counter.

"I'll have a medium black tea," she told the barista as she pulled out her wallet.

"No, it's my treat," Peter said pushing her wallet away. "For almost killing you on Friday."

"It wasn't your fault," Elinor said. But it felt a little bit like his fault.

"Yeah I know," Peter said then ordered. "I'll have a large vanilla latte."

He led them towards a table to wait.

"But I still feel bad about it," he said. "Is it always like that?"

She smiled sadly. "You just saw the pre-game show. It gets much worse. I was so glad Derek drove me home."

"How was he?" Peter asked tentatively. "Was he okay?"

"Perfect," she said, then smiled as she added. "He didn't say a word."

Peter chuckled low. "Yep. That's him."

He went to grab their drinks and when he returned she was staring off. "Are you sure you are feeling okay?" he asked, setting the drinks down. She didn't seem 'all better' to him. She seemed distant and he hoped he hadn't done anything.

"Sorry. I'm always in a fog when I come out the other end. And..." She stopped talking shaking her head.

"What?" he asked taking off the lid of his drink to let it cool.

"It's hard not to get depressed sometimes that this is my life. I mean not like in a depression, just kind of sad."

"I'm sorry. It's got to get better, right? Your doctors will figure it out. There are tons of things to try for migraines, right?"

He felt bad when he saw her barely stopped eye roll.

"Do you know it's been a year already? A year of migraines and headaches every day. I was supposed to be at Chapel Hill with my brother. I was..." she stopped curtailing her sentence and redirecting it.

"I'm sorry. You don't want to hear this. You're right. It'll get better. You are really easy to talk to," she said. "But as hard as that all is, I really wish I didn't have hallucinations or visions or whatever on top of it. Worrying I'm crazy is just too much. I wish I could talk to Derek about it. Maybe he has some answers."

Peter looked down at his coffee, thinking a moment. "Well you should start with his blog first," Peter said.

He'd thought a lot about what he should do over the past couple days since the movie. He decided to roll the dice.

"Read it. I'd really like to know what you think. Don't let him know though. Because he's *not* going to like it. He hates talking about it, even to me." Peter took his glasses off to clean them so his hands could have something to do.

"He has a blog?" Elinor asked skeptically.

"Yeah it's really good and... really bad. You'll see what I mean when you read it. Open your notes on your phone. I'll write in the website." As he held her phone he said, "Just keep an open mind. Derek's not a bad guy. He wasn't... always like he is now."

"That's all very cryptic," she said smiling as she took her phone back. "*The Morland Prince?*" she asked reading Peter's note. "Don't worry. I promise I'll be nice. I'd never criticize someone's art. It takes guts to put your feelings out there. I'm not a writer but I love to read."

"That's not exactly what I meant. But yeah, I know you'll be nice. And don't talk to him about it. He won't like that you've read it. Please tell me you won't talk to him without me," he said. When she nodded he let it go and changed the topic. He didn't want to give it away before she read it. He remembered what he had felt when he'd read the story blind. It was probably the best way to approach it.

"So," Peter said trying to keep a cool face, "I've only been texted a dozen times by the guys asking if you left a boyfriend back in Georgia."

"No," Elinor laughed, "I've never really had a serious boyfriend. And honestly I can't imagine having one now. How could I drag some guy into my migraine world? I mean what if I married him and he had to take care of me all the time. That idea makes me a little sick. I don't know that I'll be able to think romantically until I find some peace or relief."

"You know that the right guy won't care, right?" Peter said. "You know that relationships are about taking care of each other in the good times and bad? Just throwing it out there. Don't give up on love. You never know."

Chapter 11

Elinor

The Morland Prince was an unusual blog. It consisted of a dark navy background, several buttons at the top, and an ominous list of chapter names with no explanations: Home, Killing My Sister, Becoming a Prince, and The Darkness…

At the top of the page was a tab that said "Start Here." Elinor obeyed, grateful for the first step on the garden path.

"Start Here

Not sure how you found your way here. And I'm not sure what I'm supposed to say to you now. It's good you are here. You need to read this. Everyone does. Not that it's the greatest story ever written. But it's true and it's mine and you need to know what could happen to you.

People always say "What's the worst thing that could happen?" And the answer is THIS. This is the worst thing that could happen to you. So study up. I know it would have been a million times easier if I'd read a blog by someone who'd walked the path before me. But I carve me own stupid path. No one else would take this lonely path lined in blood and darkness.

Every story starts somewhere. Mine starts <u>here</u>. I'll post a new chapter every month but you really should start at the beginning. Or do whatever you want. Click <u>here</u> to go to a list of posts.

Good luck, I guess.

-The Morland Prince.

It probably looks pretentious to write "The Morland Prince" but it's not. Calling myself that is more like pleading guilty to a crime than bragging. It's not something I chose and it's not something I can run from. It is what it is."

Elinor didn't know what to make of it but she felt chills...

She went to the start of the story a chapter titled "Before" where Derek confessed to being "A soulless murdering monster." The rest of the fifteen or so chapters passed in a blur. It was a dark fairytale, not like the Disney kind where everything sorted out but the original true kind where the mermaid who has had her tongue cut out turns to sea foam or the prince trying to save the day gets his eyes pecked out by birds.

The story follows young Derek, who by climbing and hitting his head on a tree in his backyard wakes up to find himself *somewhere else*. He meets a mage and realizes he's not on Earth anymore but a planet called 'Morland'. Morland is a magic planet covered by a dark smog of Darkness, a physical manifestation of the forces of evil.

Elinor wondered if she was seeing Morland. If that was the link that someone connected them. Despite the walls she'd built around it in her mind, she wondered if Derek's tree was in the forest behind their house and if it had started everything that had broken inside her too.

Because Derek was broken. Different and worse than she was.

A few days after being on Morland, Derek's soul finds him. Where most people's souls are tucked inside, Derek's had been ripped out. His soul is a spiritual entity that only Derek can see and speak to.

Apparently their violent entry into Morland had severed them into two pieces. Derek phrased it so hauntingly beautiful when he wrote "He appeared to be all the good that was in me. He wasn't perfect but then I'd never been. He was just all the best parts of me and I was stuck being someone I didn't even like."

Each day on Morland seemed to be worse for young Derek. His mentor the mage was unsympathetic and distant. He was forced to be a child solider to which his lazy Earthling thirteen-year-old boy habits had ill prepared him.

Derek was beaten. He was alone. And he had no hope of escape.

Derek made friends and enemies. Some he betrayed and some he redeemed. But his life altered for the final time when the Queen of Morland decided she wanted to adopt seven children and somehow chose Derek instantly from the crowd to be her last son.

The Queen was a mage with control over fire and Darkness. She was not someone a lowly soldier could say 'no' to. So Derek was now a prince and it would have only been a new kind of terrible if not for Derek's sister.

Her name was Brigitte and she was written with such care and adoration that Elinor loved her a little herself. But Derek could know only short periods of happiness on Morland because the Queen had dark plans for her new children. She wanted their souls and she wanted them turned into obedient creatures of Darkness. And it was happening to each of them one by one every full moon.

When Derek discovered this he hurried to find his mentor to get advice. But... while Derek was gone Brigitte was attacked, raped, and beaten. And Brigitte full of rage went to the Queen for vengeance. The Queen happily obliged and Derek found Brigitte in the castle dungeon watching her attacker slowly die from the poison she'd given him.

From that day, Brigitte was lost to him. And as Derek waited in horror for Brigitte's full moon, he made a plan to stop her from going through with their mother's plans which would leave Brigitte empty of herself and full of evil and Darkness.

But Derek was too slow and Brigitte was too fast. She stabbed him in the side and ran into the gazebo that had been spelled for her transformation. When Derek came to from his injury, he hurried after her... hoping there was still enough of his sister to be saved.

There wasn't.

With her last dying plea, she begged him to kill her and release her from being trapped in a prison of her body. And Derek loved her enough that he did it.

Derek heard rumors and hoped that if all his siblings were destroyed his mother would finally be weakened enough to be killed.

So one by one, he hunted down his siblings and killed them all. But Derek's full moon was only days away and there was nowhere on Morland he could hide from the moon. So he went to his mentor one last time begging for a way to escape and return home to Earth. And after years of denying he had any information, the old mage finally told Derek there was a way, a magic flower. But it would cost him something. He didn't know what it would be but he told Derek it would be more than he wanted to pay.

Derek took the flower but before he could swallow it, the Queen's men came for him. He was taken before the Queen who demanded his obedience. He said no, ate the flower in front of her, and disappeared before her eyes. He was instantly back on Earth but... his soul had had to stay behind.

And then it ends. Derek is home. His soul is lost to him forever. His sister is dead and the Queen still lives.

No hope.

Elinor had never been much of a believer in the unbelievable. She didn't think Nessie was still locked in a loch. She didn't think aliens built the pyramids. She didn't think making one thousand origami cranes made a wish come true. But when she finished reading Derek's story, the truth and reality of it felt like a punch to the stomach.

So… she was seeing Morland.

It seemed to be the most logical conclusion in a pile of absolute madness. She really could see another world. There were ways to slip between the two of them. She knew a boy who was a prince in that world and she could see his soul, the soul he'd left behind as the cost of returning to Earth. The sepia shade she saw the forest world through was the layer of Darkness that covered it.

It gave her chills again. As much as she earnestly didn't want to be crazy, it was turning out to be just as scary to be sane.

It just felt like too much.

It felt like a story but heroines in books didn't have migraines. They didn't. Because girls with migraines didn't do things. They couldn't go on adventures because there were bright lights on adventures and not much napping time.

It all just felt a little cruel. What was she supposed to do? What was the point? She couldn't stop seeing Morland. And she couldn't shake the bone deep feeling that she was supposed to help. People didn't get abilities for nothing. But the Queen and the Darkness scared her. *As all villains are meant to do,* she supposed.

And Derek's story haunted her.

It was beautiful and horrible, especially the parts about Derek's siblings. She wouldn't get over that anytime soon. Maybe it was better to go through this without him. What could he possibly do to help her anyway? Did it matter if she was seeing his Morland? His link to that world didn't have to mean anything. He never mentioned anyone with her power in his blog, whatever her power really was.

And… he was not good. Something was broken in Derek and she knew now what it was. He didn't have his soul. It was on Morland. And he was here. And she could see his soul. *And this is my life now,* she thought shaking her head.

She'd thought her migraines were the random result of living in a broken world or maybe even God's way of testing her. But the truth was that somehow when she blinked her brain saw another planet and that planet just happened to be the one that Derek was trapped on for five years. What were the chances of that? *Slim.*

Seeing Derek with this new information was strange. It was like she had been completely blind before and now she saw him with perfect clarity. Derek was so dangerous. He literally oozed it. His whole manner and vibe were designed to keep people back. And it had worked before but now that she knew… There was also an unfortunate magnetic pull about him.

She couldn't stop thinking about him, about it all.

She wrestled with her decision. The desire to talk to Derek was so strong. She was seeing his soul after all. And she had been seeing his soul more often lately.

Last time it seemed like he was looking right at her. And what if Derek could help her? What if he could make her visions or ability stop? Maybe he knew what was going on. Maybe he could explain how this was happening to her. Maybe he'd had something to do with it. Maybe she had the ability to see Morland for a reason. What if Derek knew what she was supposed to do with it? But Derek was danger wrapped in electrified barbed wire surrounded by a moat of sharks. She should stay away. And she really, really tried.

She lasted until Wednesday. She decided she would approach Derek at lunch, in a public space but hopefully with some privacy. When she got to the lunch area he was sitting alone, the first of his friends. Elinor couldn't have planned it any better.

"So," Elinor said sitting a seat away from Derek. He immediately scooted three chairs over so they were on opposite sides of the table. *Great start.*

"I read your blog," she said quickly. She wasn't going to give him another chance to misunderstand her.

Derek brought his fist up to his forehead roughly. "Peter is a damn idiot," he said saying each word deliberately before turning his full glare on Elinor.

"Do you get headaches, too?" she asked noticing as he massaged his temples.

"No," he said sharply taking his hand down and flicking a crumb violently off the table. "You give me headaches."

Elinor couldn't help but flinch at that comment and lean back a little in her seat. No one had ever talked to her that way before but Derek wasn't done.

"What are you doing with Peter? Are you using him to get close to me?" Derek said. His eyes were throwing daggers at her.

"Umm no. It's not like that at all. Peter and I are just friends. He's... helping me out with something."

"With what?"

"I...I think I'll just keep it between Peter and I," she said, the feeling of stupidity was starting to settle on her. But she needed to know if it was true. He felt like her only lifeline. "Umm random question," she continued, "But have you ever had long hair? Say like to your shoulders."

If his eyes could have gotten more intense they did. She felt goose bumps rising. She should have heeded Peter's advice.

"Not in this life," he answered shoving the table hard as he stood up, sending it flying into Elinor's stomach and tipping her chair back. "Stay away from me," he said before he left.

She had just righted her chair when Peter came up.

"Hey, what's wrong?" he said immediately sensing her vibe. *Don't cry!* she coached herself. But maybe she did because Peter pulled her into a quick hug. "What is it?" he said letting her go just as quickly, as his face flushed.

"Your friend Derek is a *real* piece of work. You know that?"

"Oh no! Did you talk to him about it? About his blog? Why would you do that? You said you wouldn't. What did you say?" Peter was literally wringing his hands.

"Well I don't know why but I assumed you were overreacting," she said rubbing her sore stomach.

Peter's face paled as he took in the action. "Did he hurt you?"

"Not bad. He just tried to throw a table at me. All I said was that I read his blog." He hugged her again.

"So he doesn't know what you can do?" Peter asked earnestly pulling back to rest his hands on her shoulders.

"No, I decided to keep that little gem a secret seeing how his eyes wanted to murder me. I don't think I was quite prepared for any kind of interaction with him."

Peter took a deep breath as he sat down at the table.

"So you finished it, the blog?" he said looking up at her.

"Yeah. I was not entirely prepared for that either," she said raising her eyebrows.

"I'm sorry but I thought it would be best to let you form your own opinions. Maybe you wouldn't have believed it. Maybe it wouldn't make sense to you."

"Oh I wish I couldn't believe it. It's really horrible, isn't it? How true do you think it is? Did he embellish any of it?" she asked.

"I think it's one hundred percent true. I think there are definitely things he left out but I think every horrible detail is completely autobiographical. It's just wishful thinking otherwise." He paused for a moment. "Does it make you understand him better?"

She sighed. "I don't know. He's a soldier. Still. I don't know how I didn't see that before. It's his defining quality. His intensity. So what happened after the last chapter? He eats that magic flower and comes home and... he becomes who he is now?"

"Well when he came back to Earth, he had assumed that the same amount of time would have passed. But no time had passed here. None. He comes back in his thirteen-year-old body with none of his scars or anything. It was as if Earth had been frozen until he came back. His parents were still at work. They didn't know he'd been gone for five years. Everyone had... a hard time. They didn't believe him. He eventually lied and said he'd made it all up... It's still kinda tense.

"I met Derek a year later. His folks made him join Boy Scouts since he'd been stalking the woods behind their house with knives strapped to his legs. He never wants to go to Morland again but going there unprepared terrifies him. He doesn't take a step into the woods unless he is armed. So all of that plus not having his soul with him made him what he is now."

"So he comes back home but no time had passed? Maybe it was all a dream. Maybe none of it really happened." Elinor said.

Peter didn't smile. "Do you really think that?"

"No. No, I don't. I can see his soul. I know. I just... It's really a lot to take in, isn't it? So how did you become his best friend? Boy Scouts?" she couldn't quite keep the scowl from her question. Derek was Peter's biggest flaw.

"We... We met in Boy Scouts but we were not instant friends," Peter said, "I sought him out but he really wouldn't have anything to do with me. When my mom left us... I was different and a lot of my friends faded away. I was too angry and too sad but Derek was there. That's how I know there is still good in him. Despite everything. I know when you first read his story it's a lot to take in and he paints himself very liberally as a villain but... he's not all bad."

"How old is he?" she asked.

"Good question. So he went to Morland when he was thirteen. Comes back at eighteen but no time had passed on Earth. So he's thirteen again. Now he's been back six years. So he looks nineteen but he's lived twenty-four years. So I don't really know."

"Yeah his soul seems older..." she said, another puzzle piece settling into place. "But I think I just need to find a way to let this all go. Forget Morland. Forget Derek. Forget everything weird and just... I don't know."

"Don't you want to know more about Morland? I mean don't you want to know why you can see it?" Peter asked.

"I see it because my brain is broken," Elinor said.

93

"People's brains break every day but they don't see another world when they blink."

"Maybe. But what can we do? Derek isn't going to help and it's the most unprovable gift ever. No one else would ever believe me."

"I believe you."

"Yeah but you shouldn't. I have no proof," she said.

"Your eyes change color."

"But it doesn't mean anything."

Peter reached over and grabbed her shoulders again. "It means everything." Elinor looked up as several of the guys pulled up to the table. Peter gave her a strong look and she stopped talking about it.

She thought about her interaction with Derek all day. Her head was extra bad, a level eight and rising but she powered through her last class. She couldn't go home anyway because she had a doctor's appointment after school and she wondered if it was better or worse to come to the appointment with a bad migraine. Not that she ever had a choice one-way or the other.

The waiting room was quiet and there was only an older couple waiting. It reminded her that neurologists saw more serious things than migraines. Elinor was called back and waited in the room for Dr. Booker.

Her doctor was nice enough. She seemed like she cared. Elinor's parents were okay with her stopping supplementary treatments but they wanted her to continue to see her neurologist once every three months, as usual. She wasn't expecting much to get accomplished. She was learning to curb her hope. Dr. Booker came in with a smile, shaking Elinor's hand before she took a seat.

"So how are you feeling?" Dr. Booker asked cheerfully.

"About the same," Elinor replied.

"The same being?" she asked flipping through her chart.

"The same being bad. I have a moderate to severe migraine or headache every day. Nothing really helps."

"Oh yes," the doctor said making it to the back of her notes. "I wanted to talk to you about that. I remember at our last meeting that I wanted to look some things up. Well, I don't think you have migraines."

Elinor's eye hardened. *This was certainly a new one*, she thought.

"I think you have a headache disorder called New Daily Persistent Headache. You are actually pretty textbook. I would have told you last time but I wanted to talk to some colleagues about it first. It's much rarer than chronic migraine. NDPH is a headache disorder that characteristically just starts out of the blue one day for no apparent reason. It is a daily, unremitting headache and is very resistant to treatment. Now it can have migrainous symptoms meaning it acts like a migraine, as yours do?" She phrased the last sentence as a question. Elinor nodded.

"But they are not migraine," the doctor continued. "Migraine usually start when someone is a child and can become increasingly more frequent and intense as time goes by. Of course, they can just start suddenly but not usually. Migraine is often affected by menstrual cycle for women and is very easy to trace through family trees. The fact that yours started so suddenly and intensely is a red flag for New Daily Persistent Headache and also the fact that you have no family history of headaches.

"It can be intractable which means resistant to treatments. That's why nothing you have tried so far has worked. Now as nice as it is to know your disorder's name, there is not a lot of good news after that. Because it's a rather new classification and because it is much rarer than migraine there hasn't been much research so there are few treatments options."

Elinor just sat silently absorbing each new fact and each new blow. There were a lot of things being said that she didn't like hearing. Dr. Booker continued on, either oblivious to Elinor's growing discomfort or simple wanting to get it all out quickly.

"Sometimes New Daily Persistent Headache is self-limiting. Meaning it starts one day and can end one day just as suddenly. Unrelated to any treatments. So that's something to keep in the back of your mind. But... sometimes it doesn't go away or can last for decades. I don't tell you this to be discouraging. But NDPH is tricky. It's very difficult to treat. It may never get any better. I'm sure you'll read all about it when you get home. Now we'll have to rule out a couple things that can cause New Daily Persistent Headache but I want you to be prepared. If your spinal fluid is fine and if your MRI comes back negative, there are *no* other specific treatments." Upon seeing Elinor's face, she changed her tone to be a little kinder.

"We will continue to treat it aggressively as if it were migraine but..."

Tears were streaming down Elinor's face in full force. *This is a nightmare.* She covered her face to hide her shame at crying in a doctor's office and to keep her eyes hidden. She wasn't sobbing yet or breathing heavy. It was just a sudden burst of the dam. Words kept flying at her.

Intractable. Doesn't go away. Decades. No treatments.

She drew a few shaky breaths trying to control herself. Dr. Booker looked miserable. Elinor knew it wasn't her fault and she was grateful for the truth finally.

"I'm sorry," Elinor said after a minute, wiping her eyes and nose with the tissue Dr. Booker offered.

"I'm sorry," said Dr. Booker. "I know this is all very difficult to face. I'm going to refer you to a headache specialist who deals much more with New Daily Persistent Headache than I do. I think it will be a good fit for you. Dr. Lan is a good doctor. I don't want you to give up hope. We are going to go ahead and schedule your spinal tap and your MRA & MRV. There are still plenty of patients with this who find relief. Do you have any questions?"

Elinor took a deep breath that only shook a little bit. "When will I see Dr. Lan?"

"As soon as we can get you in but you know how hard it is to get new patient appointments. It may be a couple months. But I'll get the referral in today. And we will get your tests done so you'll have everything ready for Dr. Lan to see for your first visit. That way you won't be wasting the time in the interim." She looked at Elinor giving her a minute to think of another question.

"Um it's all a bit much today. I'm sure I'll have questions once I've wrapped my head around it and have done a little research. Can I call you in the mean time before I am transferred to Dr. Lan?"

"Of course. Just leave a message with my nurse and I'll call you back." They both stood up. "You'll get a call when your tests are scheduled."

"Thank you. I appreciate your time." Elinor said shaking her hand.

"It's going to be okay. We aren't giving up on you, so don't you," she said leaving the room.

Elinor barely made it out of the office. She kept taking deep breaths to try and keep it all inside. When she finally made it to the solitude of her car, she slammed her fists on the steering wheel and sobbed into her hands. She'd lived with the unshakeable truth in the back of her mind that this was all going to go away. That it was going to end someday. She'd heard tale after tale of how migraines were cured with this or that. Everyone had an example. But this... she was in a new club and she felt so alone.

"God help me!" Elinor cried into her hands. "My life wasn't supposed to be like this. You were supposed to heal me. No. No. No." And then words wouldn't come. It was too deep and too sharp and this new reality was swallowing her up.

Elinor replayed her conversation with the doctor and compared it with her symptoms and then with what she pulled up on her phone. There weren't many website, a dozen maybe, versus the millions of migraine ones and each site only repeated the others.

And the truth she discovered didn't change anything except making it harder to hold onto hope. New Daily Persistent Headache was exactly what it sounded like.

New: It had a beginning. It had a start. The pain hadn't always been there.

Daily: It was every day, every one of them.

Persistent: This one was the kicker. It meant that it didn't want to go away. It meant daily could become forever.

Headache: The worst misnomer of the title. People thought headaches were little things that Tylenol took away. Elinor thought her pain was closer to a nuke going off in her brain than an *ache* in her *head*.

NDPH didn't mean anything. It didn't provide any answers, only unanswered questions. They didn't know what caused it or how to treat it. They were headaches that could act like migraine but weren't. They started out of the blue one day and could last two years or forever.

New Daily Persistent Headaches was what doctors said when they didn't know what to do. But her doctor still had hope and Elinor didn't have the option of giving up. And if all her tests came back negative then they'd continue to treat it as if they were migraines, which of course they weren't. But that was all they knew to do so that's all she could ask for.

Elinor went for a walk outside her house once the sun had set to get some fresh air. No one saw her leave which was even better. Her family had handled the news just *slightly* better than she had. Colton had practically flown to his laptop and she was not prepared to face the research and treatments he wanted to try. Her parents were worried and comforting. Katie was silent and sad. Being along in the cool night air felt amazing and she let the crisp breeze wash it all away.

She didn't realize at first that she was walking to Derek's house until she was there. She sat down just watching the empty lit rooms with her back against a tree. It was really peaceful sitting in the dark watching a lit house, like a doll's house.

The whole day felt like a dream to her. She couldn't shake the taste of bitter disappointment from her mouth. She hadn't thought that she had much hope. She had always tried to be reasonable and keep her expectations down but she had been fooling herself.

Hope had been the only thing keeping her going, even if it tried to kill her all the time. She had been poisoning herself with hope every day. Hope was caffeinated poison. It made her feel rejuvenated and excited. She wouldn't realize until later that it was actually killing her. The crashing down part was like nothing else. And when it happened over and over and over, she stopped bouncing back.

It was tempting to just live down there in the depths. She told herself that hope was for the weak. It was for those without the courage to face the crap of their life and move on. Those who gave up the luxury of hope could live and breathe free. She told herself this but she couldn't make herself listen. Even in her despair, she still felt this dumb small light inside of herself saying that somehow it would turn out all right.

Hope was the thing that kept her human. It kept her going. The truth was that hopeless lives were vacant and meaningless, not strong and enduring like they advertised. They were not people worth knowing because they didn't know what they were. *Derek for instance*, she thought. He had given up all hope of living a normal life and by consequence he wasn't even living. At least she was trying. She leaned back, sighing as she flickered between two different night skies.

She liked to pretend that she was alone in her despair and suffering. But she wasn't. She'd recently read a Bible verse that rang so true that it carved itself instantly on her heart. *God has said, 'Never will I leave you; Never will I forsake you.'* The verse felt a little hollow in the cool dark night but that didn't make it less true. Because despite everything she knew that God's plan for her was for her good and that He kept his promises. She had to keep reminding herself of that every time her bitterness started to block out everything else.

My God has not deserted me. I will not let this defeat me. There had to be a way out, her treacherous hope-filled heart prayed as she turned her head south to follow the sound of a distant train sounding in the dark.

Derek

Derek thought he had imagined her. Because why would Elinor be sitting in the dark woods watching his house? Her long blond hair was caught in the breeze and she was letting it whip around. It made her look like a ghost.

"What are you doing here?" he said and it sounded loud even to his ears. She jumped about a foot off the ground.

"You scared me," she said with a hand to her heart. She was the worst spy ever if she was scared that easily.

"Why are you here?" he asked again.

"I just needed some air," she said sighing as she looked past him.

"I said stay away from me."

"Ugh everything isn't always about you. I didn't come here to see you, despite the fact that I'm sitting watching your house. That's pure coincidence," she said sullenly.

"You should go," he said standing over her. He hoped to see her scamper off, afraid of him. But she seemed to be trying to look through him. She took a deep breath and stood up to face him. He wondered if she thought she was intimidating only reaching his chest.

"I need to talk to you. About your story."

"No," he said edging towards her, wanting to see a little of the rightful fear she should feel for him. "I know the fact that someone doesn't like you is slowly destroying your perfect world but you are going to have to live with that. This isn't your teen romance novel. A midnight rendezvous isn't going to reveal my inner knight. You think having read something I wrote that it means you know the real me and now you can see past my prickly exterior. Let me ruin the surprise. There is nothing past my exterior. I have no soul and no heart," he said smacking his hands against the tree above her head, as he glared down.

"Whatever you came out here for is never going to happen," he continued when she just stared at him with nothing but exhaustion in her face. "I am not secretly in love with you. In fact, I think I hate you. If you ever seek me out again, you'll regret it."

He stormed off and expected her run away home.

But she didn't.

She ran after him and yanked his shirt to pull him back. He stared down at her small hand holding tight to his shirt in pure shock. *What was she thinking?* He was a murderer and she thought that feeble hold could keep him. But nonetheless, Derek found he couldn't quite move.

"You are so egotistical. Have that many girls really declared their love for you? I find that *impossible* to believe. You are the worst. No girl could like you."

Derek rolled his eyes. Had she just pulled him back to yell at him? He changed the subject. "Why have you been hanging out with Peter so much?" Derek needed to know what her plans were. He needed to know if she had really just stumbled accidentally into his life.

She looked surprised and released his shirt as she said, "He's my friend. He's helping me."

"What is he helping you with? Why are you pursuing him?"

She just stared at him for a moment. He could almost see the thoughts racing through her head.

"That's what I've been wanting to talk to you about since the first day of school," she said. "Derek... I have an ability. When I blink I see another world. I see Morland." He recoiled as if she'd slapped him and then before he knew it his hand was at her throat and she was sliding backwards pressed against the tree.

"What?" he growled. His voice sounded alien to his ears and a red haze of anger seemed to have slid over him when she had said *that* word. He didn't loosen his hold as he repeated, "What did you say?"

"Morland," she breathed out. "I can see it." His eyes narrowed. She probably thought she was so funny.

"I don't know what you're talking about," he said.

"Yes, you do," she said with blazing eyes. "You've been there. And I've seen your soul."

"Are you are a demon from hell sent to torture me?" he spoke low, nearly growling an inch from her face. "Who are you? Answer me. I do not make idle threats, little girl," he said tightening his hands a little and Elinor kicked wildly as true fear gleamed in her eyes.

"Good. You should be afraid. You've read my story. Well then you know I'm well versed in this activity," he said running a thumb over her windpipe. "How did you picture this ending? Did you think you could come here and lie to me and I'd just let you go?" But what if she wasn't lying? Was this the best assassin his mother could send?

She clawed at his hands. He released her a little.

"I'm not lying," she said as tears filled her eyes.

"Go home," he said making sure she was looking him in the eyes. "Never come back. And never speak to me again."

Elinor

Elinor ran home. It was late but she didn't want to go inside. She dialed a number on her phone. It rang a couple times.

"Elinor?" said Peter.

"Yes."

"What's up? It's kind of late. Is everything okay?"

"Not really," she said as her voice quivered. "Can I come see you? I need to talk to someone."

"Umm yeah. I guess you could come over here. My dad is working the night shift."

"Oh thank you, Peter. I'll be over soon. Can you text me your address?"

She told her parents she needed to grab a coffee with a friend and that her head wasn't bad and she would be out for a bit. They must have seen just enough in her face because they let her go.

She pulled up to Peter's house curious despite everything. It was small and old enough it might be historical if anyone bothered to take care of it which it didn't look like they did. Peter was waiting on the porch. She jumped out of her car and nearly ran into his arms. She couldn't keep back the tears now. How could she still have more after the day she had had?

"What's wrong, El?" he asked. He'd never called her that before.

"Oh everything," she said able to laugh a little bit as she pulled back to swat at a mosquito on her arm.

"Let's go inside," Peter said leading the way.

Peter's house was sparsely decorated. She'd gathered that he didn't have a lot of money since he was always working at the game store and hanging around there when he wasn't. She knew his dad wasn't a good guy and that his mom was gone.

"This way to my room. It's more comfortable than out here," he said motioning to everything.

His room was perfect. She hadn't ever wondered what his room looked like but it was just right. Two full bookcases crowded with books and figurines lined the wall opposite his bed. His bedspread was navy blue. The walls were very nearly covered with posters, most of which were things she didn't know.

"Very cool room, Peter," she said taking a couple full turns around.

Peter

There was a girl in his room. That was sure a first. He tried to keep his mind clear. She was only here because she was very upset about a lot of things apparently. *But still.*

"Elinor," he said gripping her arms to stop her inspection of his room. When she flinched violently and unconsciously away, his heart skipped a beat and he felt himself pale.

"I'm okay now," she said. She must have been able to read his face easily. "Derek, he... I was out in the woods getting some fresh air after a horrible doctor's appointment, which I'll get to in a minute and Derek came upon me in the woods. He said a lot of mean things and I was already angry so I told him."

She brought a hand up to her neck and Peter stopped breathing. He wanted to touch her but he made himself wait. She had hugged him earlier of her own volition. Maybe if he waited she'd let him comfort her again. When she pulled her hand away, he could see the rough red marks and his blood started to pound.

"Derek got really angry. Really fast. I should have listened to you. Especially after lunch but I just needed to make this all go away. I thought if there was any chance he knew anything that could make this all stop. Just make it go away," she said motioning to her head as a couple tears fell.

"It seemed like an okay risk. I was very wrong. He... he threw me against a tree with his hands at my neck. Peter, he is not good," she said taking his hands in hers, as if she wanted to comfort him.

"Deep down there is no goodness in him like you think. Oh Peter. What if he had? He was so close." And she finally broke. She'd told the story as fully as he needed from her and she was leaning into him crying softly. Her legs gave and he led them both to sit on the bed. She didn't let go and he breathed her in, taking deep calming breaths.

He should have never let her read that stupid blog. He felt her stop crying but she stayed burrowed into him. Being needed was like a drug to him. It filled him up and he breathed it in deep. He needed to distract himself.

"What else happened today? At the doctor?" he asked.

"Oh you are a sucker for girls ruining your shirts, aren't you?" she chuckled weakly as she pulled back and he regretted his decision to speak. She ran her hands through her hair and wiped her eyes.

"The doctor changed my diagnosis and basically said my headaches are untreatable and may never go away. It was a blow." She leaned back against the headboard pulling her feet to her chest. "Oh sorry," she said looking at her shoes that had marked his bed. "Sorry. I wasn't thinking." She started to move off the bed.

"It's fine," he said taking her arm to pull her back as he then took his own shoes off and sat cross-legged facing her. "I'm really sorry for your super crappy day," he said.

"Thanks for listening," she said taking off her shoes and nudging him with her feet. "There is no one else in the world I could have talked to."

That sentence made him feel really good and also not so good.

Maybe it was just the fact that she had no one else that made her come here. Maybe if she'd asked one the of the other guys about magic weeks ago, she'd be sitting in his bedroom right now. Peter didn't like to think about that.

"If I'd have told my parents about Derek, he'd be in jail right now," she said gauging his reaction.

"Can't say I haven't been thinking the same thing," Peter said. He felt so conflicted about Derek. He'd known deep down that Derek was still capable of this. It was why he'd tried to really discourage Elinor from talking to him about it but he also knew that Derek did have good in him. Peter was absolutely sure that Derek was really horrified at himself right now.

If Peter was a better friend, he'd text Derek to let him know that she was all right. But he decided to let Derek suffer a little longer. He deserved it.

"He really did kill them, didn't he? The other princes and princess, his siblings?" Elinor asked.

"Yes. I never doubted that he did. But you know why he did it. He had to. They were prisoners of the Darkness. It was the only way to free them."

A while later she said, "It's getting late. I'm sure my parents are starting to worry." She pulled out her phone. "No texts yet. I'm shocked they are giving me this much space. Was it weird that I came over?" she asked him levelly.

Was it weird? He wondered.

No, he'd felt such a strong connection with her since the moment they first talked. It had been... nice to have her in his space.

"No. Not weird at all. I'm just so sorry for the night you've had and the part Derek played."

"You are not Derek's keeper," she said.

"It feels like it sometimes. I know you don't need to hear this but stay away from Derek if I'm not around. I really don't think he'll do something like that again but I'd sleep better if you'd promise no more forest walks."

"Oh, I promise," she said.

Derek

Derek paced his room. There wasn't enough space. He liked his room well enough. He liked it a million times better than his room in the castle. That room had been cold and he'd always felt watched.

That was the opposite case in his bedroom on Earth. He was completely alone and he knew it. His parents rarely stepped inside and when they did it was usually just to issue an invitation to a meal. He'd made his room comfortable but not *too* comfortable. He didn't let anything in his life get *too* comfortable.

The walls were lined with bookshelves full of books and comics and DVDs that he'd read or watched exactly once. Research.

Then there was his bed, king-sized with a plain bedspread. He had two desks on opposite walls from each other. One for school work and one for other things…

He wrote on that other desk, the empty desk. He'd sat there when he'd written about Morland for his blog. He used that desk to clear his mind, to remember, or to forget, whichever was needed. It was always kept empty unless he was using it and that empty space gave him a weird modicum of peace in his life.

He paced the room like he was looking for something but he wasn't sure what. He had nearly worn a pacing circle through the carpet over the years.

Whenever he stopped pacing, he found himself pounding his hand on his thigh. He made himself sit down in his computer chair at the empty desk. He cupped the back of his neck with his hands and reclined back to stare at the ceiling. He needed to pull it together. She was probably okay. He hadn't grabbed her that hard but... She could see Morland.

What the hell? What the actual bloody hell? It couldn't be true. It must be some ploy; some game she was playing.

She'd read his blog already so she could have made it all up. What better plan to worm her way into his group? Peter would have eaten it up. He loved Morland. No matter how Derek tried to show him the truth, he was entranced.

And he'd let her read the blog! Derek still couldn't really believe it. Peter's betrayal stung. Peter *knew* that Derek liked to keep that part of himself a private from the people he knew in real life but at the first pretty girl, he gave away the state secrets.

She couldn't really see Morland. It must just be a game she'd thought of after she had read his blog. But that had been only recently. She'd brought it up for the first time today at lunch. So maybe...

Maybe this was what she had wanted to talk to him about that first day. He needed to listen. He needed to learn to keep his mouth shut. He was missing things. There were pieces he didn't have.

He wished suddenly that there was someone he could talk to who knew more than him. He frowned remembering the old mage. He might have heard of something like this, not that he would have shared that information with Derek. Was it really possible she could see Morland? What did it mean?

He sat down at the empty desk without thinking. But once he was there it felt right. He always felt better after he had written things out. His brain was too busy and cluttered to see things straight. When he poured it all out and he could see it with his eyes, then he could understand it. He pulled out paper and started writing. "Elinor. We met the first day of the fall semester at Central Piedmont Community College..."

We wrote until his hand cramped. But it was time to stop anyway. He'd started repeating himself, writing in circle, always ending up at the same knot. *Could it be true?*

He started pacing again, flexing his hand as he walked. He was never going to be able to sleep. He needed to talk to Peter, who was going to be really mad at him but he'd get over it. He always did. Derek grabbed his phone and keys planning to just show up at Peter's house when he saw a missed text from Peter.

"She's fine, you stupid a-hole."

She'd told Peter already? How long had it been? What time was it? *Just after one a.m.*

"I need to talk. I'm coming over," Derek texted back.

"What am I? A flippin hotel. Fine."

A hotel? She'd been over to his house? No one but Derek ever came over. Peter's dad was a living terror. He must be working tonight.

Derek was barely in control enough to drive. He was livid and guilty which made a terrible combination. Peter was waiting outside, pacing. He *was* mad.

"Wait," Peter said as Derek came close. "Just wait a second. I thought I was ready to see you but I'm not yet. How could you Derek? She's just a girl."

"Is it true? Can she really see Morland? How long have you been keeping this from me?" Derek asked, unable to keep the bite out of his words.

"Yeah. As far as I can tell she can. Her eyes change color from blue to green when she blinks and she approached me. She'd seen your soul. She described just what you used to look like. And no," he said raising his hand, "She only read you blog for the first time a couple days ago. I hadn't told her anything. I knew you would freak out. I tried to steer her away. But in truth I never thought you'd be *this* horrible. You were strangling her against a tree?" he asked incredulously.

"Truthfully?" Derek said sitting down on the porch steps. "It all flashed red for a second. I couldn't have been more shocked if she'd sprouted a pair of wings. It was the last thing in the world I expected her to say. When the word 'Morland' came out of her lips... I just lost it. It was my worst nightmare come true. I didn't mean to hurt her. I didn't want to."

The two guys stared silently out into the night.

"She's okay?" Derek asked.

"Barely. I don't think she'll bruise but... She'd just found out she was incurable, that her headaches were never going to go away on their own. She hoped you could help her," Peter spat.

"It would have been better if you had prepared me," Derek said sharply.

"Yeah. I completely agree with you but I had no idea she was going to talk to you again. I don't think she really did until you showed up in the woods behind her."

"I am sorry, Peter. For how it played out."

"Don't tell me you're sorry. You need to tell her. And you need to help her."

"No. I won't help her. I will apologize, if she'll hear it. But I will have nothing to do with her *powers*. It can only lead to evil. Seeing Morland... It won't like to be seen. It'll find a way to stop her."

"All the more reason you need to help her! After what happened at the doctor today, I really believe the headaches and the visions are connected. If we can make one go away the other will too."

"That is unfortunate but you cannot convince me," Derek said shrugging. "I've never heard of an ability like hers. And I don't know that I ever heard of anyone having headaches while I was in Morland. Nothing like hers at least. I know nothing that can help her and she will only cause me trouble. I won't ever touch her again but that's all I can promise you."

Peter just shook his head as he walked inside.

"You know I'm not good, Peter," Derek said after him. "You know I have no goodness in me."

"Then why do you feel bad? Why is Elinor still alive? Missing your soul doesn't make you a monster. I see the goodness in you. But if you keep smothering it with your fear and selfishness, you'll lose it. I'm done for now. Goodnight."

On the drive home, Derek remembered when Peter had first read his story. Derek had spent a lot of time on Morland looking for signs of Earth hoping to find a way home or an ally. And when Derek came home he did the reverse. He tried to find bits of Morland on Earth.

He was sure that someone else had been there or someone from there was here. Derek didn't know what he would do if he ever found that person but he couldn't stop himself from looking.

Derek read everything he could get his hands on, especially sci-fi and fantasy novels. And when he had become close friends with Peter he had gone through his collection of comics, novels, and movies. Derek would read them quickly and then give them back without a word. He never found any bit of Morland in them. One afternoon Peter had asked *the* question.

"What are you looking for?"

"I don't know what you mean," Derek had said averting his eyes.

"You are looking for something. I could save you a bunch of time by narrowing whatever list you are working from."

Derek had stared into Peter's eyes for a long moment before he'd said, "Okay. I want you to read something. But I don't want to talk about it."

"Okay."

Peter had read it in one sitting, while Derek had paced his bonus room. When he was done Peter had said, "It's good. Really good. You wrote it?"

Derek had stared then nodded.

"It's all true, isn't it?" Peter had said.

Derek continued to stare and then he nodded his head a tiny bit.

"Oh God," Peter had said rubbing his hands down the side of his face. Then he shook himself and said, "Okay well there are a couple comics I want you to skim and I'll look through my library. I'm sure someone else has been to Morland. And you need to post that online. Maybe it will draw the attention of someone else who has been there."

So *The Morland Prince* blog had been born and Derek had only regretted posting it a dozen times or so.

It still was so strange to Derek that Peter had accepted it all instantly. Never a doubt. He accepted it as truth without hesitation. And it had sealed them together.

They had never found Morland mentioned anywhere. There had been plenty of things slightly similar in stories or movies, and Derek had tried to explain to Peter how each one was just wrong enough.

Derek had said "It's like how you could see a picture of a house that's the same model as yours but you wouldn't even have to study it hard to know that it's not *your* house. Your house has a chip in the brick on the far left corner where the UPS guy backed into it and there is a dead spot in the grass from a fireworks incident and it won't ever grow back no matter the inducement. But even without those things, that other house just isn't your house."

So Morland had stayed elusive on paper and screen. She remained Derek's personal hell. Maybe he was the first to go there, but he couldn't believe it. Not that Morland was so similar to Earth but a hundred tiny facts aligned to make him believe the planets were connected.

First, they spoke English and different dialects of it. He imagined whole towns getting sucked through into Morland and each mostly staying with their own kind. What were the chances of another planet spontaneously creating the same language he spoke? Unless there was some sort of universal translator like the T.A.R.D.I.S. from Doctor Who.

Their government was also similar. They had a queen, a tyrant magic queen but still. And the people were humans. But some of them had magic. Earth had none of that. None that was real, at least. He'd seen the real stuff and could spot a fake in every show.

And most similar of all was the environment of Morland: oxygen, water, mountains, oceans. Morland's length of day and year were also very close to Earth time. What were the chances of that? What were the chances that another planet would fall into orbit around its sun at the exact same distance Earth was from its sun?

Morland years could have been twice as long or the days could have been fifteen hours long. Instead it was Earth's mirror. He acknowledged that Morland was smaller than Earth, a good deal smaller but besides that they could have been sisters. But knowing that didn't give him any clues as to what it all meant. They were connected but in a way he didn't understand.

No matter how many hours they wasted looking for something that wasn't there, Peter had been there for him.

Derek felt the guilt settle heavy on his shoulder. Peter was a really great friend. He was as different as night and day from Derek's last best friend but she was only memories now. And Derek counted himself lucky to get a chance to have another. He'd try to find a way to make things right with Peter and... Elinor.

Chapter 12

Elinor

Elinor had seriously considered skipping class on Friday. Partly, of course, because she did not ever want to see Derek again. And partly because she generally felt bad and pitiful. Being mildly strangled did horrors for her migraine. *Headache,* she corrected herself. She had headaches that acted like migraines but weren't, whatever that meant.

Thursday had been a day of pain and recovery. But she had to go back to school eventually. She wouldn't let him take that from her. And by going on today, it would say that he wasn't in control of her life, even if it felt like he was… a little bit. Peter had kept up a steady stream of communication since she'd been to his house that night.

He'd told her that Derek had come over and that he felt bad. She had scoffed. But Peter wasn't trying to play peacemaker. He hadn't tried to sell Derek's regrets. He'd just told her the facts: that Derek was going to leave her alone and she was perfectly safe going to school with him. But she doubted 'perfectly safe' could ever be applied to Derek.

On her drive to campus the rain fell steadily and her head started to escalate. She usually loved rainy days, no sunshine while everything was gray and gloomy. She'd seriously looked into Forks, WA from the *Twilight* books as a headache oasis.

But no amount of dark skies could slow her headache once it started. And it was steadily climbing. She'd tried not to count it out as she drove to school. Level six. Level six and half. Level seven. Level seven and a half.

Sometimes stress was a trigger. She was sure she had been clenching her teeth since yesterday. She took a couple deep breaths trying to calm herself. But the extra oxygen didn't slow the barreling train.

She struggled within herself. Skipping today and driving home whatever her reason was letting him win. He'd think that scaring her was the way to keep her doing what he wanted. So she pulled on her sunglasses and walked out into the rain.

He was there, of course, early for the first time ever. But she walked past him to sit in her usual seat, right in front of him.

I can't actually take my sunglasses off, Elinor realized. *This was a terrible mistake.* The lights in the classroom had turned against her. The nausea was coming now. She closed her eyes.

Level eight.

She wanted to explain her situation to the teacher but Mrs. Radcliffe wasn't in yet. Elinor hoped she'd come in before class started. She'd hate for her teacher to think she was being disrespectful. With minutes passing by from the class starting time, Elinor thought she'd caught a lucky break.

If the teacher never came she could just leave, having faced Derek but also able to escape and find somewhere dark and alone to rest. But suddenly an angry man came stomping in, leaving piles of water in his wake.

So close.

"I'm Mr. Baker. I'm subbing for your teacher..." he said pausing to look at his sheet. "Mrs. Radcliffe. She's given me an assignment so there will be no shirking."

He was all bustle and noise as he straightened his things at the front desk. He looked up at Elinor and said, "Hey 'Sunglasses at Night' what's your problem?"

Elinor was surprised and began to explain "Sorry, I have a bad headache and I'm really sensitive to light. I don't mean any disrespect."

"Yeah, my wife has headaches," he said with so much sarcasm he might as well have used air quotes. "Take the shades off."

She just stared at him. Her jaw might have opened.

"Off. You heard me."

She took them off and tried not to flinch as the light surged into her eyes like tiger claws. She kept her eyes open and downward the rest of the class in a determined attempt to not show weakness. She kept her lip strong in nearly a snarl. *I will not cry,* she told herself.

Thankfully the sub was in no mood to interact or teach students. He assigned them to read a short story and to answer the questions about it.

Elinor was mad.

Her head was pounding and her unstoppable anger only fueled it. Her temples felt freshly bruised and the pain from her eyes was shooting to the back of her head. She was counting the minutes till class was over.

Someone touched her shoulder from behind and she flinched violently. She turned around glaring at... Derek. What did he want? She turned back around without a word. She did not need to be pestered and she didn't need his pity. If he even felt any.

The moment class was over, she was packed and gone instantly. Mr. Baker might have called for her but she was pushing past the crowd running to the bathroom. She barely made it before she started throwing up. It only made it worse but it couldn't be helped. The spasms were horrible on her already aching neck. Her neck felt like it might snap in two from the violent contractions. And no relief came from vomiting because there was nothing bad that needed to be thrown up.

Once she was emptied she felt just as nauseous but less stressed knowing she wouldn't throw up down her dress. And it was only the tiniest bit of self-respect that kept her from lying down on the public bathroom floor. Her dress trailed on the floor but she couldn't care.

She couldn't quite get up from her knees so she turned to lean her forehead against the stall. She heard the door close. *Good.* Maybe she was alone now. She had no idea if there had been anyone in there to begin with.

"Elinor?" called Peter.

She could see his feet and not just his feet. Many feet.

"This is the girl's bathroom. Get out," she hissed.

The feet stepped back but didn't leave.

"What are you doing here?" she asked trying to be nice. She made herself mentally repeat her mantra: *Let it make you kind. Let it make you kind.* She hated that at the start of pain she lost all social niceties and became a monster.

"Are you okay?" asked Peter.

"No. I..." she said stopping her sentence. She was not going to cry here, sitting on the floor of the bathroom with five guys outside the stall. *Hold it together, Elinor.*

"Derek told us what happened," Peter said.

Elinor huffed.

"Yeah, Mr. Baker is a jerk," said Jerry

"No, he's an asshole," said Carlos. Then came more colorful descriptions.

She smiled a little bit.

"Do you want us to take you home?" asked Peter.

"Yes," she said and groaned as she stood up and the room shook. She smacked her hands forcefully on the sides of the stall to keep from falling. The sound was jarring and was followed by several questions all at once.

"Are you okay?"

"What was that?"

"Are you going to pass out?"

"Should we get a doctor?"

"Should we come in?"

"No! I'm fine. A little privacy might be nice though. For a moment," Elinor said.

"Oh yeah, yeah," they replied stepping back.

"See you out there," said Peter

"Don't faint," said Derek softly.

"So the girl's bathroom huh?" said Jerry as they walked out and she heard the door close.

She took a deep breath and left the stall. She washed her hands and laid a wet paper towel on her face for a second.

They really aren't so bad, she thought shaking her head and regretting it as she clutched the sink for a moment to get her bearings. Taking a deep breath, she pulled on the bathroom door but it wouldn't budge. She pulled harder and it gave a little bit.

"What are you doing? Let me out." she shouted through the door as she tried to see through the opening. It opened a little and then all the way suddenly and she stumbled into Derek. He caught her and held her upright until she pushed off, not looking at him.

"We were giving you privacy," said Peter proudly.

"We didn't let anyone in," said Jerry standing up straight.

"I needed privacy from boys. People probably thought I was being murdered in there," she said.

"So do you want me to drive you home?" suggested Peter.

She hesitated. If she went home her parents would know. Her stepmom wasn't working today. Today would get added to the list of reasons why she wasn't ready for college.

"My parents are going to freak," said Elinor. "I'll never be allowed to leave the house again."

"Okay but you don't want to stay here, right?" Peter asked.

"Yeah, definitely not. I might feel better with a Coke and a dark room."

"I know. Let's go see a movie. They are dark and have Cokes," said Jack.

"Uh remember last time," said Elinor at the same time Peter said "Last time didn't go so well." Elinor wished she had enough inside herself to turn and smile that he knew her so well. But she was using all her energy to stay standing.

"No, there will be no flashing lights or killing things. It's that movie about ocean life on the Great Barrier Reef. It'll be all relaxing and mostly blue colors and it's narrated by Jude Law who has a super soothing voice."

A breath of a laugh escaped her lips.

"Boy is obsessed with the ocean," said Carlos.

"I wish every week was Shark Week," Jack said wistfully.

"Don't we all," Elinor said. "That actually sounds like a great idea, Jack. Thank you."

"There is a showing in twenty-five minutes," he replied.

"How do you know that off the top of your head?" said Peter laughing, shaking his head.

Peter drove Elinor's car as she laid in the back seat. Peter must have remembered her description of what a perfect headache driver Derek had been because Peter didn't say a word.

When they got to the movie theater, Elinor ordered a Coke, a blue raspberry ICEE, and a box of Snickers bites. The theater was pretty empty. They went to the very top row and got settled in. Elinor ended up between Derek and Peter by chance because of the order they were in as they walked up. Peter must have been trying to make things better between them after all because when she took stock of her seat, he just shrugged looking sheepish.

She was too out of it to argue. She took her medicine, bunched up her jacket under her neck and pulled her knees up to her chest burrowing in. She closed her eyes alternating between reaching blindly for her beverages and her candy. She felt a jacket drape across her lap. She looked down and saw that it was Derek's leather jacket. She instantly pulled it off to hand it back to him.

"Just take it," he said forcing it back.

"I don't need it," she said trying to give it back.

His eyes looked pointedly down and she saw her dress was a little short in her knees-up position.

"Ugh," she said taking it back. She didn't want to offend his delicate sensibilities and she didn't want him looking at her all movie.

"I'm sorry," Derek said after a minute.

"I know," she bit back closing her eyes again.

"Apology doesn't count until she can keep her eyes open," Peter said seriously. Then added lighter. "Any better, El?"

"It will be. This really is nice," she said looking over to Jack who was sitting on Derek's other side.

"I know," Jack said winking.

The movie was so relaxing. The sound of the ocean, soothing deep blue colors, and Jude Law's beautiful British accent were exactly what she needed. She just closed her eyes and sighed. She started to drift off, a good sign her meds were kicking in, and she let it take her. She didn't notice when her head lolled to the side slowly.

Derek

Elinor's blonde head slid slowly. Derek didn't turn to look but he could see it out of his peripheral. It was as if the strings that had been holding her up were suddenly cut leaving her slumped. Her breathing turned deeper and steadier a couple minutes later.

Derek was glad she was asleep. She had been all thorns today. Not that he didn't deserve every one of them but he just wanted to get past this. Things wouldn't be good with Peter until it was back to the way it was before the forest encounter.

He hadn't been able to stop thinking about her since she'd shown up outside his house. She haunted him. A tangible link to Morland. It fascinated and terrified him.

Maybe it wasn't the worst idea to stay close, to see how this all progressed. Not that she'd ever let him around again. He'd never seen her act the way she had today even including the last time her head had been bad and he'd driven her home. That time she had been empty and pitiful. Today she was fire and prickly edges to everyone but especially himself. She'd never forgive him. What should it matter? But maybe she held some key that could free him from Morland once and for all.

He'd been watching the screen absently with his attention on his thoughts, so he hadn't noticed as Elinor's head slid lower and lower to the right. Before he could move, her head was on his shoulders. He didn't stir a muscle. What was he supposed to do? She would have wanted to be woken up so she didn't have to touch him... But she wasn't herself today and probably needed to sleep for a bit. So he left her alone.

As the movie played on and fish came and went, he felt the stirring of some strange feeling. Maybe subconsciously she trusted him. She slept soundly resting on his shoulder. Maybe she could get past it. She could have leaned to the left in her sleep, laying her head on Peter's shoulder, who couldn't have loved it more. They were getting so close.

She'd gone to Peter after... *Say it. She'd gone to Peter after what? She'd gone to Peter after I had tried to strangle her.* He'd tried to strangle her.

And yet here she was days later asleep on his shoulder. He hadn't had someone trust him so much since... Brigitte. He mentally shook himself, mechanically laying a hand on his right side where the scar wasn't. Elinor wasn't really trusting him. She was asleep and had made no conscious decision one way or the other.

She woke up when the theater lights came on, slowly shifting on his shoulder. Then she jolted up and grabbed her head probably regretting the sudden movement. She looked over at him mortified. Maybe he should have woken her.

"I'm so sorry," she said looking at him, looking around. "I just fell asleep. I'm sorry, Derek. I didn't mean to."

"Don't worry about it."

"It's good you got some sleep," said Peter looking over between the two of them. Derek wondered if he had seen. But there was no way Peter wouldn't have noticed.

"Do you feel any better?" Peter asked.

"Loads better," she said as she tried to smile but her face didn't quite make it up. "I don't feel like I might die at any second. My meds kicked in and I'm just feeling tired and sore. But numb." Then the smile came.

"That's awesome," said Peter. "What do you want to do now?"

"What time is it?" she said looking for her phone. "I can go home now. I probably look normal enough and they won't have to know how bad it was."

"Can you drive?" asked Peter.

"Umm probably. I'm a little groggy but not bad. I should be good."

"That doesn't sound very convincing," said Peter raising an eyebrow.

"I'll drive you home," Derek said without looking at her.

"No, it's fine. I don't mind," Peter said looking at him. Peter was trying to say something with that look but Derek didn't know what.

"It doesn't make sense," Derek replied. "You can drive my car back to your car and I'll pick up my car tomorrow. And I'd like to have a chance to apologize." They shared an intense look and then Peter resigned.

"Yeah, you're right. It is much easier," Peter said looking as sullen as a smiling guy could."Is that alright with you, El?"

"Yeah, it's fine I guess. I wouldn't want to make you go out of your way."

"You'll be perfectly safe," Peter said to her softly and Derek tried not to flinch at the implication.

They all walked out to the parking lot together. It surprised Derek that it was still day time. He usually only saw movies at night. He was used to seeing the stars when he came out of the theater. But the sun was shining bright and it felt nice and warm after the dark theater.

Peter stopped Elinor before she got in her car. Derek stood to the side giving them space. "Are you sure you are okay? I was really worried about you back there," he said.

"Yeah, I'm much better. It wasn't so bad. I'll head to bed early and sleep the rest of this off. Thanks for coming to the movie with me and for rescuing me from the bathroom," she gave him a hug and he held on for a breath longer than normal.

"Wasn't so bad?" he said quoting her with raised eyebrows. "You know it's okay to admit it, right? It's not complaining to tell the truth, to say out loud how bad it can be. Call me when you come out the other side, so I know you're okay for real."

"Okay," she said turning to hug Jack, Carlos, and Jerry. They were all in a hugging mood apparently. Elinor did not hug Derek.

She handed Derek the keys and walked to the passenger door.

"You can lay down if you want," he said.

"I'm fine to sit up. And I want the AC on my face."

They drove for a couple minutes in silence when Derek was distracted by Elinor. At every turn she would flip and fold the sun visor back and forth like she was trying to turn the car into a Transformer. It took him a moment to realize why she was being so idiotic. She was trying to block out the sun, her nemesis. She was crazy.

"Can we talk for a minute?" Derek said unable to listen to the clicks of the sun visor flipping around for another second. "Are you well enough?"

Elinor

"I'm fine," Elinor said too sharply and then reined it down a notch. He was trying to be civil. She should try as well. *But it is so hard to be nice to him.* "Yes. We can talk. If you need to," she added still unable to get rid of her edge completely.

"Elinor," he said and she realized he'd never said her name before. It felt like someone else's name when he said it. "I can't tell you how sorry I am about what happened. That anger came over me so strongly. You had manifested my greatest fear and I overreacted."

"Overreacted," she said hotly raising her eyebrows.

He breathed out in a loud exhale. "I'm trying to apologize," he said stopping for a moment before he continued. "I never meant to hurt you. I never wanted to hurt you. I think there is still a wild, feral thing inside me left over from Morland. I think sometimes that I've finally gotten it buried but it just shows back up. I know that's no excuse," he said lifting his hand to stop her. She'd only barely opened her lips. "If I could take it back I would. I wish I could redo that conversation."

"Me too," she said softly. She sighed. She wasn't made of grudge holding material. She couldn't hold on to blinding white anger for long. So she let it go and felt better for it.

"Then let's try again," she said. If he wanted to redo that conversation from the forest, then she'd start it. "Hey Derek, nice night for a walk." She said in a nonchalant sing-song voice looking at him pointedly when he didn't immediately respond.

Then he caught on and said "Yes. It's not strange at all that you are outside in the dark watching my house," he said sounding more like robot.

A surprised chuckle escaped her lips. Maybe he wasn't the worst *of all time*.

"So I wanted to tell you what I tried to say the first day of school when I definitely wasn't asking you out. I've got a magic power that lets me see another world whenever I blink. I mostly just see trees but sometimes you are there. Only you don't look the same. You have long hair and are wearing different clothes with a sword at your waist. This revelation makes me think I am seeing Morland, the magic world you have been to as I have recently learned from reading your blog. Which was beautiful and really horrible," she added.

"Um thank you?" he said, his turn to chuckle. "That was not alarming at all to hear you speak about Morland. I am in complete control of my feelings. How long have you been seeing another world?"

"About a year," she said, finally losing the joking tone and speaking plainly. "Ever since I moved to Waxhaw. Oh I also started getting bad headaches when that happened."

"How can you tell it's another world and not a hallucination?" he asked frankly.

"I wasn't sure at first that it was real. But the fact that I was able to see you in the woods before I had even seen you in real life is a point against hallucinations. Also whenever I blink at night I see a whole different set of stars. And hallucinations aren't usually so quick to come and go. This happens *every* time I blink. And it's not like it's just a picture of trees. It's like I'm really there. When I turn my head or when I walk it's like I'm walking through a forest. Also I don't feel crazy. Not that all crazy people do," she guessed.

"Do you know what happened to me when I came home?" Derek asked

"Umm I heard some bits from Peter. You hadn't aged a day and no time had passed since you left. And your parents didn't believe you?" she asked.

"That's putting it mildly. We can talk about that later but I bring it up to make sure you don't tell yours. You haven't yet, right?"

"No. I was scared they wouldn't believe me. Even before I knew about you. I was scared that if I talked about it would make it real or prove I was crazy. I don't know. It was really hard when no one knew. But Peter believed me instantly. I can see why you've always kept him close. It's very lonely having this secret with no one to talk to."

"Yeah."

"Have you ever heard of someone with my ability?" she asked. Now it was really turning into the conversation she'd wanted to have with him.

"No. I'm sorry but I haven't. I also told Peter I don't even remember people having headaches or anyone mentioning them in Morland. I don't know why this is happening to you or how but I really, really don't like it."

"Me neither," she said through a tight smile.

As they pulled into their neighborhood Elinor said, "Thanks for getting everyone, earlier I mean. I really appreciate it."

"Yeah,"

"Oh, what did you want in class? You tapped my shoulder."

"It looked like I electrocuted you."

"Yeah sorry. I was just so mad at the world and trying really hard not to die. So?"

"So what?"

"What did you want?"

"Oh I was just seeing if you were okay. Which you obviously weren't."

"Oh. Okay thanks."

"For what?"

"I don't know. For noticing I wasn't okay and for getting help."

"Yeah," he said. They drove the rest of the way in silence. Derek dropped her off at her house and then walked home through the trees.

Chapter 13

Derek

Derek woke up with a start, his body drenched in sweat. It sometimes felt like he hadn't had a full night's sleep in the eleven years since he'd first fallen through to Morland.

His dream had been more vivid this time. The same dream he had most nights. It lingered on him. He could still feel what it felt like to choke all the air out of her lungs. He could still see the look in her eyes as they turned for a moment from soulless-black to the dark gold he knew his sister's eyes to be.

He only ever saw her eyes in the dream. He was starting to forget her face. It was so cruel that this moment, the darkest, was the one he got to relieve.

His hands shook violently now that he was fully awake. Even though he knew he had done the right thing, he loathed reliving the worst moment of his life over and over again. She had asked him to end it. To set her free from the Darkness but... Maybe he shouldn't have. Maybe he should have joined her. At least they'd still be together.

She hadn't been the first he had killed but those deaths had been as a solider. And he had loved her so much. He shook his head and brought his hand instinctively to his right side. It was still bizarre that his scar was gone. When he'd come home a fresh thirteen-year-old, his body had been just how he'd left it.

But he had replaced the scar with his own in this world. He traced his fingers over the tattoo of her name on his right side, where she had plunged her knife. B-r-i-g-i-t-t-e. Those who saw the tattoo assumed it was the remnants of a discarded lover and he didn't correct them. His parents had not been thrilled and he hadn't even really tried to make them understand. How could he explain the loss of a sibling when in this world he was an only child? He climbed out of bed and went outside for his newest hobby.

He had started watching Elinor after he had driven her home that first night. Derek told himself that he just needed to know the truth about her. He needed to see what was real and what was a facade. He just couldn't shake the bone deep feeling that she was trouble. That she was a ghost sent to torment him. Everything she did irritated him. Everything she said made him shocked that she could be so stupid. Peter was blind, of course. *Idiot.* So were the rest of the guys. *All idiots.* It was because she was so pretty. Even he could admit that she was.

But it changed nothing for him.

People didn't get the ability to see another world for no reason. And the fact that it was Morland was laughable. He wasn't even sure that he believed her. She could have found his blog on her own before Peter. He hadn't hidden it. It was there as a calling card for the seeker, for one who had been there or would themselves get trapped. It was his guidebook.

Not that any of the comments had been from people in those categories. They had mostly been nerds who said he should publish his story. But he had no interest in that. He could not imagine having a copy of it sitting on his shelves staring at him all day and he had no desire for his parents to ever read it.

They had only *just* recovered from his breakdown and it had been six years. At first they had been consumed with him. The doctors had guessed the 'incident' was from neglect or too much time alone. His parents had always worked a lot. The doctors recommended intense family time so they had both taken a month off of work and had a mandatory family vacation at the mountain house in Boone.

And it hadn't gone well.

He'd always imagined that when he finally came home everything would be fixed. But it wasn't.

He had never felt so lost and alone as when he had finally come back from Morland. It was crazy that even though Earth had been exactly as he'd left it, it felt foreign and wrong. He felt like a traitor to his birthplace, like a brainwashed child who had been raised in the land of his enemies and couldn't readjust once he had been brought home.

He hated it.

Everything made him angry. An irrational, consuming anger. He had learned to control it, to learn what might set him off but it was always underneath his skin like a black volcano just waiting to erupt.

Boy Scouts had helped in a weird way. It had given him focused instructions and it had given him Peter. Neither of them had gone onto Eagle. Peter didn't because money was tight and he liked video games better and Derek because he'd learned everything he could and had no need for titles that weren't Morland transferable.

Because he knew Morland was coming for him. And he wasn't going to be helpless when that day came. But the Scouts had helped him to assimilate back into the world and it had helped him learn to hide his red rage.

But Elinor knew just how to pull it out of him.

He had trouble trusting anyone anyway and Elinor triggered some instinct in him that made him want to defend his turf. She was like a rival wolf in his territory and it absolutely killed him that no one else could see it. He thought her headaches were probably just punishment for whatever she had done.

But the longer he watched her, the more his feelings began to change.

The fire burning inside him hardened into something dark and impenetrable. He didn't know what he felt and he didn't like it. The mystery of her was infuriating. He had researched her endlessly. Derek knew everything about her family and her past.

Elinor's grandfather on her dad's side was an immigrant from England. He had gotten married and had Elinor's dad, George. Then one day Grandpa leaves and Grandma goes crazy. George settles Grandma in a nice care facility then and goes to college. He meets Adelle. They get married and have Elinor. Adelle dies in a car accident. George marries stepmom and brings Ryan along. Then the little kids are born. There was nothing magical or supernatural.

The only thing even a little interesting was Elinor's grandma who went crazy when her husband left her. But people leave everyday and everyone else has to deal with the mess they made. Peter's mom left one day when he was too young, when his dad had hit her one too many times. She left and hadn't spared Peter a second glance. Derek had only just met Peter and the change in him had been startling.

It was a reasonable reaction to go a little crazy. But Peter had pulled himself together and that strength was what had finally made Derek cave into their friendship. Peter was probably strong enough to handle the disastrous mess that Derek was.

Elinor's scholastic history had been above average but all premed kids were above average. If her ability to see Morland came from somewhere he wouldn't find it on the internet so... he watched her. He didn't tell Peter. Peter wouldn't have understood.

Elinor's house was only a couple away from his and he would spend part of most nights watching her. Derek didn't think Peter had any real idea of how bad Elinor's headaches must be. Their whole house was completely barricaded against the sun. Every window was covered with blackout curtains. It would have been very boring to watch if Elinor's little sister didn't fling open every curtain as soon as the sun went down.

After the first week Derek was able to almost predict her headaches.

The first thing that happened was that Elinor would go silent and still. She'd stop talking, sometimes in mid-sentence, as if she suddenly didn't have an ounce of energy for any unnecessary actions. Her eyes would go vacant like no one was home.

Then she'd retreat to what he assumed was her room since those curtains never opened. She'd be gone for two hours or twenty hours. He assumed she was laying in the fetal position sleeping it off. It was fascinating to watch. She was nearly an invalid.

Her waking hours where she was able to be mobile were so limited. He wondered how she made it through school three days a week. She obviously paid for it later. But even having a front row seat to her pain show, Derek still didn't like her.

She looked like a parasitic plant slowing spreading and killing the tree that supported it by choking out all the sunlight. Her family walked on eggshells. Their whole dynamic was centered around her.

He smiled to himself at how much Elinor hated it.

He could read her like a book. She hated their hovering and soft treading feet. She probably wanted them all to live normally but she didn't let them. Every curtain was drawn until it was dark. The little kids never screamed or ran through the house. He could see that she was pushing herself and failing. She didn't have much longer at this rate. She'd have to accept her limits or burn out.

After a couple weeks, he had to concede that she probably wasn't a threat. She was lost and broken. But she was no evil genius or master spy of the Queen's. She was just a girl. But what was it about her that made her an addiction for him? He couldn't stay away. He was running out of reasons he could admit to as to why he was still watching her. How could she know everything and even bear to look at him? He could barely look at himself some days.

Chapter 14

Peter

"Where is your car?" Elinor asked Derek one Monday at lunch. She always ended up parking a couple cars away from him in the small parking lot. Maybe they left around the same time. Peter had started parking on that side of the school also.

"It's in the shop," Peter answered cheerfully sitting down next to her and handing her an extra cookie he'd bought from Subway. He had gotten a busted lip from his dad over the weekend and he hoped it had healed enough that she wouldn't notice.

"Oh thank you," she said smiling brightly taking the treat. *Good.* Her eyes hadn't even lingered. It must not look as bad as it felt.

"I drove him to school," Peter continued.

"I can speak for myself," Derek said sharply.

"Yes, but you usually don't," Peter said.

Slowly more and more guys joined the table until it was at its usual stuffed capacity. Peter was glad to see that Elinor had really settled in. She was so used to them that she unconsciously shuffled her chair closer to Peter to make room for Jack to slide an extra chair in. She didn't even roll her eyes when Peter produced a game from his bag. *Maybe she is finally succumbing to her inner geek*, Peter thought smiling.

"Okay. Name of the game is LCR," Peter said producing a small capsule containing three dice. "It's a gambling game so dish out some quarters. You roll the dice and then do what they say. You either send your quarters to the left, to the center, to the right or you get to keep it. The game is over when one person has all the quarters." He let his smile become wicked.

They always played a game at lunch. Sometimes it was a card game like Rummy or Texas Hold 'em. Sometimes it was a board game like Scrabble or King of Tokyo which was like Yahtzee but you got to attack each other with Japanese monsters. Every once in a while when they managed a long lunch the bigger games came out like Settlers of Catan or The Big Book of Madness.

Most days there were some side Magic games going on, that is if the whole table wasn't covered with them. Elinor learned the game and would play sometimes. She seemed to get irritated when he went easy on her but if he really played he would beat her so quickly it wouldn't have been fun. She'd made a pretty strong poison deck and sometimes she could beat Jack.

Derek rarely played a game twice. Playing a game twice was unnecessary for him because it didn't further his hunt for Morland. So instead he'd scan the web or read a book with a wizard on the cover that Peter didn't even know if he enjoyed.

But whenever Peter pulled out a new game Elinor was the happiest. He loved that she was really a part of everything. He couldn't believe that she'd been so easily accepted by everyone, including Derek, who had finally conceded that she wasn't going to go away.

It helped that everyone was a little in love with her.

It *mostly* wasn't her fault.

She was petite and fragile and it went against human nature not to want to take care of her. She wasn't afraid of them or intimidated to hang around a bunch of guys. She was quick to laugh and her headaches gave her a mysterious distance that was intoxicating.

But the true seed of the problem was that she was beautiful, real life beautiful. Not stunning like a model in a magazine but so pretty she sometimes took his breath away.

Her hair was as long as an anime character's which did not help at all. It was blonde in a completely different way than his own. His hair was a light colored mop on his head, her fair hair shone.

She wasn't the sexiest girl in school by far. She dressed like a normal girl, mostly dresses and flip-flops with a jacket that usually got left behind before she dashed back to get it. Her modesty kept her from showing too much skin so he wondered sometimes where the pull came from that made her so attractive to them.

Part of it that she was nice and indulged the high scale nerdiness that was always going on. It would have been impossible not to like her but somehow Derek managed. It made Peter wonder what was really broken inside him that he saw this girl as a threat to his way of life. But then, Peter decided, it was definitely for the best that Derek showed no interest.

For Elinor's part, she didn't encourage anyone too much. She was nice while trying to stay away from 'too friendly'. Her marked preference for Peter helped with his jealousy at having to share her and it made the rest of the guys hesitant to approach her with their intentions. He knew she'd been asked a couple times if she had a boyfriend and she always said no. She usually added that her headaches were so bad she couldn't imagine dating anyone. This did nothing to dissuade them.

Most of the guys that hovered in their circle didn't grasp what that sentence really meant. They thought it might be an excuse or a ploy to divert their attentions. Derek understood, of course, for all the compassion he showed. And Jerry, Carlos, and Jack had been there for two bad incidents so they knew a little bit.

But Peter did as much as he subtly could to calm the guys and their masses of hormones from directing their attentions at her. He told himself it wasn't a selfish motivation, that it was what she wanted but he didn't let himself think too much on it. He was hoping, just like the rest of the fools, that she'd change her mind, that she'd decide that having a boyfriend to look out for her would only make her life easier.

He could make her life easier.

"When will your car be fixed?" Elinor asked Derek as she rolled the dice for LCR and gave one quarter to Jack and placed another into the pot at the middle of the table.

"What does it matter to you?" Derek bit back.

Elinor just sighed and passed the dice to Jack. Peter could see Derek's mind working. Peter had tasked Derek to try and be nicer to her. He didn't need to talk to her about Morland but to just not bite her head off every time she spoke. Derek finally spoke again.

"A couple days," Derek said.

"I don't know if you'd want to... But we could drive together for the next couple of days. Until your car is fixed," she said looking down. "It just seems like a pain for Peter to have to go out of his way."

Peter smiled. Everyone was finally getting along.

"That sounds great. Thanks, Elinor. Lugging this hulking brooder around was going to be a pain," Peter said.

"Don't I get a say in anything? I'm not some kid you two need to shuffle between yourselves. I could probably borrow one of my parent's cars."

"You could just say no," Elinor said taking the two quarters Peter slid her way after his roll.

"No, it's fine. We can drive together," Derek said almost mumbling.

"And that's a wrap you sexy devils, you," Jerry said looking at the clock as he repacked his bag. "It's time to return to our life of drudgery. Don't forget game night at my place on Saturday. Clear your schedules," he said waving as he headed to class.

"So I'll meet you at my car after class?" Elinor asked Derek tentatively.

"Yeah," Derek said walking the opposite direction to go to his history class.

See! It's not so hopeless after all, Peter thought as they headed to Sociology. Yup, it was all going to sort out.

Derek

He was waiting by her car when she came out walking with Peter. He assumed they'd been talking the whole way which had slowed them down.

"Okay see you later," Peter said hugging Elinor goodbye. "Oh do you want to go to Jerry's game night Saturday?"

"I don't know. Maybe. I feel weird going to his house. I'll call you later?" she said as a question.

"Sounds good. Catch you later, Derek," Peter said as he walked to his car.

Derek found it strange having her conscious in her car. The last two times they had been in a car together she had been out of it. They drove in silence for a couple minutes until Elinor spoke up.

"So how was history?"

"It was fine. Mr. Patterson is an okay teacher. How was Sociology with Peter?"

"Fine. It's an interesting class. I don't want to be a sociologist or anything but it's fascinating sometimes." Then taking a breath she said, "What were you like before?"

The question hit him full in the chest. How was she still so able to surprise and startle him? She was an unexpected quandary. Derek wondered what they'd been discussing in Sociology.

He didn't say anything for a moment and Elinor looked like she was about to clarify her question but there was no need. He knew exactly what she meant. His life was firmly divided into before and after. He finally spoke.

"I was different before Morland. So different you wouldn't recognize me. I was good," he said slowly. "I was carefree. I was just a kid. I played a lot of video games. They were my whole life as a thirteen-year-old kid. Just goofing off."

He stared off out the window and he wondered if that was what Elinor had expected to hear. He found he couldn't stop himself from saying more.

"My hands were so clean," he said looking down. "I was good, like Peter. You wouldn't have hated me."

"I don't hate you now," she said without looking at him. He ignored her comment. *Of course she hates me.* She was just trying to be nice. Elinor must not have learned that no lie can be kind.

"I was a good, normal kid," Derek said. "Everyone liked me. I think I was a really nice kid. I thought about other people's feelings. I felt more things, too. Not through this haze like I do now. Like the only things I can really feel are anger and fear. I don't like to think about before."

Elinor nodded and Derek wondered why he bothered. She wove a spell over him that made him say things he didn't mean. Why should he care if Elinor liked him now or if she would have liked him more then? It didn't matter. Elinor didn't matter. Nothing he had said had been a lie but he hated that he had said anything.

Elinor

Elinor focused on her driving. It was difficult enough with her forest vision threatening to consume her view every other blink. And she couldn't shake Derek's words.

They played on repeat in her head.

She wondered if everyone felt some kind of loss like that. She had thought she'd had more than her share having lost her mother so young, then to be followed by her never-ending pain. But Derek had lost something too. Stepping into Morland had cost him his future. His gentleness. His soul. Neither of them spoke for most of the drive when suddenly Derek looked over in dawning comprehension.

"You see the forest all the time," he said. It wasn't a question but she answered it anyway.

"Yes. Every time I blink my vision switches from one world to the other."

"Pull over," he said sharply putting a hand on the steering wheel to lead the car into an empty lot. She slammed on her brakes.

"What are you doing? Let go. This is so dangerous!" she yelled.

"No, *you* are so dangerous! How are you still driving? Do you have a death wish? How could your family let you drive when you are blind every six seconds or so? Get out. I'm driving us home."

She looked at him with her mouth open.

"Get out," he said again as he unbuckled his seat belt and walked around to open her door. When she saw that he was going to forcibly remove her she unbuckled herself and slid into the passenger seat. She curled her hands into fists and tried to calm down. But he wasn't done with her yet.

"How could you possibly be so stupid?" Derek said moving the seat back before pulling the car back onto the road.

"Me? You can't just go grabbing the steering wheel while someone else is driving. I am perfectly safe. I've mastered the double blink."

"The double blink? What the hell is that?"

"I try to always blink twice. So instead of blinking once and seeing Morland. I rapidly blink again so I'm always seeing Earth. I'm only impaired for a fraction of a second. Way less than if I was texting or changing the radio station. I'm probably the safest teen driver around. My attention is always one hundred percent on the road. And I only blink every ten minutes or so. I use these crazy Russian eye drops. So losing a half a second every ten minutes is not a big deal."

"Yes it is! Does Peter fall for this garbage? Do you really use this logic to get what you want from everyone? I cannot believe it works. You should not be driving. You are a hazard to everyone, including yourself. Do you drive your siblings around?"

She flushed crimson. She hated how she couldn't control her pale skin. It was her biggest tell. She had stopped driving her siblings around a month ago.

"You don't, do you?" he said smugly. "Because you know how dumb it is. So you'll only endanger yourself and all of Union county? You've been living in a dream world," he scoffed.

"I'm sorry but what am I supposed to do? Never leave my house?" Elinor said. "I have to live my life. I've found a way that works well enough. I've never been in an accident or even close. I'm careful. And how was I supposed to explain to my parents why I can't drive to school anymore? You know they don't know about this," she said encompassing her head.

"The nearest bus stop is seven miles from our house by the Harris Teeter," she said continuing her rant. "Should I walk that every day to take the bus to the campus? That's not a viable option. And what do you care anyway? It would solve all your problems if I died in a horrible car accident running into a telephone pole. You wouldn't have to decide what to do with me and your circle of guys would settle back into how they were before me which is all you really want!"

Derek

She was visibly shaking with anger. He didn't feel bad at all. He liked getting her riled up. He knew there was more to her than the gentle facade she hid behind. It almost felt like his duty to call her bluff when everyone else was scraping to do whatever she said. *Her, driving!* It was laughable. Maybe she was as broken as he was.

But what did any of this accomplish? She didn't care what he said. She was just going to keep driving around like a grenade with the pin pulled. Maybe if he brought it up to Peter he would talk some sense into her. But what was the solution? His lip sneered involuntarily when it hit him. He sighed and said it quickly before he changed his mind.

"I'll be driving you to school from now on," he said and braced himself for her outburst.

She turned her head to look at him in complete shock.

"Well," he said defensively, "we have similar schedules and it's been a waste of gas for us to drive two cars anyway. And it will be a good excuse for your parents so you don't have to tell them the real reason. Trust me I'm not thrilled with this either. But it's the only way if you want to keep going to college. I am *not* going to let you keep driving. I'm no mechanic but I know enough about cars to make it impossible for you to drive this without me," he said running his hand over the dashboard. She smacked his hand off.

"Don't touch my car like that," was all she said. He smiled with satisfaction. He had won. Then his smile slipped. He had won. He would be driving her to and from school three days a week.

This felt like the worst-case scenario.

Neither of them said anything when Derek pulled into her driveway. "Let me see your license," she said before getting out.

"Why?" he asked.

"Because I want to make sure you have one." She stared at him until he pulled his wallet out.

"You are ridiculous," he said tossing her his driver's license.

"My parents are strict with who I can drive with. They won't let me drive with someone who doesn't have a license. For all I know yours got revoked for too many DUIs. James, huh?" she said handing it back.

"Yes, that's my middle name, so what?"

"It's my brother's middle name."

"Are we good? Do I need to pass a driving exam?" he said.

"Don't tempt me," she said asking for the keys before she got out.

"See you Wednesday at nine a.m." he said as he tossed her the keys and left to walk to his house. "Oh and if you are going to Jerry's Saturday, I'll be driving you." When he heard her take a deep calming breath, he had to stop himself from whistling.

Chapter 15

Elinor

Elinor was in a great mood. The school was having a celebration for Mexican Independence day and they had provided tacos for the students. There was a band playing music and most everyone was having a great time. Central Piedmont Community College was always celebrating weird holidays and forcing the student body to celebrate by giving out goodies. Elinor loved it.

"This is way better than National Teddy Bear day last week," Carlos said pulling out his tiny teddy bear that the student government had given everyone. It was only an inch tall and had a little bow tie.

"Yeah I can tell you really hated it," Elinor said smiling as she pulled hers out and moved the two bears closer to be friends.

"Of course, he likes it better. This is the day of your people, right?" Jerry laughed as he unwrapped a taco.

"Ha ha. Even though my grandfather only lived there as a kid, I take great pride in my heritage and demand all your tacos because you don't deserve them!" he said trying to swipe Jerry's taco.

Peter came over and asked Elinor how it had gone when Derek had driven her home. She stared at him and said "Have you talked to Derek lately?"

"Um. Yes, I have… And I know you'll be mad when I say this… But he's right. You know it too, deep down. You shouldn't be driving. You could hurt yourself or someone else. If you really can't stand Derek, I could be your chauffeur."

She sighed. "I know he's right. You are right. It was just a blow. I'd kind of deluded myself that I was doing okay. That I had found a way to live a normal life. That I was doing what my family thought I couldn't do. He was right. I knew it wasn't safe." The failure wanted to stay settled on her shoulders but she decided to shake it off. It was what is was. And she was going to make the most of it and enjoy a beautiful day.

Elinor couldn't believe the mariachi type music wasn't destroying her head. It made her feel like going to community college had been a really great idea. She had texted Ryan a picture of her taco and asked if his school was celebrating Mexican Independence. Ryan replied with a long string of sad faces.

Derek was waiting at her car like he had been on Monday. He was a solitary gloomy cloud. But she smiled and didn't care that he hadn't even said 'hello'.

Derek

Her cheerful mood was radiating off her and annoying him. She didn't even have to say anything. He could almost *feel* her smiling. He'd thought they had something in common. A core of bitterness at the way their lives had played out. But she was able to shake it off and just enjoy the day. He envied her. He hated her.

The words "How can you possibly be happy?" burst from his lips before he could stop himself. She looked over, startled at his outburst.

"Today is Mexican Independence Day. There were free tacos. It is *impossible* to not be happy today. Did you not get one?" she said with a half-smile.

"Does it make you feel good to pretend that your life isn't a colossal disappointment?"

"Whoa! Take it down a notch. Or like a hundred notches. What did I do to you today? Gosh!"

"Answer the question. I don't buy your act and it just makes me sick. Just admit that your life sucks, that your headaches have taken everything from you. Your life is a dark room."

He looked over and saw that her hands were clenched and her eyes were narrowed to slits.

"I pretend everything is okay because that's how you live your life," Elinor said. "I stay strong by acting strong. That's how I keep it from breaking me. I've tried the 'give up' method that appears to be your life and it's empty and I hated it. You have to seize the moments of happiness when they come."

"That's a farce. A show. A delusion. You are just in denial," he said.

"Ha," she said barking out a laugh. "That I could deny it one second? I am well aware of this pathetic little life I'm living. But I don't let the grief overpower me and if I can put on a good enough show... If people can't tell that I'm in intense pain all day every day, then I feel like I can beat this. If only by sheer strength of will. The *show* is all I have sometimes." Tears were streaming down her face.

"And crying helps?" he said with a smirk, rolling his eyes.

"Obviously not," she bit back. "I know it only makes it worse for myself and my family. My despair only makes everything harder for everyone and plus it feels like I'm letting it win. Hope is the only float keeping my head above water and I won't let go to please you," she spat. "Just because you have accepted that your life has to be empty and futile doesn't mean it's the right choice. As much as you say you don't care, your fear possesses you. It controls every aspect of your life. If that's ever me, just kill me.

"I know my life is a sorry one but at least I'm still alive," Elinor said. "The same can't be said of you. I pity you. I pity that you have let Morland defeat you after all. I'm going to fix all this somehow and I hope there is enough of you to be saved."

They each stared out their own windows. Derek heard a pop sound and looked over to see Elinor slathering Bengay all over her head. Slather was the only word for it. The scent of menthol was sharp and filled the car. He had a feeling he was going to get tired of that smell fast.

"What is your purpose in this?" she said after a couple minutes. "Are you trying to break me? Because *you* can't. I am stronger than my headaches and I'm stronger than you. It may not look like it but I'm in the middle of a war. Every freaking day is a battle. To keep fighting when I'm so tired of it. I wish I could surrender and let it win but losing is just more of the same pain forever. Giving up doesn't make it stop. I have no plan and no one to help me. All I have is medicines that each try to kill me in their own creative way and my illusion of strength.

"You are right that it's all a show. That I'm not the sweet, nice girl I try really hard to be. Someday I'll get my softness back. I hope. But right now feelings and gentleness would destroy me. I'd be crying every single day. As it is, I barely make it through by saying over and over. 'I will not let this defeat me. My God has not deserted me.' It's so hard to fight something no one else can see. There is no proof but my word."

She exhaled like she was empty. Like she'd let a balloon go and there was nothing left now. Thank god. He couldn't have taken much more of that.

Derek looked at her out of the corner of his eyes. Her last words had jarred him. He knew only too well the invisible battle he fought. No one could really trust that Morland was real. That any of the things he said happened really happened. It was just Peter and Elinor taking his word for it. And him trying to find the strings that bound him.

Elinor was taking deep breaths as if to calm herself. He'd never heard her talk so much. He tried to stop himself from responding. He should have just let the conversation burn out into the smoking wreckage that was the two of them but the fight was still in him.

"Isn't this life you've chosen letting the headaches win anyway? Living in the dark. Letting your dreams and aspirations die. Settling for such a lesser life. You've given up a part of your soul on its altar. It's very hard to get it back," he said. He knew first hand.

When he looked over, her face was raw with emotion and as transparent as the windshield.

"There are always casualties. I just hope the good parts of me are only prisoners of war."

Elinor

"Does he do this to everyone?" Elinor said into the phone around midnight.

"Umm to some extent," Peter chuckled. "But you are getting some sort of special treatment."

"Oh goody," she said sarcastically.

"I think he finds you inscrutable. You are a puzzle to him that he's never seen. I think he's just trying to figure out what makes you tick," he said.

"I'd very much rather he didn't know. He doesn't need any more ammunition against me. His shots are hitting pretty close to the mark as it is."

"Don't let it get to you," Peter said. "The rest of us think you are awesome. And Derek hates everything and everyone so please don't put any weights to his words."

"Yeah, you are right. Time for bed. I'll see you Friday."

"Good night, El. Sweet dreams."

Chapter 16

Elinor

"Is this going to happen every time you drive me?" Elinor sighed. "I'm really not a confrontational person. You bring out this thing in me that I don't really like."

Derek had started to pick a fight Friday afternoon before they had even left the parking lot. It was like he was trying to cram in as much auguring as possible in the twelve or so miles it was between school and their houses. Thankfully, he wasn't a morning person so this cage match was only an afternoon treat.

"Are you afraid to defend yourself?" Derek said.

"Ugh! No. I just don't like fighting, but fine. I see you are just going to get more annoying if I try to avoid it," Elinor said giving up.

"So do you really honestly believe that there is a god? And if there is one, then I assure you he has deserted you," Derek said.

"Do you transcribe our conversations?" she asked and then held up her hand to stop whatever unpleasant thing he was about to say. "You are ridiculous. Yes, I believe there is a God. I know there is. And He hasn't deserted me whatever it looks like."

"Then why doesn't he heal you?"

"I don't know," she said.

She held in her sigh as once again he struck exactly where she was weakest, where she had the most struggle.

She had begged and pleaded God to heal her.

It had felt like He was behind a closed door. She imagined herself knocking over and over 'Do You Want to Build a Snowman' style. And God just sat on the other side of the door unanswering. She liked to think He kept her outside to protect her from something but maybe He was just ignoring her.

Her parents had had everyone they knew praying but nothing changed. Elinor had come to a broken agreement with God. She knew without a shadow of a doubt that He was real and that He was all-powerful. And... He was obviously *choosing* not to heal her. It helped if she imagined that miracle heals were limited and she didn't want to take one if some kid with leukemia was going to die. She wasn't going to die. So she didn't really *need* His healing.

Elinor kind of felt that it would be easier if God and her each just did their own things. He appeared to already be doing it. So she stopped begging and pleading. She stopped knocking at the door and just lived her life to the best of her ability. If she didn't think about Him too much then it helped with the bitter tide that threatened to sweep her away.

"He hasn't healed you because he can't," Derek said. "Because he isn't there. I've seen two worlds and I haven't ever seen a trace of an all-powerful god or any god. On Morland, they call it 'the Goodness' and it leaves people disappointed just like here."

"You can believe whatever you want," Elinor said, "and you'll see whatever you want to see but I know there is a God on Earth and I can't imagine a world where he isn't there. If you are honest, you haven't been looking for a god. Because if there is one, you hate him for sending you there. You hate him for Brigitte and your siblings.

"But if there was one then you'd also be eternally grateful that you made it back home. Safe and sound. Safe enough that you can contemplate how it all came to be. And I feel that people who spend the most time trying to discredit a god, are just trying to deny what they already know." Elinor took a breath and said softly, "I see the fact that you live, that I have found the one person who has been to Morland as one of the greatest proofs of my God."

She stared at him and allowed that thought to sink in. She'd found him. What were the chances that she'd ever have found the physical match to the spirit man she saw in her sepia forest? And she'd found him so easily. If he were kinder it would feel like a fairytale. But he was more like the handsome villain who the stupid heroine just won't keep away from.

Why is he so handsome! She lamented for the millionth time. *And why can't I stay away? I'm such an idiot.*

"Then why do you have headaches?" Derek continued. "Because he's not real, Elinor. Does it comfort you to believe in a god that could do this to you? Does it make you feel like there is a purpose behind it? A god who could allow the things I've seen to happen is not a god I'd want to know," Derek said with the beginnings of pity in his eyes.

Elinor shook her head softly. "Oh I know He's real and I know He can heal me. But He doesn't... It took me a while to be okay with that. To forgive him. But you know what? As corny and dumb as it may sound to you, I know that His plans for me are for my good. Maybe my headaches are the just a product of a broken world or maybe they are a test to help me grow. Either way I decided it doesn't matter. How I handle this is what matters.

"I can choose to let it turn me bitter, to let my feelings of injustice cloud my heart and turn me into someone I'm not or I can let it make me kind. Make me understanding of the invisible illnesses others suffer. I could let it make me patient and grateful for what I have. So that's what I try to do. You choose your attitude, Derek. You choose who you get to be now. Morland doesn't own you. You don't have to be that boy who went to Morland. Just like I don't have to be headache girl. You are choosing the wrong path."

"It's the only one there is," he said turning away. When they pulled up to her house, Derek said, "Are you going to Jerry's tomorrow?"

"I don't know," she said, "I'm not sure I can go another round with you. I'll text you when I decide."

Chapter 17

Elinor

"You should come," Peter said on the phone Saturday afternoon. "It'll be fun. I promise."

"Hmm. What will it be like?" Elinor asked unconvinced.

"It'll be just like lunch except longer and with better snack food. Jerry's parents are nice. They'll leave us alone after ordering a couple pizzas which is awesome. It won't be weird, Elinor, really. You should come. I could pick you up," Peter said.

"No, that's fine. My jailer has already informed me he would be driving me to Jerry's party if I decided to go. I'll just text him. It's okay, Peter. It would be silly to have you do it. And maybe one of these times Derek will cave and help me with my Morland problem."

"Good luck on that. So I'll see you at six tonight?"

"Yes, sir. Oh should I bring anything?"

"No, just your lovely self. See you soon."

Elinor had known that Derek had gotten his car out of the shop earlier in the day. So she wasn't surprised to see him waiting outside in his beat up black Toyota Camry to pick her up. She *was* surprised that he was on time. She had been hoping she'd at least get to berate him for being late. Sometimes he was so insensitive.

"Alright I'm off," Elinor called up from the foyer.

"Okay, have fun," Katie called down.

"Thanks 'mom'. I will," Elinor chuckled.

"Be sure to tell me all about the games you play," said Colton leaning over the staircase railing. "Do you need to borrow a notebook or do you have one?"

"Are you good to drive?" her dad said from the office downstairs.

"Yeah, Derek is driving me. The boy who lives a couple houses down. We have carpooled a couple times since we have our first two classes together, remember?"

"I don't know. What do we know about this boy? Where are you going again?" asked her stepmom.

"He's fine," Elinor lied, or maybe it wasn't a lie. She was getting confused on the subject of Derek. "He's driving me to a board game party at another kid's house whose parents will be home. It is the absolute safest event I could attend outside of this house. I'll have my phone and I'll text you if I'm going to be late."

Elinor heard Derek's car honk and she had to stop herself from yelling, which would not have assuaged her family.

"Okay my four parents, may I leave now?"

"I guess so," said Katie blowing a kiss.

Derek

Derek could see that she was mad already. He was glad he'd blown the horn. Making her mad was coming to be a favorite pastime of his. She had been a couple minutes late after all, so he'd had the right.

"I know," she said hotly sitting down in the passenger seat. "Sorry I'm late."

He shot her a grin and then pulled out of the driveway in one quick maneuver.

"My family is probably watching. You are going to ruin your scheme of driving me everywhere if they realize you are a maniac."

They drove in silence with Ryan Adams playing through the speakers. Derek had considered changing the music to Linkin Park or something like that but then she'd turn all catatonic and that was probably worse. He wasn't positive it was worse but there was less a chance she'd vomit in his car so he didn't change the music.

"So this is your car," she said taking stock of her surroundings. He was glad it was semi-clean. He didn't need her judgments. He cared little for cars. They got him where he needed to go and he'd made himself learn enough so he'd be self-reliant. But getting a degree in auto mechanics had no interest for him.

"Obviously," he said turning the music up a little bit. She sighed and looked out the window.

"How far to Jerry's house?" she asked after a while.

"Another fifteen minutes."

"Thank you, by the way," she said without looking at him. "As painful as it is to say, thank you for driving me. It is a relief to not have to worry about it anymore."

"It was for the safety of the community."

"Who knew you were so altruistic?"

"There is a lot about me you don't know," he said glancing at her. He was starting to feel like there was a lot he didn't know about himself.

"I know. That's part of what's so worrying," she said.

Peter

Jerry's house was nice. Peter could see it wasn't what Elinor had expected. Jerry's parents opened the door and met everyone that came in. Elinor had charmed them both instantly and Jerry had to send them back to the living room before they tried to adopt her.

Jerry had an older brother who was married with a kid or two. So his parents had given Jerry the bonus room as his personal domain. It had posters on the walls and a big flat screen T.V. The couches were pushed to the side to make room for two folding tables and six chairs.

"Ah, Arkham Horror tonight," Peter said. "Good choice." Peter turned around to see Elinor's face when she saw the complex game covering two whole tables. There were over two hundred pieces and four hundred cards. There were actually more because Jerry had added an expansion, which was why they needed two tables.

"Oh boy," Elinor said with wide eyes.

"Here," Jack said popping the top of a Coke and handing it to Elinor. "This will help."

She chuckled, "Thanks, Jack."

Elinor

Twenty minutes later Elinor had a half dozen cards she was in charge of and thought she might be able to figure this out.

"Okay so there are a bunch of different phases and you'll tell me what to do for each of them. My job is to kill monsters and close portals. And I'll need weapons and... these things," she said holding up a small round green piece with a magnifying glass on it.

"Clue tokens," Jerry said.

"Clue tokens and you'll tell me how many dice I get to roll," she said looking at the dice spread all over the tables. "Do I ever get to roll all of them?"

"When you get to be a baller like me," Carlos said moving his character token in a little dance on his space at the train station.

Elinor liked the game but sometimes the other guys's turns took so long she found herself looking out into Morland for distraction. Whenever she moved on Earth her Morland sight changed with her. So being on the second story was always a weird and beautiful perspective as she floated over the sepia trees.

She saw *him* out of the corner of her eye. She turned almost completely around to watch Derek's soul walk by. He had almost passed her when for some reason he looked up right at her and walked back. His smile was so big Elinor found herself smiling back at the invisible boy.

"I know I look good tonight but snap out of it. It's your turn," Jerry said with a crooked smile. Elinor realized with a blush that she had been staring intently at Jerry's face.

"S-sorry. Okay um we are in the otherworld phase and someone is reading me a card for ... yellow or blue," she said taking quick stock of her position in the game.

Peter read Elinor a scenario from a card and she rolled three dice to pass a strength test and was rewarded by not being lost in time and space. When her turn was done she looked back down and Derek's soul was gone. Just as well. It was too big of a distraction in mixed company anyway.

She took one last look around when suddenly he appeared right across from her floating in the air. Her surprised expression made the spirit man chuckle. She wished she could hear him.

It was beyond bizarre to be looking at Derek's soul while he looked back at her. He was identical to Derek in every way, except the ways he wasn't. Derek's soul *smiled*. His long red hair and exotic apparel made him fascinating in a non-dangerous way somehow, even though he was the one of them with the sword.

Derek's soul seemed like someone she'd want to know. His face was scruffy and his dark red hair was just past his shoulders. His smile made him a million times more attractive than the Derek at the party with her.

She made herself keep one eye on the game and one on the woods. He kept looking at her and moving his lips like they were having a conversation. Elinor wondered what he saw when he looked at her. Because when she looked down at her hands they were all mist and shadows, phantom fragments of hands. Maybe he saw mist and shadows when he looked at himself but Elinor saw him clearly so maybe he saw her clearly.

She allowed herself quick snatches of time when she looked at him with both eyes. He was talking so animatedly and she wished she could lip read. Then suddenly he reached out his hand and touched her cheek. She almost felt it and it scared her. She blinked and jerked herself back to the party.

"Hey! Watch it," Jerry and Carlos said straightening the pieces she had jostled.

"Sorry," she said. Elinor resolved not to look at the woods anymore.

It was too hard to be normal in public. *And Derek's soul is making me uncomfortable with his attentions.* And that thought made her chuckle to herself, shaking her head.

What a horrible strange thing her life was that she had just legitimately had the thought 'Derek's soul is making me uncomfortable with his attentions'. *Life was weird.*

"Something funny?" Peter asked looking a little concerned.

Elinor looked at Derek. "Just imagining what you'd look like in five years with a beard and if you could actually smile." Peter and Derek immediately got her pointed looks and scanned the room like they'd be able to see him. The others probably thought she was raving mad. She made up for it by diving into the game with fervor.

"This is a very fun game, Jerry," Elinor said as they were closing the final gate. "Thanks for letting me come over. Sorry I was distracted at first."

"Me casa es tu casa," he said taking a half bow. "I'll be sure to host again."

It was nine thirty when the game was over but everyone was restless and unwilling to go to their respective homes. Derek looked at Elinor maybe to gauge her mood. Elinor smiled trying to tell him that she was fine for whatever. She had taken a couple pills as a precaution when the pizza had arrived and she was game for pretty much anything.

"The night is young. What is our next activity, game master?" Peter said looking at Jerry.

"Alright. Awesome. Well we have the Wall of Games," he said gesturing to two bookcases packed with more board games than Elinor even knew existed. "Or the gaming systems. But the only game we'd all be able to play at the same time would be like a dancing or sports game. Or we could watch a movie." Jerry had two couches against the walls that he must have moved to accommodate the game tables.

"Vote?" asked Jack.

Carlos wanted Xbox. Jack wanted Cranium. And the rest voted for a movie.

"The lady of the hour picks," Jerry exclaimed leading Elinor to his cabinet with rows of DVDs.

"No pressure," she said under her breath.

"It better not be dumb," Derek said.

"I'm sure whatever you pick will be fine," Peter said.

"Of course it will because I don't own dumb movies," Jerry said.

As the guys debated that, Elinor felt a knot in her stomach. How could she possibly choose a movie all the guys would like? The two movies she'd seen with them were *Blood Bomb* and *Great Barrier Reef Adventure*. Two more different movies did not exist on the face of the planet. She decided to let fate decide. She picked a row, closed her eyes, and grabbed a movie.

"Supernatural, season one," she announced.

"Classic," Carlos said. Elinor beamed. She had finally done something that didn't make Carlos growl at her for being a dumb girl. She exulted in her victory. When Elinor turned around she was faced with a new dilemma. The couches had replaced the tables but... They were full.

Jerry, Carlos, and Jack sat on the large couch while Derek and Peter sat on the smaller love seat. Everyone shuffled a little as though a seat could be made if they adjusted correctly. Elinor decided on the third option. She grabbed the decorative Death Star pillow from behind Peter and sat down in front of him preparing to lay down on the carpet.

"I can't have that," Jerry said standing to give her his seat.

"No, really it's fine. I usually lay on the floor at home. It's sometimes best for my head. But I wouldn't say no to a blanket or a throw."

"Done, my lady," he said handing her a fluffy blanket from inside a cabinet. "Any other takers?" he asked handing out the extras.

After a couple minutes of arguing about which episode to start on, they finally decided on number ten. The lights went down and Elinor adjusted her pillow to rest it against the couch and incidentally Peter's feet. She turned around to apologize but his face was right next to her. "Are you sure you are okay down here? I really wouldn't mind trading," Peter whispered.

"I'm great," she said. "Sorry for squishing your legs. I can scoot down."

"Nope. You are fine," he said scrunching his eyes.

Peter

Peter tried so hard not to stare at Elinor lying at his feet. Her hair splayed out on the pillow as she turned to lie on her side to watch the Winchester brothers kill demons. Her right hand rested under her pillow and ended up next to his foot.

162

He didn't dare move.

As the show got scarier, he watched as she curled up tighter. She visibly jumped whenever something scary happened. By the middle of the next episode, she was sitting up pressed into his knees hugging the pillow. Whenever the suspense grew she would lean back into his legs trying to get away from the show. Peter could not remember what the episode was about. Her nearness and need of him were so intoxicating.

Elinor

Peter's knees bore into her back. She didn't care. This show was very scary.

She'd only seen snatches on the CW when the little ones were asleep. In truth, she knew she had a very low scary tolerance and the episode they picked about the mental asylum was really pushing her luck.

She didn't want to tell Derek that she wanted to go home because when the show wasn't terrifying it was so great. She was definitely crushing on both Sam and Dean Winchester, even if they were fictional characters. It was a strange thought to think while she had her back pressed against Peter.

He rested a hand on her shoulder for a moment and she turned around to give him an awkward smile showing all her teeth.

He chuckled. Without really thinking, she brought a hand around to rest on his ankle. Elinor decided that Peter was a great scary movie partner. He was so solid and protective of her. He would definitely protect her if demons tried to set her on fire on the roof or kill her in a harvest ritual.

Peter felt like… like nothing very bad could happen while he was there. She was starting to feel that it was exactly what she needed in her life. She needed something solid to rest against that would have her back and keep her from being afraid. Peter was like taking the weights she carried and letting someone else bear it for a bit while she caught her breath. Maybe that wasn't enough but she couldn't move away from him.

Derek

Elinor was proving him exactly right. She was only a leech and Derek couldn't stand to watch another moment.

She was the exact opposite kind of girl Derek would have picked for Peter. She was so needy and broken. And Peter couldn't help himself! He didn't need to take on someone else's issues. But maybe it made Peter feel like a hero. Maybe letting her lean on him made him feel stronger. Derek didn't think so and he didn't like it. When the next episode ended, he stood to turn the lights on. He was glad to see Elinor move away from Peter.

"It's getting late," Derek said gathering his things.

Derek waited in the car, not wanting to watch her goodbyes to everyone. He was ready to let her have it the second they pulled out of the driveway but she surprised him again.

"Your soul tried to touch me tonight," she said nonchalantly looking out the window.

"What?" Derek said unable to process what she had said. He was having trouble changing tracks from pure rage to calm talking about his lost soul.

"He was there while we were playing the game. Sitting in the trees with me. At first he was walking on the ground and then he saw me and was up floating with me in the trees. I got my first really good look at him. He looks like you in five years. A little older. Face all stubble. And he does this strange thing with his face. He smiles," she said raising her eyebrows at him.

Derek huffed, "Yeah alright. He's the best. I am well aware. You said he tried to touch you? Do you think he can really see you?"

"Oh, yeah. He could definitely see me. When he hopped up in the trees and startled me, he laughed. I couldn't hear it, of course, but he was reacting to me. Then he started talking a bunch." She held up her hand. "I have no idea what he was saying because I can't hear Morland and don't know how to read lips. But he was cheerful. And then suddenly he reached his hand out to try and touch my cheek. It... it startled me and I stopped looking at Morland. It was just too much weird for one night." Derek decided he would process what that all could mean later. His anger boiled back quickly.

"What was all that about back there?" Derek said in a near growl.

"What was all what about? Seeing your soul?"

"No. You being all over Peter."

"Hold your horses. I just leaned against his legs. Nothing inappropriate."

"Uh huh. You are an anchor, Elinor. Peter is going to do great things. He doesn't need your headaches or Morland keeping him down. He needs to get out of Waxhaw and go do something."

"By including Morland and Waxhaw you know you include yourself."

"I know. I'd shake him off if I could," Derek said truthfully.

"You need him too much? Maybe I'm starting to need him too."

"Don't," Derek said simply.

"Why? He is as good as they come. I really like him. Mostly as a friend but it could be more."

"You are toxic, Elinor. You are this broken mess that needs fixing. Peter needs a girl who will take care of him for a change. He's always been on his own. You are just another thing he needs to take care of. Don't you see that? You are not good for him, Elinor."

"I think you are wrong. Peter deserves to be happy and to like who he wants."

"Maybe you are right," Derek conceded, "But think about it. Are you really enough for Peter? Are you the best there is? Shouldn't he be with someone healthy and happy?"

As Derek slowed the car in front of her house he said, "I'll help you with Morland. We can talk about it next week." She must have heard the unsaid bargain because her lips moved into a sneer.

"So good of you," she spat getting out of the car without looking at him.

Peter

Peter was so curious as to what Derek and Elinor were talking about as they drove home. Were they talking about him? Was Elinor talking about him? Derek had been radiating disapproval. Peter had tried his best to ignore him. Elinor made him happy. He'd never felt that way about anyone. She was a source of light in his dark world. She gave him something to look forward to. Something to hope for.

And Derek was seriously jumping the gun. All Elinor had done was lean against his legs. The most platonic form of physical contact there could be. Nothing R rated. Nothing even PG-13. Until her hand slid around his ankle...

He'd never thought that an ankle was a particularly sexy part of the body until then. It stilled his breath. But it was more that she had initiated the contact with him. Maybe it didn't count because she had been scared. He'd have to wait and see how things were now.

But when he felt his phone vibrate, he felt his heart drop to his feet.

Elinor texted "Peter... I'm sorry about tonight. I messed things up with us. You already give me too much of your time. I'll see you at school on Monday."

It took everything in him not to call, not to drive to her house and throw rocks at her window. His instinct was to get as clingy as possible and demand answers and to vent about all the thoughts that had been swirling in his heart. But... after reading the text ten times he thought he detected an influence other than her own.

Derek... Something had happened on the drive home.

Peter was not cool headed enough to call now or see her. He couldn't lose her. He wouldn't. Peter wouldn't let Derek break this.

Peter couldn't leave the text unanswered and since he didn't know what poison Derek had spewed he didn't know what antidote was needed.

So he texted back. "You are wrong. See you at school :)"

Chapter 18

Derek

"What did you say to Elinor last night?" Peter said throwing open the door to Derek's bedroom on Sunday afternoon.

"Well 'hello' to you to," Derek said pulling a shirt over his head. He'd slept the best he had in a while.

"What did you say to her? You ruined it somehow. I need to know exactly what you said so I can fix it."

"What did she say to you?" Derek said curious. Maybe she wasn't a child idiot. Or maybe he'd made the temptation too sweet. Either way a smile crept up.

"Ugh. There you go. That's as much of an admission as I need. Why Derek?"

"Does it matter now? It sounds like things have ended."

"Oh no they haven't because you wouldn't let them even start. You kill me, Derek. You think because you've lived five years longer than me that I need you to protect me. She's not some scary monster. She's a girl and I really like her. Isn't that enough to make you play nice? I've done so much for you. I have always been there. I'm your best friend and you couldn't let me have this? Why? Because I'd give her too much time? Because she can see Morland and it scares the hell out of you? Because your goal in life is to be miserable to atone for your sins and you don't think anyone else should be happy either? Why Derek?"

"Several reasons."

When Peter just stared at him Derek continued, "Because she could be dissuaded. Because she gave you up just because I was harsh with her. She doesn't deserve you. She is a broken doll and you are addicted to trying to fix broken things. I want you to be with someone healthy."

"Her headaches have nothing to do with this," Peter growled. He really was mad.

"Oh yes they do. They are slowly becoming her defining quality. She lets them define her. And she needs you too much. She's a weight dragging you down. You deserve a girl who'd get you the hell outta Dodge and away from this town with your father in it. You'd be trapped here with her. All I told her was the truth."

Peter was fuming as he paced up and down Derek's room. But Derek wasn't worried. Peter would calm down and see reason. Elinor really wasn't that great.

"You do not have the final say in this," Peter said, "And who said I was gonna marry her? Who said this would ever be more than a fling? You've told me about the fun you had in Morland. I can't even remember all the girls's names. Maybe that's all this would be with Elinor. Who are you to judge me and decide who I can be with?"

"You talk a big game. But you are already in love with her. Maybe you don't even know it yet," Derek said raising an eyebrow. "Also you are incapable of being a bastard. It's your most horrible flaw. You'd never use her and leave. Of course you would marry her. You've probably already envisioned your dumb little family of blond brats. You are the most loyal creature on the planet. You are my friend after all! If she ever showed you the slightest affection you'd never let her go."

"I can't even believe you, Derek. I can't," Peter said with clenched fists as he headed for the door.

"Hey wait. Come on, Peter."

"No. I need a little space. I'll see you at school."

"I agreed to help Elinor."

Peter laughed, a bitter grating sound. And walked out the door.

Peter

170

Peter wished Derek had been watching as he left his house and drove straight to Elinor's. Peter was his own man and he needed to see for himself where everything stood. Her house looked a lot like Derek's, red brick on all sides with a nice green yard in front and woods as a backyard.

When he knocked, a small girl answered the door.

"Yes?" she said. Her hair was long like Elinor's but it was darker in color.

"Hello, Katie. I'm Peter. Elinor's friend from school. Is she home?"

"Elinor!" Katie yelled up.

"What Kat?" Elinor said stepping out of her room in a short dress with her hair wrapped in a towel.

"Oh hello," she said blushing pulling the towel free, letting her wet hair trail down her back. "Why don't you come up?"

"I don't know," Katie answered for him. "I don't think you are allowed to have a boy in your room."

Elinor smiled, "I'll keep the door open. Peter is a gentleman, I promise."

Eventually Peter was allowed access and he climbed the stairs to Elinor's bedroom.

"Thank you, miss," Peter said nodding to Katie who stood in her own bedroom looking wary.

"Sorry. They are a little protective," Elinor said motioning for him to sit on her bed as she sat at her makeup desk.

Her room was different than he had imagined. He'd though it would be kind of frilly and soft but it was bold. The walls were a deep rusty pink and the bedspread was a patchwork of silks and velvets in pinks and purple. She had thick heavy golden and purple curtains that blocked every trace of light and her makeup desk looked like something an old Hollywood star would have used.

She had a bookcase that was filled with books and pictures of her with large groups of girls. And he wondered where they all were. Maybe they got left behind in Atlanta or maybe just from the pain. He'd lost friends when his mom left. His feelings had been too raw and he'd been too hostile. It had just been too much for casual acquaintances. Only Derek had stuck.

She never mentioned talking to those girls or having friends visit. He could almost see it in his head. She moved away, then her headaches start, and her friends were too far away to understand the monumental thing that had happened to her, that shaped her whole life now.

They'd only known healthy Elinor and they couldn't possibly understand her illness and what had gone wrong with miles and miles between them. Maybe they'd gotten irritated when she never called them back or when she wasn't able to come back to visit. And then slowly they would have stopped calling leaving Elinor alone, in pain, for a whole year until she'd met him.

It struck him that she'd had no one when she'd walked to him that day at lunch. But she had him now. He could be enough.

"I know the feeling," Peter said looking around. "I've just come from visiting my buddy, Derek."

"He's a charmer," Elinor said running a couple of products through her hair without looking at him.

"Elinor," Peter said moving closer, taking a knee in front of her so she had to look at him. "He is not the boss of me. Or my keeper. I don't know what he said to you last night but please ignore it."

"It wasn't just that," she said turning so she was eye to eye with him. "I was too forward. I'm not usually like that. I didn't like that I did that without talking to you. I forced us into this place we are in now. I should have let *us* decide where this was going because I have no idea what I really want."

"Do you like me?" Peter asked.

"Yes," she said without hesitation.

"More than a friend?"

"A little, yes. I think," she said and Peter felt a full smile spread across his face. "But Peter, I don't know about this. Derek was right."

"Derek is rarely right," Peter interrupted.

"He said I was a broken mess. That I would hold you down. And he's right. I'm just another thing for you to take care of."

"El," Peter said looking at her levelly, "*I* am a broken mess. I don't know how you both have managed to raise me to sainthood but I'm just as lost as both of you are. My mom left us. Did you know that?" She nodded her head.

"I never heard why she wasn't around," Elinor said.

"She left me with that... with my father. She knew what he was but she bolted. Don't you think that could mess a kid up? Even my own mother could leave me. I don't say that to get your pity. I just think that the more you get to know me, the more you'll see that we are actually a perfect fit."

He didn't like to think about *her* and he succeeded most of the time. He liked to pretend that his mother didn't exist. He was sure he'd learned some of his avoidance issues from Derek. What kind of mother leaves her young son with that man?

173

He felt a thread of anger weave through him and he stuffed it down, stuffed all of it down. *She* didn't matter. Elinor mattered and if proving to her what a messed up guy he was would stop the distance between them then he'd tell her the whole stupid story. About how his dad would beat up both of them and how one day his mom had said she was done and was gone. And then there was only Peter for him to vent on.

"Are you getting proposed to?" Katie said from the door. Her mouth was wide open. Elinor quickly pulled Peter up by his shirt and said, "No, Katie. I am not getting proposed to."

"Elinor, you are getting proposed to?" Colton asked peeking his head in. "Like right now? In your bedroom?"

"No. No one is proposing to anyone," Elinor said exasperated, "Peter was just sitting down next to me talking."

"He was on one knee," Katie told Colton.

"Hmm. Are you sure he wasn't proposing? That is how it's traditionally done," Colton said.

"I am one hundred percent positive," she said looking to Peter for confirmation.

"Yup. No marriage proposing going on here. Just two friends talking. Nothing weird," he said but he was sure Elinor could see he was barely keeping his laugh in.

"Oh, get out of here you two," Elinor said shooing them.

"Is she allowed to have a boy in her room?" Colton asked Katie.

"My goodness!" Elinor said sitting down on her bed. "Do sights like that make you thank the heavens you are an only child? I'm sorry. They are... precocious to say the least."

"Well now that they mention it," he said getting down on one knee again. "Elinor 'whatever your middle name is' Lirdin will you..." he said and was interrupted as the little ones came back.

174

"See I told you," Katie said nudging Colton.

Elinor stared at Peter shaking her head in disbelief. "I'm going to get you back for this. You don't know what you have started in this house. Peter, you need to go now. He's just leaving," Elinor said pushing him out the room and down the stairs.

"Elinor and Peter sitting in a tree," Katie and Colton sang from the railings.

Peter let himself have a full laugh.

"You can't avoid me now. It would be suspicious. Your reputation would never recover from jilting me at the altar," Peter said winking.

"I'll talk to you later," she said trying to finagle all his limbs outside the front door.

"I look forward to it," he said kissing her cheek before he bolted.

"Ohhh he kissed her!" Katie said as Elinor banged her head on the door.

Elinor

Elinor had been unsure of the whole Peter thing after she had talked to Derek last night. In truth she'd been avoiding the whole situation since she'd met him.

She knew it would be easier if she could forget he was a boy and just think of him as a friend. That was what she had needed at the time. She had been so lonely and felt like she might just disappear. She had armed herself with the excuse of not wanting to involve Peter in her pain but she had practically been dragging him through it since they had met.

Peter was so comfortable and safe. He was like taking a deep breath after being underwater. But she wasn't in love with him... yet. She did like him more than anyone she knew. She wanted to be with him all the time but... she would know if it was the right thing, right? It would feel like lightning. Maybe she wouldn't be able to feel that even if it was happening.

She felt like there was an emotional blanket over her sometimes that dampened what she could feel. Her pain seemed like an armed solider that only allowed approved feelings to pass: worry, anger, loneliness. But she would be lying to herself if Peter didn't stir something in her. She smiled to herself recounting his interactions with her siblings. She was charmed. And she couldn't help it. She did wonder if Derek would still help even if she didn't let Peter go.

Chapter 19

Elinor

She heard the voice of reason this time as it told her to just *leave it be*. Who cared if she would have headaches forever? She should not approach Derek. She heard that voice but she ignored it. He'd said he would help her, even if it was a veiled blackmail.

Elinor held the phone in her hand like it might be a snake. "Can we talk?" she asked him.

"No. What?" said Derek's sharp voice.

"I want to talk to you."

"Just because I'm not actively trying to kill you doesn't mean I want anything to do with you."

"You drive me to school every other day and you most recently agreed to help me with Morland."

"That was just to keep Peter away, which is apparently futile."

"Why do you care who Peter sees?"

"Because if Peter sees you, then you'll always be around. You and your eyes that can see it."

"I'm sure you wish you were the one who could see your home."

"Do you ever listen? *That* is not my home! *This* is my home. *That* was a five-year purgatory," he fumed.

"You are right. I'm sorry. Can I come over? I'd like to talk to you."

"We are talking now. Fine. My parents are gone. Come over."

She walked the short distance between their houses feeling more nervous by the step. Even though things were better between them, slightly, she didn't really want to go to his house. But she needed to be able to see his face, to tell if he was lying.

The front door was left ajar and she walked in calling for him.

"Over here," he said from the kitchen. She was glad they weren't going to his bedroom.

"So," he said just staring at her.

Derek

"I... I want you to help me," she told him, staring up with her big doe eyes for added effect. He didn't think he could have stopped his eyes from rolling, even if he'd wanted to.

"What could I possibly do to help you?" he said biting out every word. "I know nothing of headaches or your magic. I would be just as useless as every doctor you've seen. I don't know why you got your powers or how. What do you want from me?"

"I don't know. You were the one who said you'd help me with this Morland stuff. Why all the attitude now that I've come to collect?"

He sighed, "I'd really like to back out. But I won't. Peter is still... upset with me. And I know this would make him happy. What is your plan?"

"I wish I knew why I was tied to Morland. I feel like if I went there, it might..."

He interrupted her with a growl followed by a bitter sardonic laugh.

"You don't know anything. That's the stupidest thing you've ever said and there is quite the competition. But please finish that sentence. If you went to Morland, it might what? Help you understand yourself? Cure your headaches? Give you all the puzzle pieces you are missing from your life? Ha! Going to Morland would do nothing to help you. Morland is incapable of helping anyone. Especially you. Just look at yourself," he said with raised eyebrows.

She looked at him, clueless. Then she appeared to be taking invisible stock of herself. He didn't mind filling in the blanks.

"You are pitiful! You can hardly be in a room that's not curtained against the sun," He said motioning to the large windows that she had strategically put to her back. "What good would you be there? If I were to ever go back, I would never take you with me." *But it doesn't matter,* he added to himself because *I am never ever going back.*

"I," she interrupted

"Morland would kill you. Do you understand?" he paused "You've read it and yet you still want to go?"

"Yes"

"Then you are an even bigger idiot than I thought which did appear to be impossible. Is your life so horrible that committing suicide is your only option? Is the pain really so unbearable that you'd give *your soul* for the chance it might stop? Morland isn't a fairyland with unicorns and rainbows. It's worse than every fantasy novel you've ever read because it's real. With a real life Witch Queen who wants to suck out your soul. You are as bad as Peter. You can't see it. And what was he trying to accomplish by letting you read it?" He closed his eyes. "Can you just forget all this? Can you try to live your life as if all this isn't happening?" he asked.

"No," she said reflexively, then stopped to think. "Maybe if I didn't have the headaches with it. If it was just some weird visions... But no. I know myself. A healthy Elinor probably couldn't leave it alone either. It would seem rather fantastical and enchanting, if the headaches didn't make it so real. But they do. I don't think this is a fairy tale like you think I do. I know I apparently come off as a silly, shallow girl but that's just because I'm too good at hiding my pain. I'm barely holding it all together. I don't want this. Any of this." She gestured around including herself and the forest and maybe Derek also.

"This was not supposed to be my life," she said and had to stop because it looked like her eyes were welling. She took a deep breath and continued. "I don't want this to be my life. Can you just help us end this? There has to be a way to make it all stop. Please. Please just think about it."

She walked away slowly without looking back and Derek stared at the back of her head unflinchingly.

"Okay," he said and he wasn't sure she heard him but she stopped and nodded without turning.

Elinor

He agreed to help but it didn't make her feel any better. Maybe part of it was that she didn't really believe him. Derek didn't want to help. He didn't want anything to do with her and that really was a good thing. She'd forgiven him but she didn't trust him.

Unfortunately, fear of him didn't lessened the magnetic pull he had on her. She really hoped he didn't notice because there could *never* ever be anything between them. He was a soulless monster and she wished she never had to see him again. She also wished she could just combine Derek and Peter.

Peter had the personality and kindness she wanted but there just wasn't that spark. He was good looking, handsome even with messy blond hair and glasses. But she just didn't feel that *something*. Maybe she felt it with Derek because her adrenaline was always kicked into fight or flight around him. But even if she could merge them she didn't want to. She didn't want a boyfriend. She didn't want to go on a date or get married. She just wanted her head to stop hurting and that meant spending time with Derek which was a dangerous hobby. But it also meant spending time with Peter and he was quickly becoming her best friend.

Chapter 20

Derek

"Why do we have to go to breakfast?" Derek complained as he waited in his driveway. The morning air was crisp and clean and it did nothing to lessen his bad mood. This was the worst possible way to spend a Saturday. "Isn't it enough that I'm giving her a full day?"

"I think we need to take a breather and start this adventure on a friendly footing," Peter said. "And you need to back down your attitude. You agreed to help. No one made you. So we are going to breakfast and... Good morning, Elinor." Peter walked over to hug Elinor as she came into view. Derek couldn't decide if it was good or horrible that she lived only a few houses away from him.

"Good morning, Peter," Elinor said. "And Derek," she added when Peter lightly elbowed her. "So what's the plan?"

"Breakfast!" Peter said opening Derek's passenger door for Elinor. "Food then adventure. That's my motto."

"What are you a giant hobbit?" Derek said.

"Just because I'm almost six feet doesn't mean I don't associate more with hobbits than elves. Maybe I've had Ent draft. Ever think of that? See you don't know everything," Peter said sitting in the back seat. "Music or no music today, El? How is your head?"

"Um it's not too bad. We can do music as long as it's pleasant. No screaming or electric guitar solos." Elinor said.

"So like Enya?" Derek said sarcastically.

"No, let's do..." Peter said reaching between the two of them to plug in his phone.

"Perfect," Elinor said when the music started softly. "I love Death Cab for Cutie."

"Of course you do," Derek said.

"Hey, no more snapping you two. We are all on the same team today. To breakfast," Peter said tapping the side of Derek's seat like it was a carriage roof as he reclined back. Derek barely concealed his grunt and drove them to downtown Waxhaw.

Elinor

As soon as they made a left out of their neighborhood, Elinor knew where they were going. The Old Train Diner was one of a few restaurants in downtown Waxhaw. Which was the tiniest, cutest little downtown Elinor had ever seen. When they'd lived in Atlanta, they'd lived *in* Atlanta not in a suburb. There was nothing tiny or cute about Atlanta downtown. It was a million humans and traffic no matter what time of day and that was one of the reasons she loved Waxhaw.

There was never ever traffic and half of the houses looked like they might be haunted which thrilled her a little bit. Downtown was the last vestige of Providence Road, one of the biggest roads in Charlotte. It slowly trickled down southward, got renamed a couple times, and dead-ended in front of a school.

No building was over three stories tall and everything was a beautiful aged red brick. There were four restaurants, a coffee shop, a bike shop, a yarn store, three antique stores, and two pet supply stores. The train tracks ran straight through downtown and Elinor liked to have a visual for the distant train horn she heard most nights.

The Old Train Diner was on Providence road shortly after it became N Broome Street. It had its own little building with six official parking spots and another half dozen gravel spots. They parked and seated themselves, as the sign instructed, at a booth near the large window and urged by Derek's impatient look they ordered when the waitress came the first time.

"What can I get for you, dears?" she asked.

"Umm. I'll have two scrambled eggs, sausage and hash browns. Oh and an orange juice and hot tea," Elinor said.

184

Peter ordered a large stack of pancakes, sausage, and bacon. Derek ordered a loaded omelet and a black coffee.

"Be out in a minute, kiddos," the waitress said walking away. They waited in silence for her to bring their drinks and after Elinor picked her tea out of a little wooden box, they finally turned their minds to the mission.

"So what are we actually going to do today?" Elinor asked. She was glad that Derek was finally willing to help but she didn't know exactly what Derek's 'help' looked like.

"We are going to drive around," Derek said.

"Why?" Elinor said.

"Because you can see Morland," Derek said.

"Yeah… So," Elinor said.

"Okay great communicating, guys," Peter said giving everyone a thumb's up. "Let me just speed this along. We are driving around today because as you move on Earth your vision moves of Morland. Right?"

Elinor hadn't really thought about that too much. But yes, she didn't always see the same ten trees wherever she was. When she was driving in the car the Morland trees zoomed past. Before she'd gotten her eye drops and learned to double blink, it had been kind of scary seeing a sepia tree slam into her chest. She couldn't feel it, of course but it was hard not to flinch.

"Yes, as I move it's like I'm walking on Morland and my vision moves at the same pace," Elinor said. Now that she was thinking about it, it would be really weird if when she blinked she was looking at the same place like it was a still photograph. Or what if her Morland sight moved much faster. It was all so weird and she was kind of glad it wasn't a worse kind of weird. She'd forgotten that there always could be one.

185

"So our goals are: A. Find a clue as to *where* you are seeing in Morland. B. Maybe find information of the state of affairs. And C. Have a great team building day." When neither Elinor or Derek responded to that Peter continued. "So where should we drive?" Peter asked.

"I was thinking we could drive north, into the city," Derek said sipping his coffee. "You've seen a good bit of this area with your everyday driving so I think we need to go somewhere you haven't been."

"Sounds good to me," Elinor said.

"Okay can you give Elinor any ideas as to what she should be looking for?" Peter asked as he stacked the jellies and jams into a pyramid.

"Well anything man made. Let me know if you see a clearing or anything that gives you a vantage point that would let us know *where* you are seeing in Morland."

"Why don't we go up in one of skyscrapers in Uptown Charlotte. Are there any that let tourists on the roof?" Elinor asked. "We'd be able to get a quick vantage point from there."

"Great idea, Elinor!" Peter said.

Derek just nodded.

"Okay, so let's meander our way to Uptown and then try to figure out how to get up one of them. But what would we do next, Derek? Once we knew where we were," Peter asked knocking over his condiment architecture to make room for the plates the waitress brought.

"I don't know," Derek said salting his omelet. "That will depend on what Elinor sees."

"Well I've only ever seen trees and … you," she said to Derek, "I mean the Morland you. Maybe there isn't anything else to see."

Peter

They finished their food quickly. They were all suddenly in a rush to get it started or get it over with, as in Derek's case. Elinor sat in the passenger seat as Derek drove. Peter was in the back seat with a notebook ready to sketch a map or write down her narrative descriptions. *This is so exciting!*

"Keep an eye out for roads. They'll look like a dirt path to you," Derek supplied as they all buckled their seat belts.

"I'm not an idiot. I know they won't be paved with cement," she grumbled. The two of them were hardly trying and it made Peter sad. He just wished they could get along and realize what a fun thing this was. They were driving around looking for clues. He felt like frickin Sherlock Holmes, although he was obviously the Watson to Derek's Sherlock. And that meant Elinor was Molly or was she Mary? It would be amazing if she turned out to be the Mary.

"Okay here we go," Derek said then looking vaguely at Elinor he added. "Let me know if you see *him*." She nodded and they drove.

"Is it hard to see Morland on purpose?" Peter asked. She'd spent so long trying to avoid it he wondered if her body would be fighting her now.

"Oh, it's easy as pie," she said turning to look back at him with green eyes that instantly blinked to blue. "Seeing Morland on purpose is strange and easy. My body wants to see Morland, I think, and finally giving into it is relaxing. It feels like I'm flying," she said blinking her now green eyes at him. "Flying through the woods."

"Does your head hurt less when you are looking at Morland?" Peter asked.

"Hmm. I don't really know. Let me think about it," Elinor said and then after a moment added. "No. It's not a magic cure to look at Morland but it does get worse if I blink a lot. So there is some link. But it's impossible to stop blinking, I've tried. So even if seeing Morland made it better that would be an impossible lifestyle to maintain."

187

Elinor studied a world unseen to him and he was mesmerized watching her. She was seeing another planet right now. He was equal parts jealous and excited. Derek was decidedly neither. Even if Elinor couldn't see him, she could *hear* his periodic sighs at her lack of progress. It took them forty-five minutes before she saw anything but trees. Elinor was growing dejected, Derek was growing cross, and Peter remained unwaveringly optimistic.

Derek remarked for the fiftieth time that he wished he could see because he would have figured out where they were by now. Elinor responded crisply that he must have been very bored in Morland if he knew every single tree there, because that's *all* she had seen so far. When suddenly she grabbed Derek's arm and her head turned around to watch what they had passed.

"Wait," she said and when she turned to look at Peter she saw right through him with her green eyes. She scanned back to the right. When the car pulled to a stop she got out of the car and bent down. She tried to touch something but, of course, she couldn't. She could only see Morland. She couldn't hear or touch it.

"What is it?" Peter and Derek asked together.

"I'm not sure. We are in a small clearing. It looks natural not man made. But there is a bit of metal that caught my eye. Peter give me the sketch pad." She turned back startled as her eyes turned blue and she noticed they were suddenly so close. She took the pad wordlessly and sat on the ground with one eye fixed on the object. She drew a broken circle.

"Part of it is buried in the dirt," she said as explanation. "It's bronze I think. There is a thick border all around the edges and there is an image in the center," she said as she leaned close looking with both eyes. "It's a circle with a "c" inside it, the "c" shape is raised and there is a star in the right corner. Does that mean anything?" Elinor said turning back to look at Derek.

He was shaking his head. "What are the chances?" he said grabbing his mouth and shaking his head.

"Do you know where we are in Morland?" Peter said trying to pull Derek back to the moment.

"I know exactly where we are." He almost chuckled, it was a strange empty sound. "We are standing on my oldest brother's grave." He kept shaking his head. Elinor and Peter looked around. Elinor took a couple steps back from the object and Peter took a couple steps back from a world he could not see.

"What are the chances" Derek repeated, "that in all of Morland we'd find this place? Felix was out of town when I... when Milena, Riley, and Jermaine died... When I killed them," He finally said, as if he needed to say if out loud as a punishment. He wouldn't allow himself to skirt around the truth.

"He was away and he didn't even know yet. I mean he would have felt it I guess. The others... said they had felt something, that the Darkness bonded them in some way. Felix was really strong. The death of the others had weakened him a little but he was big. That's why she chose him first. He was her hound. And he was consumed with the Darkness. He had had it in him the longest. He had been her first."

Derek bent down as if he wanted to get a closer look at the object, which of course he couldn't see. "It was a gift from her. It's not a 'c'. It's a crescent moon and a star. One star because he was first. Gabriel's had two... Mine would have had seven I guess." Derek was silent for a moment. And then heaving a sigh that seemed too old for his twenty-four-year-old soul and his nineteen-year old body he rose to his feet looking away.

"The crest had fallen off in the fight and I found it afterwards. I don't know why I put it there. It's not like it was a proper marker. It's not like anyone would know where to look for his grave." A wave of sadness fell over the group but when Elinor stirred slightly, Derek pulled back sharply as though she had slapped him.

"He would have killed me," Derek said. "The Queen did not give him the same order to not harm me. He hadn't been back since Riley stabbed me." Derek couldn't stop his hand from shaking a little.

"Felix had disarmed me and grew careless. He was coming down slowly when I grabbed the spare knife from his boot and... What do you guys care? You didn't know him. You don't know me."

He turned around and started to the car. The loud engine shattered anything that had been building, anything sacred. Elinor laid a hand on the ground a moment before she left, as a prayer? As an apology? Peter didn't know.

When Derek turned around Elinor dared to break the silence by asking "Are we not going to Uptown?"

"No need. I know exactly where we are. An aerial view of here would tell me nothing of the state of things. The palace is six days to the northwest. I'll look into my maps when we get back and we can make a plan for a short trip to wherever that is in our world. It'll be a good chance to scout around and see what kind of activity is going on at the castle." Elinor and Peter murmured sounds of assent.

Elinor

It had been a strange, strange day and Elinor really didn't know what to expect when she felt her phone buzz late that night. It was a text from Derek to her and Peter.

"We need to go to Boone. My parents have a place."

"When?!?" Peter texted.

"Sorry why are we going to Boone?" Elinor sent.

"It's my guess to where you might be able to see the capitol. And we'll leave in two weeks. We have a three-day weekend for fall break. No class that Monday. I'll check with my parents."

Peter's response was a nonsense stream of happy looking Emojies.

Elinor texted, "Okay." But she didn't feel okay. She was so confused and scared. She was really seeing Morland and she'd just seen where Derek had buried a body there. It was real, all of it. And they were going to go look for more.

Chapter 21

Elinor

"I know just what to do with these," Elinor said packing up a dozen of Katie's experiment cookies. "Katie, do you mind if I drop some of these off to Peter?"

"Peter, your fiancé? We never see him anymore," Colton said without looking up as he wrote in a notebook.

She didn't honor him with a reply.

"Yes, that's fine. Take him three of each batch. And find out which one he likes the best," Katie said.

Elinor tried not to chuckle. Each batch of cookies was nearly identical. Katie was always trying to perfect her chocolate chip cookie recipe that was already perfect. Elinor thought it might be a way for Katie to know their grandmother. It was their dad's mom's recipe and Elinor liked that Katie still used it, tweaking it and making it her own. Keeping her memory alive with every cookie.

"You sure know how to have a wild night," her dad said kissing the top of Elinor's head. "Have I told you lately how grateful I am that your idea of a fun Friday night is baking cookies with your siblings and then delivering them to your fiancé. What's his name again?"

"How do I make everyone in this family have selective amnesia?" Elinor asked Colton.

"Hmm. Maybe some sort of trauma that represses all recent memories."

"Tempting," she said as she walked out into the garage, "Very tempting."

She knew she shouldn't be driving but going against Derek was a little thrilling. And she was only driving a short way. Peter only lived ten minutes away. It took her too long to realize that there was a second car in Peter's driveway. When she finished her third knock a large man slammed the door open and said, "What is it?"

Elinor took a step back. Did she have the wrong house?

"Um excuse me, sir. Is Peter home?" she managed to squeak out. The man was as tall as the door and nearly as wide. He had a cigarette in his sneered mouth and Elinor was a frightened. She started backing away before the man even replied.

"That idiot? Yeah, he's around. What's it to you? He's got work to do around the house. He doesn't have time for..." he said looking her up and down with a look that Elinor did not like.

"Oh, okay. I'm... I'm sorry." She almost ran back to her car but then she heard him.

"Wait, Elinor," Peter said from his opened bedroom window.

"What do you think you are doing? Close the damn window," the man yelled at Peter. "Do you think air conditioning is free? And you aren't going anywhere with this…" His cruel description of Elinor was cut off as the window slammed shut and she heard running footsteps.

"You don't get to talk to her like that!" Peter shouted at his father. Elinor had never heard Peter yell and she hated it. He wasn't built for it. He should never have to do it. But he did. For her.

"Oh, is your little *girlfriend* too good for us? She *is* whatever I say she *is*. And you don't ever get to tell me what I can and cannot say in my own home. You are nothing. Do you hear me?" he said pinning Peter against the outside of the house by a hand at his chest.

"Get back inside," he said as he slammed Peter's head against the doorframe and then threw him inside without looking.

"Get off my land. I better never see you here again," he said flicking his cigarette butt at Elinor. She didn't need to be told twice.

She couldn't stop herself from crying as she drove home. She'd heard all the guys talking about how horrible Peter's dad was and she'd just assumed it was an overreaction. When would she learn to take people at their word? When would she learn that sometimes the world was a really horrible place? She kept assuming the best and she was always so horribly wrong.

She pulled over at the first gas station she found and parked, trying to calm down. She pulled out her phone. No messages from Peter. She didn't know if she should wait until he reached out. Maybe she'd only make it worse if she called. But in the end she couldn't stop herself. She texted him.

"Peter. I'm so sorry. I should have called before coming over. I'm sorry. Please call me when you can." She stared at the screen willing a response but one didn't come.

Maybe Peter was hurt.

Elinor felt sick. She couldn't go home. She was too upset and she wasn't far enough away from the event to be able to hide it. So she called the only person she could think to call.

He picked up quickly, too fast. She'd hadn't thought what she was going to say.

"Hello? Elinor is that you?" Derek said.

"Yes, it's me sorry. Can I come see you?" Silence. She continued. "I just stopped by Peter's house without calling first. Oh Derek, it was really bad. I messed up."

"I'm not home."

"Yeah, sorry. I shouldn't have assumed. Bye."

Before she could hang up she heard him say, "I'm at the game store. Peter will probably be here soon. You could come if you want."

"Okay. Would it be worse? He probably doesn't want to see me."

"He will. Come."

She pulled into the game store and rested her forehead on the steering wheel for a minute. She needed to charge up before she faced Derek. What did she know about hardship? So what she would have headaches forever? She'd just seem a glimpse into Peter's life and it left her shaking. She had the best family in created history. She was so smotheringly loved.

Peter's dad... How could a mother abandon her son in that house? How was Peter still so sweet? How was a smile his face's resting expression? It was a harsh reality check to see how often she despaired of her situation and how much better she could be handling it. She finally lifted her head to see Derek looking at her through the window of the store. She sighed, checked her face in the mirror, and headed inside.

She'd been to the game store many times since she'd first met Peter. They'd met there originally because Peter worked there and it was an easy place to work on a group project they'd been assigned in Sociology. Elinor's house had been out because her siblings would assume Peter was her boyfriend which had happened anyway. And Peter's house hadn't been an option for exactly the reason Elinor had walked right into. She exhaled shakily and started into the store.

She'd been surprised that such a store existed. It was lined with board games and action figures and posters of scantily clad elf maidens and burly men in fantastical armor. It was an interesting place. She'd felt very uncomfortable the first time but Peter had this magic way of smiling and making everything better.

Since then she'd come to the store at least one night a week usually with Derek driving. Peter was always there and it seemed like the easiest job ever. He got paid to play Magic and sell energy drinks and consult on board game purchases. She liked it there.

The owner, Nick, gave her a wave when she came in and she smiled back. He never made her feel out of place or like she didn't belong there as much as everyone else did. But Derek's quick glare brought her back down and she walked over to his table.

Derek

Elinor sat down across from him without saying anything as she dropped a container of cookies on the table.

"Did he hit him?" Derek asked.

"He threw him around a bit. He slammed his head back onto the door. I don't know what else." She looked sorry enough that Derek had to stop himself from berating her more. She seemed to know what she had done. But he had to make sure she wouldn't put Peter in unnecessary danger again.

"And you will never go to his house again?" Derek said it like a question.

Her lips started to tremble and he wished he hadn't spoken. He should have just left it alone. Now she was going to cry all over the game store. *Ugh.*

"I feel really bad, Derek. I know I made a mistake. It was all my fault. Seeing Peter get pushed around..." She covered her face with her hands.

"And you know you shouldn't have driven yourself. Now you see what comes when you do stupid things. Pull yourself together. He'll be here soon." Derek said looking at his text from Peter.

"Game store. Dad."

Derek watched her pull out her phone and then close her eyes. He guessed that Peter hadn't texted her yet. Maybe it was a mistake to tell her to come.

"What's going on over here?" Jerry asked sliding an arm around Elinor's shoulders. "Is big bad Derek making you cry?" When Elinor instantly stiffened, Derek had to stifle a chuckle. Seeing Elinor uncomfortable was one of the most entertaining things he ever saw. She flushed red and tried to squirm away from all physical touch with Jerry. She could have been really rude around it. She could have told him to go to hell. But she was just too nice. There she'd ruined it. His only source of entertainment.

"Back off, Jerry," Derek said.

"Oh is she yours now?" Jerry said wryly. Elinor looked in physical pain from the embarrassment and he had to stop himself from smiling again. It just confirmed what a sadist he knew himself to be.

"I'm not anyone's," Elinor said standing. *So she has a spine after all*, Derek mused. Jerry was about to say something smart when Jack came over with an armful of supplies.

"Hi Elinor," he said setting everything down on the table. "Want to play Ticket to Ride? Want a sour straw?" he said offering her a green sour candy.

"Yes and yes," she said smiling. "Only I don't know how to play."

"Uh girls!" said Carlos sitting next to Derek. "How can you not know how to play this game?"

"I don't know. We mostly play family games at my house. Like Cranium or Yahtzee."

"Baby games," Carlos judged. "Now it's time to play a real game with real men."

Jack chuckled, "Only Derek can grow a beard."

"What?" Jerry asked studying Derek's face. "Then why don't you have one? Why would you shave if you could grow a beard?"

"They are too itchy," Derek said avoiding everyone's eyes. Elinor smiled and he wondered if she was seeing him with the scruffy face he always had in Morland. Shaving was too big a pain for everyday there. And having a beard now only reminded him of his other life.

"Okay I'll explain the game," Jack said, "It's not so hard. You'll be fine."

On their fifth round, Peter came in. Derek had been wondering what Elinor would do. Would she play it cool so he wasn't embarrassed? Or would she make a scene? Derek decided for her, which was for the best, because when Elinor saw the shiner on Peter's right eye she was speechless.

"Finally," Derek said, "Take my spot. I have a paper to finish and I got wrangled into playing this dumb game." Derek didn't wait to see what Peter would do. He just grabbed his bag and moved to the next table.

He did have a paper to write which was why he had brought his laptop so the excuse was believable. Derek hoped Elinor would take his hint and not bring up his eye. The other guys were trained enough that they ignored it. Hopefully Elinor wasn't the stupid doll she looked like. And when she kept her peace, Derek nodded to himself.

Chapter 22

Derek

Derek stood in the kitchen slowly eating his breakfast. His parents buzzed around him putting coffee in to-go mugs and papers into briefcases. And everyone kindly ignored everyone else. He wondered if all families were like this. He wondered if his family had been like this before.

"Hey wait," Derek said as his parents headed to the garage. "I want to take some of my friends up to the mountain house this weekend. We have a long weekend because of fall break. Is that alright with you guys?"

His dad looked floored. Derek rebuked himself. How long had it been since he had initiated anything with them? His dad spoke after a heartbeat. "Yeah that's fine but you haven't been up there in years so we are coming too."

Derek said, "Okay," as he walked back up to his room.

"Are we really going on a family trip and he's the one who brought it up?" asked his mom with a smile in her voice.

"Calm down. We are only joining as an afterthought."

"But still."

Elinor

"Oh Ryan. That'll be great. Everyone will be so glad to see you, especially Elinor," her stepmom said as she looked over smiling and pointed at the phone. Elinor and Colton nodded and continued watching a show. Colton had several serious electrode-like things attached to different parts of Elinor's face. She had pads on her checks and temples as well as little clamps on her ears that did some buzzy thing. She was sure she looked like Frankenstein's bride.

"So, Ryan is coming this weekend. That'll be fun. Speaking of fun, how much longer, good doctor?" Elinor asked.

"Umm," Colton said pulling up the timer on his iPad. "Thirty more minutes."

"What?" Elinor asked as she started to disentangle herself.

"Hey! Hey now! Stop that. You gave me free reign, remember? When you decided to not go to doctors anymore I was understandably upset. So you, in your infinite wisdom, agreed to try *any* at home remedies I wanted."

"Yes but I didn't think they'd be so numerous and weird."

Colton smiled all the way up to his eyeballs. "Well then you don't know me at all."

"Ha ha. You are so funny. Fine. I'll be your good little guinea pig but you have to tell mom to back off a bit. She's hovering extra low lately and she's driving me bonkers. I only need one doctor in this house and apparently I let him lightly electrocute me."

"It's not electrocution," Colton sighed dramatically. "It's called a TENS unit, which stands for Transcutaneous Electrical Nerve Stimulation. And yes I'll see what I can do about mom. And this is not that bad. Wait till I get the seaweed samples next week. Oh boy they look interesting."

"Uh huh. Oh boy."

Katie came into the room skipping, per her usual, and stopped mid step to burst out laughing.

"Oh Elinor. When are you going to figure out he's just messing with you? The family has bets going to see what it takes to make you tell him no," Katie said unable to stop laughing for several minutes. Colton huffed when Elinor chuckled.

"Well you tell me when and I'll make sure you get the cash you need for your new DS."

"What level today?" asked Katie sitting next to her and taking her hand.

"Um currently a six. You'd think having my brain microwaved would be worse but you never can tell with these things."

"Here is my journal if you need to consult it, Kat," Colton said lifting up the empty box for the TENS unit to reveal a moleskin notebook. Elinor was pretty sure there were a thousand of those hidden all over their house. This one contained a daily log of headache levels on a scale of one to ten and any exerting factors Elinor attributed to that particular day. Katie picked it up, skimmed it, and set it down. It was a dry read. Elinor didn't blame her.

"It's not one hundred percent accurate," Colton added unable to help himself. "Because the patient was not very compliant for a stretch there."

"Yes master," Elinor said raising one shoulder and speaking like Igor. "Please no more punishing."

"You are almost done. Stop your griping."

Elinor's phone buzzed and she read a text from Peter.

"Mountain is a go :) :) :) :) :) Talk to your folks! Fingers crossed."

Elinor wasn't sure how to convince her parents to let her go on a weekend sleepover with a bunch of boys she hardly knew. One of which had actually choked her pretty recently. She hadn't told them about that but still it was a stretch even without that. Then she remembered that Ryan was coming home. Her parents would definitely be okay with it if Ryan came with her. *Yes, that could work,* she thought.

She texted Ryan. "Hey favoritest older brother."

"What do you want? :)"

"College has made you so smart, huh?"

"Yes. I have transcended to an intelligence that is almost precognition."

"*Rolls her eyes dramatically*"

"What's up?"

"Can I ask a favor?"

"Maybe... Katie just texted me a photo of your current predicament. Is your favor that I don't post that on the Internet because..."

Elinor looked over at her sister and said "Katie... Did you text Ryan a picture of me all rigged up?"

Katie's eyes went wide like a startled forest bunny and she was bounding out of the room before Elinor could grab a limb.

"Don't harm the child. She's just keeping her end of the bargain. Keeping me posted." Ryan texted.

"You are lucky that she is so darn fast."

"So favor?"

"How would you like to spend this weekend that you were planning on spending in our boring dull house at a cabin in Boone instead :) :) :)"

"For real?!?!"

"Yeah. Some new friends from school are going this weekend and I think mom and dad would let me go if you went."

"You probably don't need a babysitter. Or is it a chaperone?!?!?!? Details now!!"

"Ugh! I don't think you need any more college. You are too smart already. So the reason you should come is that I've only made friends with... boys. NOT BOYFRIENDS. It just happens that all my friends are of the male persuasion. So will you come?"

"HAHAHAHAHAHAHAHAHA"

"Ryan!!"

"HAHAHAHAHAHAHAHAHA"

Elinor was not amused. Maybe it was better if Ryan didn't come. She'd probably have to fill him in on the weird things going on and he *hated* weird things. He didn't read books about magic or watch sci-fi flicks. He was really content with his normal ordinary world. Maybe that's why he was studying political science, a clinical lack of imagination.

"Sorry," Ryan texted back when she didn't respond, "that may have been an overreaction to the information. Yes, I'll come with you to an awesome mountain cabin with your numerous lovers. JK JK Sounds really cool."

"Really?!?! Yeah! Thanks, brother."

"And I promise to be cool around your 'boys' that are just 'friends' hehehe."

"The 'hehehe' makes me doubt your truthfulness."

"Cool as a cucumber. hehe."

"Hilarious. I'll text you when I know more details," She set her phone aside when Colton's timer went off.

"Okay you are free. But let me take them off. We don't want to crimp the cords," Colton said.

"We don't want to crimp the cords because we'll be doing it again?" she said as a question.

"You are impossible. Yes. You can't just try things once. That's not scientific. So how do you feel?"

"The same."

"So a level six. And other sensations?"

"Nope. Am I free to go?" she asked as she grabbed his neck, tickling him into submission.

"Fine. Fine. Get out of here you maniac."

"Thank you," she said kissing the top of his head as she headed to her room.

Elinor called Peter right away.

"Hello," Peter answered

"I can probably go. My brother said he'd come!" she said without preamble.

"Sorry. This is Elinor?"

"Yes, Peter. It's me. I knew my parents would probably have a problem with me going on a weekend trip with strange boys but…"

"Hey," he interrupted, "I'm not a strange boy."

"You are a stranger to them and I've only known you a little while. Maybe you could still be an axe murderer."

"An axe murderer? With these wimpy arms? Maybe a poisoner or the boss who tells the bad guys who to kill."

She found herself laughing.

"Yeah, that's not who parents want to send their invalid daughter on a vacation with. So anyway, my brother is coming home this weekend and he said he would come with us. By the way, I'm inviting my brother."

Now Peter was laughing. "I'm sure that will be fine with Derek's parents. Does your brother know about…"

"Um no. He's been gone and he doesn't like weird things. Like how you love weird unexplainable magic things. He does not. But he'll be cool. You can't not like Ryan. Unless you are Derek and hate everyone probably."

"When are you going to ask your parents?"

"Tonight. When would we be leaving? And where exactly are we going? Details might sell my case."

"We would leave Saturday morning probably and come back Monday evening. And I'm not sure exactly where it is. I've never been. Oh and Derek's parents are coming too. They wouldn't let Derek go alone."

"That's great! My parents will have no problems now. Yeah! We are going on an adventure."

Chapter 23

Derek

Derek couldn't believe that he was going on a trip with her in a few days. This whole thing felt like it had spun out of his control. His original goal had been to make her just go away. Then somehow he'd ended up being her personal chauffeur and now he was taking her to his family cabin for a weekend trip. He blamed half of it on Peter and the other half on Elinor. But blaming others didn't fix the situation.

He was able to somewhat ignore her in their first class together. English was a pretty solo experience and they only rarely had to peer review each other's work and Elinor never turned around to partner up with him. So they could each pretend they didn't know each other but in their second class together it was different.

The seats they'd chosen their first day had been their permanent seat assignments. Elinor's seat was across the aisle from him and he had thought that would be far enough. But this first aid and CPR class was a very partner intensive class. It could have been alright.

Elinor had a girl at her table and they would be partners and Derek would either perform the task alone or just pick a different group to work with for the day because he had no table mate. But fate enjoyed nothing more than laughing in his face and Elinor's table mate dropped the class after the second week and being the only two partner-less students they were assigned to each other.

It was made slightly more bearable by the fact that Elinor hated it as much as he did. If she had enjoyed it, then it would have been intolerable. But her suffering made him almost cheery some days. They didn't speak beyond the required script for assessing if someone consented to care or to check for unconsciousness but even without speaking some things were too intimate.

Elinor currently had one arm snaked up along his chest while she stood pressed to his side. It would have been romantic if not for her other arm which was pretending to pound aggressively on his back to dislodge the imaginary thing he had been choking on. She did it correctly and professionally but she was too close. When she was close like this the scent of her shampoo drove him a little mad and he found himself fighting to lean into her. He was relieved when it was his turn to be the saver and her turn to be the dummy.

Elinor stood in front of him and waited. There were two different procedures to dislodge an object from someone's throat, back blows and abdominal thrusts. Elinor had done the back blows and he decided it would be safer to do abdominal thrusts. He wrapped one arm around her placing his fists just above her belly button then he wrapped his other hand around that one and gave a soft in-and-up motion.

Elinor's breath came out in a soft whoosh and she said "Okay. I think you've got it." Derek was about to release her when the instructor called out, "Your patient has just gone unconscious, walk them to the floor and begin CPR." Elinor sighed and slowly collapsed. Derek was ready for her and as she sank back he laid her down softly.

They'd only done this a hundred times.

He tilted her head back to open her airways as he lifted her chin and brought his face close, close enough that Elinor's eyes shot open and locked into his. He just stared at her for a second, his thoughts leaving his mind as he looked into her green eyes that couldn't see him. By the time she blinked and her eyes were blue again, he had removed his hands from her face and reached up for his textbook on the table, pretending to consult it. Elinor sat up and didn't look at him.

Derek mentally shook himself. What had he been thinking? Had she felt something too? A charge? A strange pull between them? He decided not and that he would forget it. The class had to be over soon and they would each forget that this past hour had ever happened, they always did. Derek wished for the millionth time that her partner hadn't dropped the class.

Elinor

She couldn't look at him. Something had happened in class and she didn't want to think about it. Peter was waiting for them at their usual lunch table and Elinor hadn't even noticed that Derek was walking in front of her until he sat down at their table as well. Elinor sat on Peter's other side and didn't look at Derek. Why were they partners in class? Why was there so much touching? The teacher should not have allowed boy-girl pairs. It wasn't professional or appropriate.

Elinor had never been that close to a boy before. She'd never had a boyfriend. She didn't like that the farthest she'd ever gone with a boy had been during a health class. Peter watched her curiously and wisely didn't ask. He knew that they didn't like to discuss each other or their classes together. She made herself forget it and focus on her lunch and the news around the table.

If Derek hadn't been so good looking it would have all been easier. It wasn't her fault that she was responding to him on some biological level. Because he was not a good man. He wasn't. It wasn't too long ago his hands were at her throat and he might of... Best to forget Derek even existed. Peter was the one who deserved her attention. He was good and kind and always there for her. If there was someone who should make her heart beat faster, it should be Peter.

Chapter 24

Elinor

"Why do you *really* want to go to Boone with these nerds?" Ryan asked Elinor as they waited on the driveway for the Jensens to pick them up. The early October morning was crisp and Elinor pulled her scarf tighter around. She let the question hang for a moment trying to decide what to say.

"A couple reasons. Partly because I need to get away. I need a little space and an adventure. The other things is... It has a little bit to do with that tree we found when we first moved here," she said thinking that was the easiest way to prepare him. She hadn't thought about that tree much since that day but it had been a weird experience and Ryan had been there.

"You haven't been messing with it, right? You told me you wouldn't go back there without me."

"No, I haven't but there are some other weird things going on and I think going to Boone might help. Do you need to know more?"

"No, I don't," he said which was exactly what she had expected. He was missing the curiosity organ. "You know how I feel about 'weird things'. I have to say it's probably best to just let it all go but I see that stubborn streak rising from here. Fine we'll go but I'm going to be watching that you don't do anything stupid."

"So the usual," she said grinning like a Cheshire as an SUV pulled up their driveway.

"Oh and which boy do you like?" Ryan asked failing to keep a straight face.

"Neither!" she said blushing.

"Both?" Ryan said laughing as he started to load their things into the car.

Elinor sat in the sideways seat at the far back of the SUV. Derek's parents had tried to make Derek sit back there but it was too small for him or any of the guys and she didn't mind.

Mrs. Jensen was peppering everyone with questions and by the clench in Derek's jaw he could hardly stand it. Elinor grinned.

The scenery progressed as the roads grew windier. Trees were bursting with bright fall colors. The light dappled through the trees sending green flickers of light and shadow through the car. It was beautiful but... The flickering shadows and winding road were making her head pound and her eyes sting. She could feel the nausea rising. Elinor thought maybe she should rest her forehead against the seat back of the boy's row and close her eyes.

Eventually Derek's parents ran out of questions and the radio came on. Sometime later Mrs. Jensen's voice cut through the music.

"Elinor?" asked Mrs. Jensen "Are you okay?"

"Mmmm. I'm not feeling so great," Elinor said raising her head.

Peter jerked his head around "Is it the...?" he said blinking his eyes exaggeratedly.

"No, it's just regular car sickness from all the hills and sharp turns plus my headaches," Elinor said.

"Nathan, why don't you pull the car over there at that stand?" said Mrs. Jensen.

"No. I'll be fine," said Elinor in vain.

"Don't worry about it," said Mrs. Jensen. "We'd talked about wanting boiled peanuts anyway. We'll put you up front and put Derek in the back. I don't mind sitting in the middle."

Derek

Elinor was asleep in the guest bedroom. She had barely made it there in time. It amazed him that she was still alive. Natural selection was failing.

Derek looked out on the view of the valley and exhaled. This place brought back strange memories of his parents trying to fix him, to mend their relationship. He felt the belated guilt for how it had played out. His parents weren't bad people but he knew it couldn't have gone any other way.

He remembered the moment he had come home with crystal clear clarity. He hadn't been in his backyard but the cars and houses told him he was on Earth. He had asked for directions and had found he was in Waxhaw, close to where he'd been born. He had then walked the five miles to his current house. His mind had been racing. Would his parents be there waiting for him? Would the neighborhood be covered in missing posters? He'd started running.

When times had been hard in Morland, he had clung to the hope that someone was looking for him. His parents would find him. Even though he hadn't known exactly where he was he knew with the certainty of a child who had never been let down that they would find him and bring him home. They would never stop looking for their only child.

But then years went by. *Years.* And they hadn't come. He had learned with a bitter coldness, that others could not be trusted. He could count on no one but himself. *He* had to find a way home. That is, if he still wanted to go home. He hadn't allowed himself to remember the good times with his parents or the ease of the technological world. He would remind himself of three facts when he found the longing unbearable. *They hadn't come. They didn't miss him. They didn't care.*

He had repeated that to himself as a mantra. *They hadn't come. They didn't miss him. They didn't care.* He had repeated it on those cold winter nights when had had nothing but the cloak on his back to fight the chill of frostbite. He had repeated it when he had trained at the citadel and had been beaten for being too slow. He had repeated it when he had been chosen by the queen. He had repeated it when his siblings had each turned to Darkness. Because missing home had been too horrible a feeling to feel.

Trust no one. Trust nothing but yourself. And it had given him strength. It had made him self-reliant. It had made him unbeatable.

When he had finally returned home, it had only taken him an hour to realize that no time had passed. That it was still the same day he had disappeared on. That *no* time had passed. His parents were still at work. It was only three forty-five p.m. and it was still June fifteenth.

No time had passed.

No time had passed.

Rushing to look in the mirror he had been shocked to see his juvenile face. He was thirteen again. His scar from Brigitte's knife and every other scar he'd earned in Morland had been washed away and he was thirteen again. Who ever wanted to be thirteen again? But then it had hit him. He hadn't missed his life. He was getting a second chance. No time had passed. The last five years had happened in an instant. It had really been too much for his brain to grasp.

Had his parents been home when he returned, things might have been different. Things might have been repaired between them. But they had still been at work for another two hours. They weren't aware their thirteen-year-old son had left and returned a man.

Even though he knew he hadn't been gone but a moment in this world, it didn't lessen the pain of the abandonment he had felt for five years. It was actually just as he'd always envisioned it; he'd realized with a bitter laugh. *They hadn't even noticed he was gone.* He'd thought he would be able to hold it together but when he saw them pull into the driveway, he'd run outside and collapsed in his mother's arms.

"How could you not know I was gone?" he had sobbed into her neck.

Derek then got committed to an insane asylum for a while, a month. They didn't call it an asylum, of course. They called it a 'pediatric psychiatric ward'. Part of the problem had been his British accent. He had had trouble dropping it after five years. It had been his first and most important piece of armor for his deep undercover life but the doctors and his parents had seen it as a sign of something seriously wrong.

He had come out renouncing everything and was talking like a good American boy, if not quite a Southern boy. But in his heart he still knew it all had happened. He had never doubted that it had been a dream or just his imagination. But that's what he had told them. Then they'd all come to Boone to become a family again.

He had been too angry and bitter. He had changed and become a man, a bad man. He couldn't turn back into the son they'd known.

By the end of the month vacation they had found a semblance of a routine. Derek had made himself try. He'd made himself forgive them. Over and over. Every time the red rage had threatened to overcome him he had made himself forgive them. He forgave them for not knowing he was gone. For letting him suffer in a prison world for five years. For not believing him when he had needed them so much.

Staring out at the porch as a grown man, he forgave them again. It saddened him that he couldn't be what they wanted.

His mom came out and leaned against the railing next to him. Being back in Boone reminded him that he hadn't done a very good job at being a son. He resolved to try again. They both looked down on the tiny town below them that looked more like a painting of a town than a real place. There was the required tiny white church and the hazy mountains behind serving as the backdrop. He could see the hotel on top of one of those mountains that had been a big scandal when it was built. It was the one manmade mark on the mountain peak.

"I've really missed this place. It was a good idea to come here," she said. "And I like your new friends. Especially Elinor."

215

"Yeah, she's bearable when she's unconscious." Derek said looking down at the small toy town below him. He wondered what Elinor would see from this vantage.

"I like her," said his mom.

"Oh please stop, Mom. There is nothing there," Derek responded exasperatingly.

"I'm just saying you've seemed a little happier, a little less in your own head lately. I wondered if it had something to do with her."

"She is just Peter's friend. Stop okay."

"Just think about it."

Derek didn't want to think about it. But Elinor filled his mind just like always. He told himself it was because she was a threat or an asset that needed to be watched. It was nothing more. He still hated her. He was sure he did.

Chapter 25

Elinor

Elinor woke up feeling groggy and disoriented. She wasn't sure where she was but her head hurt so... it was like home. The room was dark with the last remnants of the day shining through the cracks in the curtains.

She was in Boone at Derek's cabin.

She stretched her sore arms and legs as far as they would go, a nice benefit of being short in that it didn't push her off the bed.

It was so interesting how the after effects of her headaches felt like a full body beating. Colton would have enjoyed discussing it, she thought smiling but then stopped suddenly. Her facial muscles were excruciating to move. They were always the sorest. It was like her whole head had been trying to contract itself into a singularity and upon failure settled for seeing how long it could hold its tight twisted pose.

Elinor sighed and blinked.

And gasped.

The castle. It was right there before her. She was on a roof of some kind of shop or house. The castle loomed above her and the setting sun lent an ominous red background to the view.

From her position on the roof she could see below her to shops and houses. Awnings and roofs made it difficult to see much of what was going on but she could see shapes of people walking below.

She looked back up to the castle, unsure how she could get a closer look. Their current cabin was near the top of a mountain but there were many small mountains in this mountain system. One neighboring one would surely get them in closer. That would be tomorrow's problem. The sun was setting quickly and there would be nothing to see in Morland and no chance to navigate the Boone woods or mountains in the dark.

Elinor made herself presentable and headed downstairs. She was starving. When had she last eaten? Yesterday night? She hadn't had breakfast. She went down the stairs to see the guys playing something on the Xbox. Only Derek's side look acknowledged her entrance. Mrs. Jensen was in the kitchen fixing dinner.

"Oh Elinor, it's so good to see you up and about. How are you feeling?" she said setting down a bag of salad to come give Elinor's arm a rub. "Is there anything I can get you?"

"Thank you, Mrs. Jensen. I'm better. I'm so sorry to be such an inconvenience. Can I help you with dinner?"

"Absolutely not," she said smiling, patting one of the stools at the island. "You can sit right here and rest a bit more." Derek's mom had his bright red hair but it was the smile that divided them. It was so warm and so open. It made Elinor feel instantly at ease.

Elinor took the chance to really look around the cabin. It was stunning. Derek's parents must make a lot of money doing whatever they did. Every inch of the place was decorated impeccably to make it look cozy and still fashionable. There was a long dining table that looked like it had only yesterday been a large tree. She could have counted the rings if she'd wanted to.

The large fireplace was supposed to be the focal point of the living room but the boys were facing away from it as they sat on the designer couches playing what she could now see was Halo. But even with the sounds of simulated murdering, she could see herself wanting to stay here for a week at least but she knew better. The large A-frame window had no curtains and was going to shine so bright in the morning. She was already anxious about it.

"Can I get you something to drink?" Mrs. Jensen asked.

"A water would be great."

Mrs. Jensen set the water down in front of her looking at Elinor with kind pity on her face. Elinor sighed and smiled weakly.

"I'm really better. That's just how I am."

"Yeah, your brother was telling me earlier," she said resuming her work in the kitchen. "It's such a sad thing in someone as young as yourself. Have you tried being gluten-free? I remember seeing something on Dr. Phil about that, maybe."

"Yes, I have tried it." Elinor said trying to keep her sigh internalized. People *loved* trying to fix her and she reminded herself again that it only came from kindness. "There isn't much I haven't tried. My younger brother keeps very detailed lists. I'm trying to come to peace with it. It is what it is."

"Do you get like that very often?" she said and Elinor wondered how such a compassionate woman who seemed kind and attentive could think her son was a crazy liar committing him to a pediatric hospital. But maybe her parents would do the same thing to her if she told them. Maybe it was the only option if your kid really believed in magic and other lands.

"Yes. It's like that all the time. I have a moderate to severe headache every day. It started a little over a year ago. It's bad like that, incapacitating, maybe ten days a month."

Mrs. Jensen stopped mixing the salad and turned to look at her. Elinor turned away calling to the boys, "Are you guys just going to sit there on the couch all trip?"

"Hey, you're up," said Ryan turning around.

"Oh yeah. Let's go do the thing," Peter said leaving the game and this controller as he hurried to the kitchen.

"Well dinner is all ready if you guys want to eat first," said Mrs. Jensen.

"Sounds great honey," said Mr. Jensen coming in from the porch. "It's a really pretty night tonight. You all should be sure to go in the hot tub."

"I think we should wait to go exploring until tomorrow," said Derek. "It's dark and we wouldn't see anything anyway."

"Great idea," said Mrs. Jensen smiling.

Derek

Derek was the first one changed and in the hot tub. Peter was shortly behind him.

"This place is sick, Derek. Why do we not come here every month? Why have I never been here before?" Peter said settling into the water slowly exhaling at the heat. The air was crisp and clean and Derek let it clear his head.

"I don't know. We haven't been here in a while," Derek said.

"Do you really think she'll see anything tomorrow?"

"I don't know. Maybe she has seen something already."

"Do you hope she has?" Peter said looking at Derek levelly.

"Yes and no. It would be great and terrible to know what's going on. But I still keep hoping she's just making it all up for attention. So tomorrow will be a test. I didn't describe the castle in that much detail in my blog. I'm very curious to see what she says," Derek said.

"She sure is taking forever," Derek said after a while, unable to contain himself. He couldn't help himself that everything she did annoyed him.

"I think her and Ryan got held up talking to their parents on the phone. Derek, what's your deal with her? For real? I've never seen you dislike someone so much, which is saying something. You'd think her life's goal was to infuriate you. I mean I hope it is but that's just wishful thinking."

"You know why," Derek said.

"No, I don't think I do," Peter said. Derek's eyes darted inside watching Elinor come down the stairs with a towel as her only cover. Her pale skin almost glowed in the dark. Derek looked back to Peter and Peter's eyes grew huge as he said, "No way! You like her."

Derek didn't have time to answer as Elinor and Ryan came outside.

Elinor

There were so many stars, in both skies, and Elinor just leaned her head back and sighed. The Earth city below shone like a little tinsel town and her Morland sight was pitch black. The castle had no lights to illuminate it. It was almost ghostly how it looked like nothing was there. It was like a wolf watching from the dark woods.

But nothing to see meant she was off the job, so she allowed herself to enjoy the hot tub and the cool breeze caressing her face.

"Hot tubs are pretty great," she said. She'd been nervous to be in a bathing suit around boys who were not her brother but being in a hot tub when it was chilly outside was a dream come true. Her head was cold and the rest of her was toasty warm. She could alternate between heating her neck in the water and cooling it off to numb it. "I think we need to invest in one of these at home," she told Ryan.

"I'll see what I can do," he said looking skyward as well.

"How are the stars looking tonight?" Peter asked Elinor.

"You can see them yourself," Derek said

"No, the other ones," Peter said and was promptly elbowed by Derek.

"The 'other' ones?" Ryan asked. "Do I want to know? Is this the weird stuff you were talking about, El?"

"Yup. Super weird. You'd hate it," she said not looking at him. "And they look amazing, Peter." Ryan groaned.

"You came on this trip without knowing why?" Peter asked.

"Oh I know why I'm here," Ryan said and Elinor looked over quickly hearing the mischief in his voice.

"He's here because he's a really great brother, who would never say dumb things to embarrass his sister," she said with raised eyebrows. Ryan just shrugged but made a sign to show Peter and Derek that he'd be watching them.

"I'm mostly here to just make sure she comes back alive. I think I got stern instructions from every member of our family about making sure you don't die. Colton wanted to give me a checklist and a handful of notebooks," Ryan said and they both started chuckling because it wasn't a joke.

"So what's the plan for tomorrow?" Peter said looking excitedly to Derek.

"I figured we'd just take a hike up to the peak. We'll see what we can see and go from there," Derek said.

Elinor's eyes were drawn from the sky to Derek's voice and then torso. She couldn't help but stare at his tattoo, his sister's name written across his side, snaking up his ribs. *Brigitte.*

Chapter 26

Elinor

After the hot tub, Ryan and Peter returned to their spots on the couch with their controllers. Derek was off somewhere. His parents had settled into their room for the night and Elinor had tried to read in her room but she felt too energized. She had slept for a long time earlier and she felt restless.

She headed downstairs and made herself a cup of tea as she grabbed a quilt to sit on the swing on the back porch. It was just the most stunning starry view. She heard the door click and a shape came out and sat beside her in the dark night.

"May I?" Derek asked after he was already sitting down.

"Sure. Your house," she said laughing awkwardly without looking at him. She set her drink down in the cup holder.

"What do you see?" he asked. She felt more than saw the energy behind his request. He'd probably been itching to ask her the moment she got up.

"The castle is that way," she said pointing straight ahead. "Though I can't see it now. It's like it disappear after nightfall. There are no lights to mark its presence. Are there curtains in every window? Does she keep it dark inside on purpose?"

"Yes and yes," Derek said and then was silent waiting for more.

"Right now we are on a roof of somewhere... The city is layered, right? Three layers that rise up, like it's all built on a mountain. Well we are in the middle layer. There are shops and houses below us. There are dim lights lit and every once in a while I see someone walk with a lantern. All seems quiet enough from here."

Derek exhaled. "It's really true then, huh?"

"Did I pass the test?"

"Yes."

"Are you happy?"

"Never." His words hung suspended like the stars. Neither of them knew what to say next. They swung in silence in the dark.

"Elinor," he said after an untold amount of minutes, time had no meaning out there.

"Yes."

"I want you."

"You what?" she coughed. The words he said made no sense. Had he really just said what she'd heard? He wanted her?

"I've been fighting it. I didn't even really know until Peter accused me earlier. But don't be confused. I don't *love* you. I don't even really like you. I just... want you."

Elinor stood to rise and Derek gripped her wrist somehow seeing in the dark.

"Let me go," she said snaking her wrist free as she went for the door. Derek was faster and pressed her back against it before she could open it.

"I would never take you," he said pressing his face to her neck and breathing her in. She made an inarticulate sound.

"I'm not that kind of girl," she said pushing against him to no avail. He was made of granite. She couldn't help but breathe him in. He smelled like the fireplace.

She would not lean in.

"I'm not asking for anything more," he said using a soft voice she didn't know was in his repertoire. "I just can't get you out of my head. You are a cancer in my bones and a song stuck on repeat. I want you and I need to be free of you."

"Please, Derek. Let me go," she said weakly but he held her fast.

"Tell me you haven't thought about me and I will."

"Not like that," she said.

"I don't believe you. Tell me you aren't attracted to me."

As she stayed silent he said, "I see you can't. I don't need a commitment from you. And I promise I'll be nice."

As if to prove his point, his arms snaked around her back and a gasp escaped her lips as shivers follows his hands. Her whole body was on fire. He ran a hand through her hair and she had to stop herself from arching into him.

All she could think about was how good it felt. It felt so good to have Derek holding her. He pulled her closer and she stopped fighting for a moment. Everything else just slipped out her mind.

Derek noticed when she stopped pushing and moved his face from her neck to look at her. But as he opened his mouth to speak a cool breeze caught Elinor's face and her senses returned.

She worked an arm free and felt for the handle. She fell back hard on the wood floor as the door crashed open under their force and Derek stumbled on top of her. She was about to yell for her brother when Derek got, whispering, "Just think about it. I won't touch you again unless you tell me to."

"You okay?" Ryan yelled over the couch without moving his eyes from the screen.

She wasn't but she said "Yes."

Elinor nearly ran to her room and locked the door. And then propped a chair under the handle. She paced the room. She had never been so confused in her life. It had almost been worse than the last time his hands had been at her neck. Derek speaking to her like that... It was something she hadn't imagined was possible.

He couldn't really care for her, she knew. It was just a gross proposition. It would have been better if he wasn't so handsome. She'd almost wavered for a moment. Thank God she'd stood firm. She felt like a fool that she had ever felt torn between Peter and Derek. Derek was not good. The absence of his soul made him more monster than man.

Why had she come here with him? How could she ever trust him again? She and Ryan should leave in the morning. She wasn't sure she believed that Derek would stay away. She jumped when a note slide under the door. She picked it up like it might burn. It was a folded piece of paper. Inside it read:

"I'm sorry. That was a mistake. I scared you. Can you believe that I'm sorry? It really won't happen again."

When she huffed out loud she heard a faint laugh from the door and she retreated to the bed. After a couple more minutes pacing she decided to go to bed. She looked in the bedroom and the bathroom but her toiletry bag wasn't there. She contemplated sleeping in what she wore but decided against it.

The amount of supplies she needed to sleep was laughable. She went downstairs and saw her things on the floor. Derek's bedroom door was closed.

On her way upstairs her eyes caught on a painting in the hallway. It was entrancing. It was of a house covered in snow. There was a soft yellow glow coming from the windows and there was a swing on the tree out front. It felt like the kind of painting you'd want to hop into Mary Poppins style. She leaned closer to see if there was a signature on the painting and when she blinked she saw something, a shadow in the Morland woods.

What was that? Elinor thought as she looked from side to side. There it was again. Elinor squinted into the darkness and suddenly a creature loomed before her. She covered her mouth to stifle her scream. It was a thing of billowing blackness. It had claws and moved like a fog. It looked like death itself.

"Hey guys," she called out to Peter and Ryan but her voice was a mere squeak. She didn't dare take her eyes off the creature. It scanned the area and then fixed right on her.

"It's looking at me," she said and took a step back as it came closer. She tripped over something and blinked back to Earth sight.

"Ryan. Ryan," she called.

He said "huh?" without looking her way.

She didn't want to yell and wake Derek's parents up. She could hear the sounds of gunfire and explosives coming from the T.V. She knew she shouldn't look again without telling them but they weren't listening. So she blinked.

All she saw was the creature. So much closer. Its eyes locked onto her in an instant and it lunged at her in one bound. A color caught her eye: red. She looked down and saw so much blood. It was pouring out of her stomach. She grabbed it and blinked.

She said his name only once, "Derek." He came running around the corner.

"A creature," she said, still holding her stomach as she passed out.

Chapter 27

Derek

"Turn off that stupid game. Now!" Derek growled as he lifted Elinor and carried her into his and Peter's room downstairs. Peter and Ryan looked in time to see Elinor's head hanging like a golden curtain over Derek's arm.

"What the?" Ryan said dropping the controller on the couch. Peter turned off the system and followed.

"Hey stop that! What's going on?" Ryan yelled seeing Derek pull Elinor's shirt up. Ryan pulled it hastily down.

"I have to look. You need to move." Ryan did not move.

"What's going on Derek? Is she asleep?" Peter asked.

"She saw a creature. She called me and when I got there she was holding her stomach and then passed out. Let me see her stomach," he said forcefully.

Ryan moved.

There was no discernible injury. Derek rolled her from side to side checking everything as Ryan growled. There was nothing until suddenly there was something. A white line drew itself across her stomach. It looked like an old healed scar. Then two more lines appeared only slightly fainter.

"What is that?" Peter and Ryan said together.

"Something bad," Derek said.

Peter and Ryan started firing questions at Derek, which he ignored as he sat down in a chair staring at the lines. Were they getting thicker? Was this tied to what happened earlier? When he'd lost control? He knew it wasn't. His failed seduction of Elinor wouldn't elicit an attack from Morland.

Eventually the guys stopped questioning him and Peter took Ryan downstairs for a drink and to fill him in, Derek supposed. Later the two of them fell asleep, Ryan in the other chair and Peter in Ryan's room but only after receiving a promise that Derek would wake him when she woke up.

Derek knew he should get as much sleep as he could but he paced the living room. Stopping for a moment where Elinor had been attacked, he wished not for the first time that he had the ability to see his demons as she did. He rested his hand on the wall. "What do you have waiting for me, Mother?" he whispered. When he walked toward the bedroom, Elinor was stirring.

"Derek," she said. Her eyes were full of an emotion he didn't want to name. He couldn't find anything to say to her.

"What happened Elinor?" he finally said.

Elinor

Elinor sat up slowly. She blinked and looked down at her stomach.

"Ohhhh," she said softly. There was a lot of blood. Caked and oozing.

"Elinor. What is it? What happened to you?" She blinked to look at him and the blood was gone.

"I was downstairs looking at the painting of the cabin in the snow. I blinked without thinking and I saw something. A creature. It was horrible. It had claws and it moved like smoke. It was the scariest thing I have ever seen.

"I tried to get Ryan's attention but he didn't hear me and I didn't want to wake your parents. When I blinked it was on top of me. Its claws were in my stomach. I was bleeding but when I blinked to see Earth again I wasn't bleeding. That's when I called for you."

She looked down at her stomach and saw the white lines. "Do you know what that creature was?"

"I... I'm not sure. My soul could see them. They are creatures of the Darkness. They haven't ever bothered him but he kept far away from them. I didn't think they could hurt anyone."

"What are these?" she said looking at him as she traced the lines.

"I'm not sure either. When I first brought you up here you didn't have a mark on you but then the lines appeared like someone drew it with a marker. I don't think it's changed much. Maybe they are thicker? But I can't be sure. How does it look in Morland?"

She answered without blinking. "Bad. There is a lot of blood. It doesn't hurt. I can't feel it but it doesn't look good."

"Elinor. Can I please apologize? Can we ever put it behind us? I made a mistake. I gave into my desires. It will never happen again."

She looked at him. "Would you have stopped?"

"Yes. I swear. If you had wanted to go, I would have let you."

"How can I trust you?" she said

"I don't know. But I wish you would. I give my word if that means anything," Derek said.

Elinor studied him and decided she could trust him *enough* to handle whatever had gone wrong. The rest she could figure out later.

Ryan stirred and upon seeing that she as awake, he roused himself completely.

"Elinor!" he said hugging her and he pulled back to examine her. "Are you okay? What happened?"

Before she could answer, Peter came hurriedly in. "You told me you'd wake me when she woke up," he said to Derek.

"She's been awake a total of two minutes," Derek said.

"What happened? Are you hurt?" Peter asked.

"Um yes and no," she said. "Derek and I were just hashing out the details. Things are going to get weird," she told Ryan. He nodded and smiled a thin smile.

"Yeah, I know some of it," he said. "Peter filled me in. It's weird, El. I don't like it and I don't know that I believe a word of it. Your headaches have been giving you visions?" he asked.

"It's hard to describe. When I woke up at the hospital I started to seeing a forest whenever I blinked. My vision kept switching between the hospital and the forest. I thought I'd finally gone crazy but then I saw a man in the forest. He looked a lot like Derek. Only I hadn't even met Derek yet. Long story short, I'm sure Peter told you the long story. The forest I've been seeing is Morland. A different planet. And the Derek-looking man is his soul. He is there because that's where Derek left him five years ago. On another planet..." Ryan did not look amused.

"Okay sure, sure whatever. What happened tonight?" Ryan asked.

"Well I blinked and saw Morland but there was something there. A creature. It attacked me and I started bleeding. Well only the part of me that I can see in Morland is bleeding. This new development is especially confusing."

Ryan sighed and settled back in his chair. No one seemed to know what to say after the facts had been laid out.

"Tell me about the wound," Derek said.

She blinked hesitantly and said, "There are three of them. The center one is the deepest. The other two are really only lacerations. But the center one is deep," she said probing her stomach, "I can't seem to touch my Morland self. When I run my fingers over the wound I'm only feeling my unscathed skin. Weird. Okay," she said measuring with her fingers, estimating an inch at a time.

"The large one is four inches long and half an inch wide. I don't think any of my organs are pierced. It's just barely past all the layers of skin. But it is still bleeding. A steady ooze I'd call it. Bleh. The ones on the side are an inch shorter and not as wide," she said blinking to look away. "I can't handle my own blood."

"Okay what do we do?" Peter said looking at Derek. "Can we bandage it or pack it with something?"

"She can't touch anything, remember?" Derek said.

Elinor moaned as she leaned back down. "I do not feel very good," she said closing her eyes as she exhaled a deep breath.

"Is it your head?" asked Peter and Ryan.

"Yes. It hurts, of course. But I feel ill and tingly. Like when your leg falls asleep. Mmmm," she moaned. "This is bad. This is bad," she repeated.

"How long has it been?" Peter asked pulling out his phone.

"Two hours," Derek said without looking. It was probably just past two a.m.

"You are the expert on all this magic stuff right?" Ryan said standing up to look Derek in the eyes. "You need to fix this."

"I don't know. Let me think..." Derek said, "Okay so I'm just making guesses but maybe Elinor isn't seeing Morland, part of her is *going* there. She has been *projecting* her spirit into Morland. Across how many billion miles. She's somehow sending a part of herself to Morland. A spirit form but present enough that those creatures can see it. It would seem that your spirit being wounded is not a good thing." Derek was rubbing his left wrist as he spoke but he stopped when he saw Elinor watching.

"No duh, Einstein," Ryan spat. "How could you guys bring her here? Did you not think about the risks?"

"We are all figuring this out as we go along," Elinor said. "I didn't know I was in any sort of danger. We were just coming here to look around. Get a little information." She looked down and wiped her hands on the bedspread. "Why can't I wipe the blood off my Morland hands?" she said looking at Derek. Her misty hands were covered in bright red blood. The mist and blood seemed to layer and bleed into each other. It was a disconcerting sight.

"There is blood on your hands?" Derek asked.

"That's what she *just* said," Ryan said.

"So you *can* interact with your body... Maybe this will help us. If you touch the wound can you get more blood on your hands," Derek said.

"Umm," she said trying. "Yes."

When she closed her eyes she could almost feel how slick they were. "But I can't touch anything. I can't bind it or anything."

"Is it better or worse laying down?"

"Better. It's getting squished when I sit up."

"Okay, okay I've got an idea. You can't interact with your surroundings at all and you can only really touch your Earth body but what your Earth body does your Morland body does also. First things first, we need to do is stop the bleeding. So we bind one of your arms firmly around your stomach. It'll apply constant pressure while also making sure the wound doesn't open and close whenever you move. Yes, that could work." Derek said leaving the room.

He was back in a moment with a large first aid kit. He pulled out several rolls of bandages and a triangular bandage.

"It'll be easier if you stand for a moment," he said. He lifted her shirt as it slid down. "Calm down everyone I just need to make sure we position her arm where the wound is."

He had her wrap her arm tightly around her bare stomach. "Okay, keep your arm firmly wrapped around. As tight as you can make it."

"You remember how to do this, right?" Elinor asked.

"I don't remember this exact example in the syllabus but yes I remember the principles."

"Okay," he said a couple minutes later as he tied the triangular bandage in a sling around her body and then added gauze ties on top.

"You are going to want to move this arm as little as possible. The goal in this is to use your arm to force the wound to clot and stop bleeding. So any movement could really impair your body's ability."

"Thank you," Elinor said. "I was really worried. I thought I might bleed to death."

"You still might. I don't know what would happen to you if your spirit died but nothing good."

Elinor stared down unable to stop looking at her blood.

"Stop looking at it," Derek said sharply. "It might see you again. Don't look until we leave. Do your dumb double blink or just keep your eyes closed." Elinor nodded and laid back down moving in tiny slow movements until she was settled.

"So we need to stitch it up, don't we?" Peter said. "I mean this is not a permanent solution. We'll need to go to Morland. Fix it over there where we can touch her."

"Bloody hell!" said Derek sharply turning on him. "You are loving this, aren't you? I can't even be in the same room with you." He stormed out of the room.

"What's all that about?" said Ryan.

"Sometimes I'm not very sensitive about his past," Peter said.

"His past being what? His time in Juvie?" Ryan asked.

"It's so much to explain at once. Okay so we are getting into weirder things. Things that can't be explained with evidence. But you are doing pretty well, aren't you?" Peter said smiling. Elinor smiled. It was good to have that smile diffuse a tiny bit of the tension in the room. It felt like she was a live bomb.

"Have him read the blog," Elinor said closing her eyes. "It'll be easier." Peter loaded the website on his laptop and left the room to find Derek.

Around three o'clock Ryan finished. He stirred Elinor awake.

"I finished it," he said.

"And?"

"Elinor, you should have brought me into this earlier. You should have told our parents."

"Why?" she said looking at him steadily. "What can anyone do for me? They would never believe me. You don't even really believe me. You are just trying to get through tonight."

"You should have told someone because Derek is dangerous. He's bad news in the worst way. You've read it?" She nodded. "Then how could you be so stupid? How could you be so reckless? I think he's a sociopath."

"That's only because he doesn't have his soul."

"Do you even hear yourself? I just don't get it, El. I don't. And not just the magic stuff but teaming up with these two. I'm not saying anything but are you sure this has nothing to do with all the meds you've been on."

Elinor was too tired to be as angry as she should have been. Instead she turned on the bedside lamp. "Ryan, look at my eyes." He leaned in unsure and she blinked. Slowly she blinked both eyes and then one at a time deliberately. His eyes grew wide but he kept watching. After a minute he sat back down with his head in his hands.

"So it's all true then?" he said looking at her with the saddest expression she had ever seen on him.

"Yes. But I wish to God that it wasn't."

"They all made me promise to take care of you this weekend. What am I going to tell them?"

"Nothing. Ryan, this isn't your fault. None of this. It's not your fault. I know you've always tried to protect me but whatever this is," she said waving to her body and the room and everything, "Whatever is happening to me is not your fault. It's not anybody's fault. I don't know what it is. But it is really nice that you know and believe me."

They sat in silence for a couple minutes.

"We found it that day. In the woods. Didn't we?"

"Maybe."

"So we'll have to go there to fix you, right?"

"Yes, I think so."

Peter

Derek and Peter came back into the bedroom to check on things. The night was still, black, and silent. And Derek was a barely contained mass of red rage.

"Okay so Derek and I have been talking but with little headway. Obviously this," Peter said motioning to Elinor's bandages. "is not a permanent solution. But the question is how do we treat your spirit. It's in Morland and we don't know how to get there. Derek thinks he might be able to find the portal eventually. There aren't infinite trees behind your neighborhood."

"Um Elinor and I were just talking about that and we know where the…" Ryan said as Elinor tried to motion him to stop talking.

"What are you talking about?" said Derek stalking toward Ryan like a solider.

Ryan looked over at Elinor annoyed. "We found what we think is the portal. I fell into it when we first moved here."

"What? You've been to Morland?" Derek said charging toward Ryan but Peter reflexively stuck out his arm to protect Ryan from strangulation.

"What is this? Who are you?" Derek yelled with his hands in fists at his sides.

Derek's eyes were so cold and dark. Peter realized that Derek thought this was some kind of trap, a betrayal. That they were the Queen's men. Elinor opened her mouth to speak but the fear and raw anger emanating from Derek silenced her.

Ryan oblivious or fearless, spoke without hesitation.

"Yeah. It was an accident. Elinor said she saw this light and I climbed a tree to look at it. I fell into something and neither of us could see each other until she pulled me out. I thought it was a trick of the light, that's what we told each other anyway. "

Elinor looked at Derek. Her eyes were pleading. Peter hoped she could diffuse the situation. Derek was only letting himself be restrained. If Derek changed his mind...

"We have never been to Morland. We didn't know what we found that day. I have never met anyone from Morland besides you," Elinor said, "Ryan leaned into the portal and his torso disappeared for a moment. We both thought it was strange but Ryan convinced me it had been a trick of the light. I honestly forgot about it with everything that was going on. I wasn't purposefully keeping it from you. Ryan and I just talked about it a couple minutes ago and concluded that it was probably the portal."

No one spoke for a minute. Ryan had finally grasped the hornet's nest they had walked into and he'd slowly been putting himself between Derek and Elinor. Peter was thankful. He didn't think Derek would do anything but...

"We need to get to Morland soon. By tomorrow night at the latest," Derek said suddenly. Peter felt his jaw actually fall open. "We should leave tonight, now," he continued.

"What?" Elinor said. She looked exhausted, so drained.

"We need to get back to Waxhaw, to the portal, to my supplies."

"But we came in one car. It's the middle of the night. How do we explain this to your parents? Oh they are going to be so sad..." Elinor said.

"Don't you think they'd be more sad, if they found you dead at the end of fall break?" Derek bit back.

"We have no plan," Peter said. "Maybe we should sleep tonight and we'll leave in the morning. It doesn't matter if we were in Waxhaw right now, we don't have any idea what we'd do right?"

"I agree with Derek," Ryan said, "Let's go. Let's get her to Morland. Do we really need a plan? Derek, you can sew her up right? You were in first aid with her?" Derek nodded and Ryan continued, "She said it's deep. She looks worried and she never lets on how worried she is. So the plan is to get back to Waxhaw, find the portal, pop in, sew up her stomach, and come home. I don't know what more of a plan we need."

"I think we need to sleep," Elinor said. "I think I need to sleep and I want to give my arm a chance to stop the bleeding before I'm bumping around on a windy road for hours. And we are going to want to go to Morland the second we get back and I don't want a Derek who hasn't slept in a couple days sewing me up. Can we just sleep until the sun comes up, then we'll wake up you parents and leave? We'll tell them I've got a bad headache and I need to see my neurologist. Nothing serious. I don't need to go to the urgent care but I need to go home. Deal?" she said looking around.

Peter nodded. Derek shrugged. Ryan still didn't look convinced.

"She'll be fine to wait a couple extra hours?" Ryan asked looking at Derek.

"Probably," he said. "I mean, I haven't seen it but yeah. Let's go to sleep. Oh and Elinor?" Derek asked. "What phase is that moon in tonight?"

"I don't know what it's called but the moon was full a couple days ago," she said.

"Well that's something at least," Derek said.

Chapter 28

Elinor

Elinor had no trouble making a show of having the worst headache of her life, because she wasn't too far off. Even though her stomach didn't hurt she just felt ill, worse than a usual headache. She was lightheaded and dizzy.

They all waited for the Jensens to finish locking up the house as the sun made its way into the sky. They hadn't wanted to explain why her uninjured arm was in a sling so she wore one of Ryan's hoodies and kept her arm inside. Mrs. Jensen came out first. She noticed Elinor was moving to sit in the back and insisted she sit in the front seat again.

"Thank you, Mrs. Jensen. But I think I'd do best if I could be horizontal. Hopefully I'll just sleep the whole time. Again, I'm so so sorry to ruin..." But she was interrupted which was good because Elinor was starting to cry.

"Please, honey. You can't control it. My aunt has migraines. I understand. This just means you'll have to come back," Mrs. Jensen said.

"Of course," Elinor said as brightly as she could as she opened the passenger door.

She settled into the middle seat and laid her head on a pillow on Ryan's lap and draped her legs over Peter. It was the only way to keep her back flat on the seat. She fastened herself in and tried to stay as still as possible. She was hyperaware of her arm wrapped tightly around her middle. She tried not to move it.

"Peter?" Elinor asked. She was trying not to make this a big deal but it kind of was.

"Yes."

"I'm buckled in pretty well but I think you should hold my legs tight to keep me from sliding." She couldn't quite look him in the eyes. It felt so intimate.

He didn't say anything but just wrapped his arms around her legs and smiled.

Ryan

Elinor was finally asleep. Ryan didn't move his hand from her shoulder. She needed to keep still. He was finding it almost impossible not to fidget. He was so angry about everything. How had any of this happened? And how had it all gone so poorly? He needed more information. He needed all of it. He pulled out his cell phone and handed it over his shoulder to Derek who was huddled in the sideways seat.

"Put your number in it," Ryan said casting him a quick glance.

Derek obliged and handed the phone back. Ryan started a text.

"I don't even know what to say to you," Ryan sent. He watched the three flashing pips that meant Derek was writing back.

"I don't know what to say."

"I read your story," Ryan heard a soft curse from behind him. Peter looked over wanting to speak but he glanced down at Elinor and kept out of it which was good because Ryan was almost madder at him.

"It's slowly becoming a best seller," Derek wrote.

"I don't think you are funny. And I don't trust you."

"You probably shouldn't."

"Then why am I letting you come to Morland with us? I could Google how to sew her up myself."

"If you've read my story then you know that you'll need me if things go south."

"It seems that if you don't come, there is less of a chance that will happen."

"Maybe."

Ryan waited sensing Derek had more to say.

"Ryan, none of this is my fault. I didn't give Elinor her visions or her headaches but... I'm really sorry for everything that's happened. But I have to come with you to Morland. I never thought in a million trillion years that I'd ever say that sentence. I wish I could just let you all go without me. But the thought that Elinor might die or suffer some unknown horrible fate is too much. It's too much for me."

Ryan was stunned.

He'd pegged Derek as a narcissistic sociopath, unable to acknowledge the pain and suffering of others, some kind of robot. But somehow his sister had gotten through to him. Ryan didn't particularly like that. Derek was the last friend Ryan would have picked for Elinor but the truth was she did that to almost everyone she met. There was something about her that seemed so fragile and soft, so unequipped for the world and it made people look out for her. Relatives. Neighbors. He'd seen random people at the grocery store go out of their way to help her.

Ryan had fallen under her spell the first time he'd met her. She'd been so lonely and sad. She'd brought out a protectiveness in him he hadn't know he had. When she lit up under his mom's attention, Ryan was done. He'd been all in. At first he hadn't cared either way for George Lirdin. But Elinor was it. She was his sister. No matter who either of their parents were. He'd always look out for her. So Ryan totally got it. He just wished Derek had been immune.

"How do we even know that the portal will be able to bring us home? And how do you know that we'll be able to fix her stomach in Morland?" Ryan wrote.

"1. We don't know for sure but the portal's power hasn't been the problem. It's been that I couldn't find it. But we'll sew her up within sight of it and with her sight I'm sure she'll be able to find it if we were to lose it somehow. But whether it works or not Elinor doesn't really have a choice. 2. When Elinor looks down at herself while looking at Morland, her body looks see-though and misty. I assume that when Elinor goes to Morland we'll be able to fix her injuries. But that's just a guess. I have literally no idea."

"Sure. Great. Now tell me the worst case scenario," Ryan typed.

Elinor

They were back in Waxhaw before she really even knew they left. She must have slept the whole way. She was wide-awake and suddenly nervous. She looked around and saw the boys were all on high alert. She wondered if they had slept at all. She looked down at her stomach and exhaled. The bleeding had finally stopped. Although that wasn't always a good sign.

"Peter, should we drop you off at home?" Mr. Jensen said turning around. "We pass right by it on the way."

"No thanks," Peter said trying not to look conspicuous. "Derek can drop me off later. We have some... schoolwork to do since... we are back home early anyway."

"Yeah," Derek added, "You should stay over and watch that movie. I'll take you home later."

"Yeah. Okay," Peter said. They drove in silence for the last twenty minutes. Elinor could see that Peter was itching to talk to everyone. He was a nervous ball of energy.

"Okay. Here we are at the Lirdin house," said Mr. Jensen.

"Oh wait, Mr. Jensen," Elinor said, "could we stop by your house first? I think I left my cell phone charger there. I'm going to need it."

244

"Yeah, no problem," he said as he drove past.

Everyone started piling out of the car and unloading their things and carrying them inside.

Elinor grabbed Ryan when they were in the kitchen. "We can't go home. We won't be free to leave until tonight. Everyone thinks we are still at the cabin until the end of the weekend. We'll pretend to walk home and meet the guys in the woods."

"Yeah. Good idea. I was worried about that too," Ryan said.

Once everyone was in the kitchen, the goodbyes started.

"I'm so sorry we couldn't stay all weekend. I feel just sick about it. Thank you for coming back early," Elinor said

"Next time," said Mrs. Jensen hugging Elinor. "And don't be a stranger," she added.

"I'll give you two a ride back," said Mr. Jensen.

"Oh No. We'll walk over," said Ryan.

"No, I insist."

"No, really. It's only a couple houses away and I'm feeling a little car sick. It would be good for me to walk," Elinor said.

Elinor hugged Peter whispering. "See you in ten minutes in the woods between our houses. We aren't going home."

Elinor hugged Derek also. "Ten minutes," she said. He nodded.

Once they were in the woods alone Ryan said, "That was quick thinking. It was going to take a long time till we could both get out to the woods alone if they had dropped us off at the house."

"Yeah, especially if Mr. Jensen mentioned we came home because of my headaches." They both shook their heads. They sat down for a couple minutes before Ryan and Derek came into the clearing.

Derek walked right past them saying, "This way to get my stuff."

Derek

"You guys already have stuff?" Elinor asked looking at their new backpacks, as she and Ryan dragged their bags through the forest trying to keep up.

"Yeah, I have food in my bag and Derek has the first aid kit. We told the Jensens we were going to spend the rest of the weekend camping, like when we were scouts. So they didn't think it was weird," said Peter

Derek pulled a false front from a tree and began pulling bags from inside.

"Do you guys need anything from your house?" Peter asked noticing they only had the bags they took to Boone.

Ryan and Elinor looked at each other.

"Um we can't go home. Otherwise we won't be able to leave again until it's dark, until everyone is asleep," Elinor said.

"And," Ryan added looking at the array of weapons that were being laid out on the ground. "I doubt there is much we could bring that would help. Also I thought we were just popping over for a quick sew job."

Derek stared at him for a second stilling his hands as he said, "I hope so," and then continued his busy work of moving things from one bag to another.

He'd slowly built his stockpile after he'd returned home. He knew one day he would be back in Morland and he had wanted to be ready with the right skills and equipment. He had started martial arts and later krav maga. His parents thought he had been getting in fights at school but none of the kids messed with him. He thought that they could tell that he was different, that he was still a little wild around the edges.

He'd trained to keep his skills up. He knew only too well the laziness of being a teenage boy in a technological world. He had no intention of wasting his years of training to level up an avatar while his muscles deteriorated. But he'd also needed weapons.

Derek had worked at a pawnshop after school when he was eighteen and was able to score a couple of weapons under the table. Preparing for Morland was his only long-term plan. And he was finally doing it, finally facing his fear. He didn't pack light even if it was only for an hour's visit.

Ryan and Elinor each added some clothes and necessities to the food bag. The three of them just watched in silence until Derek had sorted everything to his satisfaction. He handed Ryan a large duffle bag full of weapons and assorted equipment. Peter had the bag of food and water.

Derek handed Elinor his backpack of first aid supplies but Ryan took it from her. There were still several weapons on the ground unpacked when Derek began putting everything back into the tree hideouts. He put the sword on his left hip and the gun holster on his right torso. And he held a quarterstaff in his hands. He carried no bag.

"Okay girl, take me to your portal." Derek had a good idea the general direction the portal would be in. He'd never ever gone looking for it but he thought he'd know it when he saw it. But he didn't.

Elinor walked with a purpose as an unseen compass guided her. And once again every bloody tree looked exactly the same. It would have taken him a long time to find the right one but Elinor saw it clear as day.

Elinor

Elinor had been secretly nervous that she wasn't going to be able to find the portal again or that it would be gone. But there it was shining away like before.

"There it is," she said pointing at a "y" shaped tree.

"I kind of remember," said Ryan looking at it as if he was trying to imagine a portal.

"I'll go first and I'll help you guys through the other side. Elinor, you'll need to go last in case they can't find their way," Derek said.

He started for the tree but Elinor pulled him aside. "You don't have to do this," she said. She had noticed that he had been acting strange all morning, even strange for him. She could only imagine how scared he must be. She was scared and she had never actually been there. "I could probably stitch myself if I had to. I hate to make you go back there for me. I want you to come and we need you but make sure you are okay with coming."

Derek was silent for a moment staring at her like he did often. He then turned to talk to everyone.

"I've thought about this a lot. Before this weekend and on the drive home. Hopefully we'll just be there thirty minutes, if not... If things go bad... If she is waiting for me... If we are captured and... I'm prepared for that and you need to be as well. Elinor doesn't have a choice. I don't know what happens if your spirit dies but nothing good. You two..." he said motioning to Peter and Ryan.

"This is no picnic. Morland is hell. It's the worst place you can imagine. And you are going there with me. The worst tour guide possible. If the Queen is still alive... Peter, you know but for some reason you think this is some kind of dream come true. But we might not come back. Or what if it's five years? Are you prepared for that? No. You should stay. We'll go in there alone. Peter, I'm asking you not to come. Ryan, you too."

Ryan spoke first "She's my sister. I'm coming," he said shrugging. "We'll figure the rest out."

"Derek, I'm coming," Peter started.

"No, why do you need to come? Why?" Derek shouted at him.

Peter stared at the ground a moment. "I know that I've always been pretty excited about magic being real and other worlds and stuff. But I also believe the bad stuff too," he said looking Derek in the eyes before he could interrupt again "And that's the reason I'm coming. You're my best friend. And you aren't going in there alone this time. So let's go."

"Fine. I'm first. Then Peter. Then Ryan Then Elinor last."

"Come through this way. It's between the "y" part of the tree. Yeah, like that," she said as Derek started to climb. "Oh and Derek," Elinor said tugging his pant leg before he went through. "Don't hit your head this time."

He gave her a ghost of the smile and then jumped.

Derek was there one moment and then his legs were gone and then the rest of him disappeared in one swift jump down.

"Weird," Peter said.

"Is that what it looked like when I fell in?" Ryan asked.

"Yeah," Elinor replied

"Must have freaked you out," Peter said

"It did."

"Can you see him?" Peter asked.

Elinor blinked. And there he was safe and sound. *Right?* She thought.

There was a young man scouting the area. He had red hair to his shoulders and he was wearing armor. She couldn't see his face. But it had to be him. She ran around to the side to catch a glimpse. She could hear Peter's voice growing worried.

"Elinor, is he there? Is he?" Peter asked as he grabbed her good arm. And then the man turned. It was Derek all right, just not the Derek from North Carolina.

"Yes. It's him. But he looks different. Peter, go see if he's okay. Give me a thumbs up when you get through to let me know you are okay."

"No. Jump down and then come back through. I need to know that it's a two-way door," Ryan said.

Peter jumped through the invisible portal without a thought. He landed hard on his butt then he climbed back up the tree to stick his head through. "We are good to go," he said impishly. "Come on in the water's fine." He then ran over to the man who looked like Derek.

Elinor waited a minute to see what Peter would do but it must be Derek because they were talking easily. "Okay let's just do this. Go on."

"No, what's wrong with Derek? Did he lose it or something? We can come back later, you and me."

"No, he's fine, I think. He just looks different. Long hair, armor on. He looks like his other self. Everything is fine. Peter is laughing. I can't hear anything, so let's hop over and find out. You remember, right?"

"Yeah but it's a little unnerving knowingly jumping into an invisible world, isn't it?"

"Yup."

"See you on the other side." And he was gone. He landed in a hard crouch and gave her a thumbs up. Now it was her turn. Her heart was pounding but not just from her headache.

I should have taken some medicine before this. Of course, I'd have a headache on an adventure, Elinor thought tragically. *Derek did say he would never bring me to Morland and this is exactly why.*

"Oh here goes," she said to herself as she climbed up the tree. It was awkward going with only one free arm but she made it up and jumped, landing hard on her butt.

She felt it instantly. She didn't realize how the boys could be laughing and joking with each other. She felt like she was suffocating. The dark haze that made everything real life sepia was the Darkness. The real Darkness. It was all real. All of this. She leaned back against the tree, taking deep breaths that felt like thick smog. But her overall body pain brought her quickly back to why they were there.

"Don't you feel it?" she said.

"Feel what?" Ryan said not looking at her as he started walking to Derek and Peter. "I feel like a million bucks. I feel really good. So what's the deal with Derek's hair?" Ryan said turning his head as Elinor struggled to walk up to the boys.

"Whoa! That's a lot of blood, El. We should start now!" Ryan said.

"Hmm," Peter said looking her up and down.

"What?" she said. She wondered for a second if her body was all misty but she looked down saw that she was solid. She was wearing different clothes. She was wearing boots, pants that could only be called breeches and a linen top. It might have been cute except it was all covered in blood. Her arm was bandaged to her stomach under the shirt.

She looked at the boys. Peter and Ryan clothes were changed too. No longer jeans and t-shirts, they now wore linen pants, shirts, and vests of different colors. And Peter's glasses were different.

Elinor noticed that Ryan's scab was gone from his elbow but it had probably just healed since she'd seen him a month ago. But Derek was the most changed. His hair was to his shoulders. He was wearing armor and leather. He was hard to recognize. She felt wary.

"It is you, right? It's not your spirit self," Elinor asked the Derek-shaped man.

"Ha," Derek laughed. "Trust me. You'll be able to tell us apart. It's still me. Apparently Morland has a memory or a cruel sense of humor. Also, it's as I suspected. There is some sort of item conversion. We can't bring over items that haven't been invented yet. See my gun is now another sword." Elinor hadn't noticed but he now had two swords, one on each hip.

"It's a nice sword at least," he contented pulling it out. "Oh," he said suddenly pulling back his armor and lifting his shirt on his side. "What is here?" he asked frantically pointing to his side.

"A large ugly scar."

He smiled. The biggest smile any of them had ever seen. He pressed his hand against it and bent his neck to try and see it himself. He then looked up and noticed everyone watching and pulled his shirt back down.

"So Morland remembers you?" Elinor asked.

"I guess so. This is definitely the body I was in when I left."

"Where is your other body? Your Earth body?" she asked looking down at her own a little worried. But that was probably because it was leaking blood. Ryan and Peter both looked at themselves and Ryan rubbed his elbow. Maybe he'd bumped it on the way down.

"I have no idea and who cares?" Derek said "Let's just do this. We'll do it here. I don't want to lose the portal. You can still see it right?"

Elinor hadn't thought about that. She turned around quickly and then exhaled. There it was shimmering away.

"It's still there. I see it," she nodded.

"Okay then. Let's take a look at this."

Elinor started to undo the bandages that had tied her arm in place binding the wound closed. She hated looking at her own blood. She was feeling faint already. "I think you should take over from here," she said to Derek before laying down.

"And you told me to stay behind," he scoffed as he lifted her shirt a bit, more gently than she had expected. She locked eyes with Derek. He was serious now.

"So this is Morland," Peter said grinning as he walked around, somehow still finding the joy in their situation as Elinor's blood pooled around herself. *Good for him, I guess*, she thought.

Elinor didn't much care what Morland looked like at the moment she was mesmerized by her blood that was slowly leaving her body and flowing onto the ground. The blood didn't pool on the ground. The soil drank it up like it was in a drought. Elinor looked to Derek and saw that he was also watching the blood.

"Yeah, this is Morland, alright," Derek murmured. "Let's get this over with."

The End

This book series can be enjoyed in two orders.

Magic Headaches > The Morland Prince> Morland Blood

or

The Morland Prince> Magic Headaches> Morland Blood

Enjoy excepts of each book below.

See you in Morland

The Morland Prince

Megan Allen

The Morland Prince

Before you follow Derek into Morland you need to know what happened last time.

This is the story of how a boy
became a prince who
became a monster.

Morland has a way of turning a person into the worst version of themselves. Derek knows that better than anyone. He hardly even remembers the scared, naive thirteen-year-old version of himself who fell through a portal in his backyard in North Carolina and ended up on the other side of the universe. But Derek had made the most of it.
He soul is outside his body. (Convenient and also irritating)
He kills for the Queen so he's not killed. (Unpleasant but unavoidable)
And his only hobby is trying to find the portal home. (Addictive and infuriating)

Morland is a lot of things (mostly obscenities) but it's never boring.

Derek's story is enhanced with illustrations, charts, maps, and more. Morland has never felt so close.

Please enjoy the first chapter.

Welcome, I guess...

Not sure how you found your way here. And I'm not sure what I'm supposed to say to you now. It's good you are here. You need to read this. Everyone does. Not that it's the greatest story ever written but it's true and it's mine and you need to know what could happen to you. People always say "What's the worst thing that could happen?"

And the answer is THIS.

This is the worst thing that could happen to you. So study up. I know it would have been a million times easier if I'd read a story by someone who'd walked the path before me. But I carve my own stupid path. No one else would take the lonely path lined in blood and darkness.

Good luck, I guess.

So kind of gloomy huh?
This is how he introduces his readers to his blog.
shakes head
Derek is not known for his optimism.

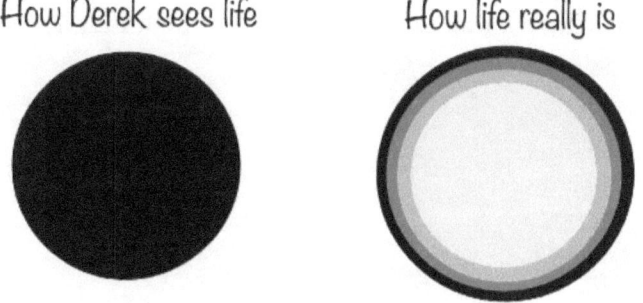

How Derek sees life   How life really is

Before

My life is very clearly demarcated by a before and its after. Most people's lives aren't like that; I've found. Most people's befores and afters are a smudgy business, blurry guesses containing many small events that lead a winding path from the land of before to the nightmare of after. My before is written in **bold**. It's spelled out in fireworks. It's a crack that spans my whole world.

I write this because I have to, because the weight of it hangs like an anchor around my neck. I know this won't help. I know it doesn't change anything but maybe I'll sleep a little better. And I haven't had a good night's sleep in so many years. Maybe the people who read this will remember the missteps I took if their fates lie along a similar path to mine. I wouldn't wish my past on my worst enemy.

Well, actually I would.

I would wish it on *her*. I'd wish what happened to me times a thousand over on her. I guess that makes me a monster but I already know that. And it's good that you learn it now. It will help you not feel sorry for me when you read what's coming.

Hello, my name is Derek and I'm a soulless murdering monster.

If this were a support group, it would be your line to say "Hello, Derek."

But you wouldn't want to know me without the safety of these pages to separate us. Enjoy the story. I hope you don't have too many nightmares. I know I still do. Ten years seems like a long time ago but nightmares have a way of staying fresh in the mind, don't they?

Hello, my name is

Derek

soulless murdering
monster

He's not sooo bad. Most of the time.
Sometimes. It's, uh, complicated?

Hello, my name is

Peter

best friend

Don't think about what kind of person is
best friends with a murderer.
Move past it.

I hope you enjoyed the first chapter of The Morland Prince.

Here is a sneak peek of the final book in the series.
Morland Blood

Megan Allen

MORLAND BLOOD

Morland Blood

The Darkness is worse than she imagined...

...and just as terrifying as he remembers.

Derek is back on Morland, something he vowed he would never ever do. But sometimes a girl turns a guy into an idiot. Morland is the worst and it has been patiently waiting for him. His mother, the Queen, wants to resume her dark plans that end with a soulless Derek and unimaginable power at her fingertips. But this time is different from the last time Derek was trapped on Morland. This time he isn't alone. He has friends with him. He has Elinor.

Elinor thought her ability to see Morland was a pointless curse but as soon as she stepped onto Morland soil everything changed. Her magic has blossomed into something she doesn't understand and can't control. Danger and Darkness seem to follow their every step as Elinor and her friends try to find some way to free Derek from the Queen's grasp. Despite everything, Peter still thinks Morland is a dream come true while Ryan just wants to survive this nightmare and bring his sister home. When they find a secret group of people hiding from the Queen, Elinor starts training like all of Morland depends on it...which it does. Because the Goodness has been waiting a very long time for a girl like her.

The clock is ticking. The full moon is rising. The Goodness and the Darkness will battle for Derek's soul and the very fate of Morland rests in Elinor's hands. Headaches or no headaches, the task before her seems impossible. Thank the Goodness she isn't alone.

Chapter 1 of Morland Blood

Elinor

Elinor took several deep breaths as she watched Derek pull a knife from the first aid bag. Her arm was wrapped around her stomach and held tight by layers of bandages and blood, both old and new. Using her arm to keep the wound closed had been the only option they had had at the time and she was nervous to see the damage that lay underneath.

Derek met her eyes and then sliced the bandage off. The bandage didn't fall off like she'd thought it would. It *stuck* and he had to *peel* it off. She let out a deep breath when he lifted her arm off the wound. She was glad she was already laying down.

"It's..." Derek said looking from the wound on her stomach to her face. "I'm surprised you didn't go into shock. It's deep, like you said. And obviously there was a lot of blood. Man, this must hurt."

"It's coming to me now," Elinor said trying, and failing, not to look at the claw marks that stretched across her stomach. The creature that had done those was the stuff of nightmares. It was impossibly made of both smoke and claws and had somehow attacked her from a world away, Morland. Elinor's magic ability made her able to *see* the magic planet of Morland but this was the first time something from Morland had been able to see her.

And now they were *in* Morland. She had climbed a magic portal in a tree in Waxhaw, North Carolina and was now on another planet. But only for a short trip, an hour tops. Derek would treat her wound and then they would be safely back home via the portal in the tree. Because Morland wasn't a place to linger.

The man gently touching her shredded stomach was so different from the Derek she'd seen just moment ago. His short hair had turned long. His jeans and t-shirt were now leather armor accessorized with swords. Studying him distracted her for a moment. He was somehow more handsome than before but also so much more dangerous. Elinor made herself take a couple deep breaths and calm herself. The blood loss was making her a little lightheaded.

"Oh man. That's bad," Ryan said sitting down next to her and reaching for her hand. He was such a good brother. Elinor was infinitely relieved to have him with her. "It's really bad," he said frowning. "Can you fix this, Derek? Is there someone else we can take her to?"

"Ha," Derek said simply. "Have you listened at all? The point of this whole reconnaissance is not to *see* anyone or be *seen*. Also, there is no one I trust." He paused a moment in thought and then said, "And yes, I'll do a good enough job. I've got more experience than just our first aid class." He started to look through the bag and then he was throwing things on the ground as his search became more frantic.

"Bloody hell," he muttered after a minute, shaking his head.

"What is it?" Peter asked. "Did you forget something? Can we still do it? Do you need me to go get something?"

"Oh, I can still do it," Derek said, his voice a thick mockery. "It's just a matter if our little princess can do it."

"What?" Elinor said. "What do you mean?"

"The nice local anesthetic I packed for you is gone. In its place is this," he said holding up a red plant.

"What is that?" she asked.

"Bloodroot."

"Of course it is," Elinor said rolling her eyes. "What does it do?" The pain was making her snippy. She could take her pulse from her pounding wound now that her arm wasn't the stopper over the claw marks on her stomach.

"It'll make you unconscious for a couple hours. Or it would if I ground it up and brewed it into a tea."

"A couple hours!" Elinor said. The plan was to only be in Morland for a couple *minutes*. She knew enough of Derek's history with Morland that the idea of staying longer made her *very* nervous. This world seemed to have a way of taking a person and changing them into their worst possible self.

"How is this going to work? I don't know," Elinor said shaking her head. "If I was unconscious you'd have to drag me up that tree and then dump me over or worse we'd have to wait it out here. No way!"

Derek stared at her a moment.

"Yes, those are our options," he said. "Not taking it though... I don't think you could handle it."

Elinor felt torn. She *hated* being a burden. "I don't want to slow us down..."

"Why don't we just take Elinor and the bloodroot back through the portal, shoot her up with the local anesthetic, and then bring her back?" Peter said.

"It's too late to move her," Derek said looking at Peter. "The wounds are bad and we've opened them up. For her to stand up, climb the tree, jump down, and then do that again would be too much. Also we might only be injecting her Earth body. And then it would all have been for nothing."

"Okay. Then make the tea. El, I'll carry you up that stupid tree myself when we are done or we could make a pulley system to carry you up and down to the other side, okay?" Ryan said.

"Can we just try it without first?" Elinor asked.

Derek looked visibly relieved.

"Yeah. I'm glad you said that because making the tea would mean making a fire and... I'll be very gentle. Alright, here we go," Derek said. "Oh, remember to breathe."

Elinor closed her eyes and tried to think of anything else. When Derek cleaned the wound with water and clean cloths, Elinor hissed through closed teeth. *I can do this*, she told herself, *it can't be worse than a headache*. But the pain of the needle diving deep in her sensitive, angry wound made her lose herself for a moment. She arched up as a single solitary scream burst from her lips. Derek did not hesitate. In one powerful punch, he knocked her unconscious.

Ryan

"What the hell?" Ryan yelled as Derek continued to sew. Derek was a maniac and Ryan was an idiot for trusting him.

"I commend her for trying," Derek said. "But I couldn't have her yelling the whole time and now we get the effect of bloodroot without making a fire. Win-win."

And then Derek actually smiled.

Ryan extricated himself from Elinor and had to take a couple deep breaths.

"You are such an asshole. You know that?" Ryan said pacing around the clearing. He didn't want to yell at Derek since he was sewing his sister's stomach back together so he turned to Peter. It was as much his fault anyway. "I don't get it, Peter. You seem like an okay guy. How can you be around him and not want to kill him all the time? When we get out of here..."

"Hey. Just calm down a minute," Peter implored, following Ryan as he paced.

"He punched my sister in the face," Ryan said.

"She was screaming," Derek said matter-of-factly.

"You could have made the bloodroot tea," Ryan said

"We are not making a fire," Derek said without lifting his eyes from his work.

"She already has bad headaches every day. She didn't need a knock-out punch," Ryan said.

"Then she'll probably hardly notice any difference when she wakes up," Derek said with the hint of a chuckle. Ryan started to see red.

"Derek..." Peter groaned.

"You..." Ryan said coming towards Derek.

"Shut up," Derek said

"What!" Ryan growled.

"No, shut up," Derek said standing as he dropped everything. He stood completely still. His hands were covered in Elinor's blood and he just listened. The sight made Ryan's heart stutter and he listened too. Then he heard it: noise and the shout of men. Derek brought a finger to his lips. He knelt down to Elinor and frantically tried to finish. He motioned for Ryan to come over to start wrapping her torso with the bandages he had laid out.

"How is your Scottish accent?" Derek whispered to them

"I don't know. You tell me," Ryan said in a jilted whisper.

"You dunna have to worry about me, laddie," Peter whispered with a wink.

"Okay, neither of you say anything. We are from the South. Traveling home after some bad luck trading with the nomads. Bind her wound quick, doesn't matter how." Derek said as he stood to face three armed men walking towards them.

Derek

It took an effort for Derek not to sigh. Of course, they had been found. What had he really expected. He *knew* that Morland was the worst. He'd been trapped on this stupid, garbage, magic planet for five years. And he'd allowed a pair of doe eyes to drag him back. He deserved everything that was coming for him.

"What have we got here?" said the first man. He was all muscle and just as tall as Derek. But his uniform named him a low born, nothing to worry about. One of the other men was just a solider as well but the third one was dressed well and bore himself well. He had brown hair pulled back to his neck and he looked at Derek keenly. He was the one to worry about. Derek nicknamed them Dumb Muscles, Other, and Officer Trouble.

Derek didn't relax his right hand from the hilt of his sword. The other two men stayed back watching as the first man kicked their bags around until he came to Ryan binding Elinor's stomach.

"Is this the scream we heard earlier? You all having a little fun? Since she's asleep she wouldn't mind three more, I don't think," Dumb Muscles said laughing as he tugged at his belt.

"Don't touch my sister!" Ryan growled in a thick Scottish accent. Derek glared at him.

"Oh now," said Officer Trouble as he walked closer, his interest piqued. Derek silently cursed. *Bloody hell.* He'd made some mistake. "What do we have here, indeed?" the man said.

Derek kept his pose with difficulty. This man was a highborn officer, not some hired muscle that joined the army. Someone with family, money, clout. Someone he might have known, who might have known him, who certainly knew the Queen. If she was still around...

"Now what are boys from the South Coast doing here? Or anywhere?" the officer laughed. Ryan looked at Derek helplessly. Derek hid his confusion. He'd thought picking to be from the South would be a safe bet. It was far enough away from where they were that no one would know enough to doubt them.

And the South was a big port so even though the natives were mostly dark skinned there were so many merchants and visitors that it would be impossible to keep track of who came and went. But something must have happened...

"We are on our way home. We had bad luck trading and we are heading back south," Derek said falling effortlessly into the brogue.

"Trading with who?" the officer said with narrowed eyes.

"Bloody nomads."

The officer's face blanked and then he burst out laughing. The other two soldiers looked on unsmiling. Peter and Ryan looked about to wet themselves. Derek made himself take a deep breath.

"Now, now," the officer said still laughing softly as he shook his head. "If I don't kill you for lying to an officer of the Queen. I may recommend you as court jester," he chuckled again. "And you did it so straight-faced." He tapped his finger to his chin. "What should I do with you?"

"You could let us go?" Derek said with a wicked grin. *Hide it. Hide it,* Derek told himself as his fear, panic, and confusion rose to take control. He could find out what happened later. Something was wrong in Morland and he felt chills rising up his spine as he waited for the next blow. And the Queen was still alive. Of course she was.

"Ah no," he said without taking his eyes from Derek. "The General will want to speak with you. You'll be coming with us. And where would you go anyway? The whole South Coast is just ash after all. You could have thought of a better story... and nomads. Who can even find two nomads to rub together, let alone trade with?" He barked a laugh as Derek felt his heart drop to the floor. There it was.

Officer Trouble motioned for Dumb Muscles and Other to collect them. Derek didn't move. The two soldiers moved to fight him but Office Trouble laughed again.

"Such spirit. You might be able to take these two but," he said as he raised his hand to his ear, "there will be five dozen men passing by soon. Shall we make this fight a bit more challenging? How many more would come if she screamed again? A dozen? All of them? I am accompanied by the General and I am one of his men. You may be good with that sword but not that good. No one has ever beaten him. And none of your other companions are even armed and your girl is still unconscious. What did you do to her anyway?" he said raising his eyebrow.

"Come," he said with no humor this time. "Carry the girl," he said to Dumb Muscles. Ryan protested and received a sharp punch in the stomach as the man lifted Elinor into his arms.

For more information, check out

www.MeganAllen.com

If you enjoyed this book, please leave a review on Goodreads and Amazon. Thank you!

The Magic Headaches Series

Book Club Discussion Questions:

1. Has chronic pain affected your life or the life of a loved one? How so?

2. Would you want the ability to see another world? If yes, would your spouse/parents believe you if you told them? If no, would you believe a loved one if they told you they could see another world?

3. If you HAD to share your true life story on a blog would it be exciting or horrifying to let people know you that well?

4. Which main character do you most relate to? Elinor, Derek, Peter, or Ryan?

5. How do you handle big disappointments? (ex: Elinor not being able to go to Chapel Hill for premed) Does your faith play a part in how you react when things go terribly wrong?

Bonus Question: If you had to marry one of the three main male characters (Derek, Peter, or Ryan) which would you pick and why?

And now, what you came here for...
Personality Quizzes

Instructions

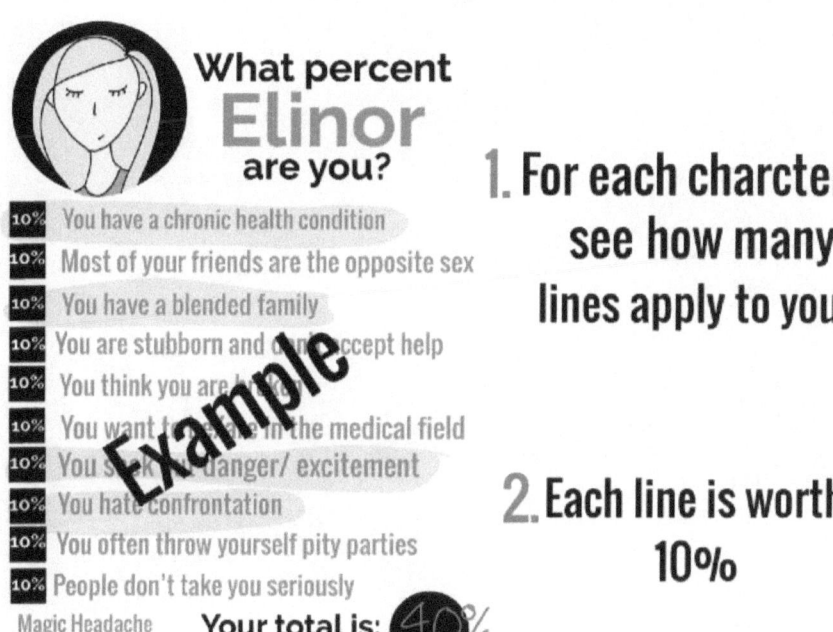

What percent Elinor are you?

- 10% You have a chronic health condition
- 10% Most of your friends are the opposite sex
- 10% You have a blended family
- 10% You are stubborn and can't accept help
- 10% You think you are (...)
- 10% You want to (...) in the medical field
- 10% You seek (...) danger/ excitement
- 10% You hate confrontation
- 10% You often throw yourself pity parties
- 10% People don't take you seriously

Magic Headache
@megan_allen_books

Your total is: 40%

Example

1. For each charcter see how many lines apply to you

2. Each line is worth 10%

3. Add the up and you are ___% that character

Share your results in comments

What percent
Elinor
are you?

10% You have a chronic health condition

10% Most of your friends are the opposite sex

10% You have a blended family

10% You are stubborn and don't accept help

10% You think you are broken

10% You want to be/are in the medical field

10% You seek out danger/ excitement

10% You hate confrontation

10% You often throw yourself pity parties

10% People don't take you seriously

Magic Headache
@megan_allen_books

Your total is:

What percent
DEREK
are you?

10% It's often a struggle to control your temper

10% You do not have a favorite color

10% You are (currently) an only child

10% You need to write out your feelings

10% You believe in fate

10% You rumminate on past mistakes

10% You don't make friends easily

10% Things seem to just happen to you

10% You want to avoid too much notice

10% You are a night owl

Magic Headache
@megan_allen_books

Your total is:

What percent
Peter
are you?

10% Once you make a friend you don't let go

10% You love to read fantasy/sci-fi

10% You are always smiling

10% You wish you lived somewhere else

10% It takes a lot to get you mad

10% You do not want to talk about your family

10% People don't know when you are struggling

10% You want evryone to just get along

10% You will patiently wait for the right time to do things

10% You love board games

Magic Headache
@megan_allen_books

Your total is:

What percent
Ryan
are you?

10% You do not want adventure

10% You feel very protective of your family

10% You prefer nonfiction books

10% You do things you don't want to do easily

10% School/work sucess comes easy to you

10% You very rarely lose your temper

10% People often come to you for help

10% Your family sees you as the golden child

10% You just want everything to stay the same

10% You love to tease your family

Magic Headaches
@megan_allen_books

Your total is:

Dedications

First, all glory goes to my God.

I want to thank my husband, Matt, for living with my headaches with grace and kindness. And for giving me the space to get Elinor out.

Thank you to my mom & Brittany. Your love of this story helped me to finish it and write two more besides.

To Kelli, you so selfless gave me your time and love to read my giant manuscripts. Your advice and encouragement were precious to me.

To Lauren, for reading my books more than anyone and giving them away as gifts and making all your book clubs read them.

To Sheila & Bri, you are chronic pain warriors. You showed me how to do it well and how to laugh when it is all going so poorly.

To Candace and Aunt Brandee, you didn't have to love my stories but you did. I couldn't ask for a better family.

To Autumn, it's an honor to be your friend and create with you.

To Heather & Teresa, you read these books with babies asleep in your arms and toddlers running amuck. Your time was precious and you gave some to me.

Thank you to Natalia Suellen for my beautiful cover.

About the Author

Megan Allen lives in North Carolina with her husband, daughter, and two giant Ragdoll cats, Poppet and Moxie. She writes books about magic, headaches, and magic headaches. She draws a funny blog about her battle with chronic headaches.

Come find her here:

Website:
www.MeganAllen.com

Instagram:
Megan_Allen_Author